MISERERE

MISERERE

BY
CAREN J WERLINGER

CORGYN
Publishing

Miserere
By Caren J. Werlinger

Copyright © 2012 by Caren J. Werlinger. All rights reserved.
Published by Corgyn Publishing, LLC.
Printed in the United States of America.

Print ISBN: 978-0-9886501-1-4
eBook ISBN: 978-0-9886501-0-7

Scripture readings are taken from the *Jerusalem Bible*, copyright 1966
by Darton, Longman and Todd Ltd., & Doubleday and Company
Inc. Used by permission.

Cover photo by Erica Helm
Cover design by Patty G. Henderson

E-mail: cjwerlingerbooks@yahoo.com

* * *

* * *

This is a work of fiction. Names, characters, places, and incidents are the product of the author's imagination or are used fictitiously, and any resemblance to actual persons, living or dead, businesses, companies, events, or locales is entirely coincidental.

DEDICATION

For Beth

Acknowledgments

This story was born from a distant memory of a house that our family looked at when I was about nine and we were having to move. It was much as described in the opening chapter of this book and I, of course, thought it would be a wonderful place to live and at last have a horse. My parents felt otherwise. But, my fascination with that old farmhouse has stayed with me all these years — what kind of stories could it have told? — and it only took a little imagination for the rest of this tale to come together. To Roxanne Jones and Annabelle Lamarre of L-Book, for believing in this story prior to Roxanne's tragic and untimely death and the unfortunate closing of L-Book. Their support gave me the impetus to publish this story myself. The process of publishing this book on my own would not have been possible without the generous and unselfish assistance of fellow authors Patty G. Henderson, Catherine M. Wilson, Q. Kelly, Lynn Galli and Beth Mitchum. Other people's assistance was immeasurable as well: Karen Follett for her technical assistance and Erica Helm for her generous permission to use her photo for the cover. My sincere thanks also to Marge and Marty for their reading of the early draft, and providing their proofreading and feedback.

And to Beth, for reading, for believing I could do this — and for putting up with endless hours of Celtic music as this story came together.

PROLOGUE

10th May 1855

"Caitríona! Where are you?"

Orla Ní Faolain cast about, looking for her younger sister. The sudden wind whipped her long, black hair sideways and brought rare color to her normally pale cheeks as she held tightly to the halter of the stout Connemara pony pulling her cart.

"Shhh, Connor," she said soothingly as he tossed his head, his eyes wide.

"Where are you?" she moaned again, glancing worriedly at the black clouds roiling in from the sea.

Without warning, Caitríona ran out from behind a small hillock near the dirt lane. There were brambles tangled in her wild red hair, and she had dirt smeared across her freckled cheek. In her hands, she cradled a small mound of red fur.

"Look, Orla!" she exclaimed excitedly as she scrambled over the stacked rock wall rambling along the lane.

Orla, with a reserve born of experience, cautiously looked to see what her sister held. A tiny fox kit blinked up at her.

"Isn't she beautiful?" Caitríona murmured, entranced.

Orla sighed in exasperation. "Aye, she's beautiful, but Mam will have our hides if we don't get the cart home before the storm."

She wasn't sure Caitríona was listening as she bent over the fox kit, stroking its soft head and murmuring to it.

"Put it back where you found it," Orla said gently, casting another glance at the ominous clouds. Her sister was always finding stray and injured animals. Or they found her. Even the wild ones came to her trustingly, seeming to know that she would do them no harm.

Reluctantly, Caitríona carried her small burden back to the gorse behind the hillock. She ran back to the cart and took the pony's halter on the other side as together they urged him into a trot.

They arrived home as the first fat raindrops began to fall. Connor trotted right into the three-sided run-in that served as a barn, its rock walls chinked with clumps of sod so that the stones looked hairy. Because the storms here on this peninsula were so fierce, the thatched roof was reinforced with strong cords anchored by more rocks, swinging wildly now in the wind.

The girls unhitched the pony, and Caitríona put him in his stall next to the milk cow. Hastily, she put a few handfuls of sweet hay in his feed bin and gave him a pat before putting up the boards that closed his stall.

"You'd better be hoping Da doesn't see that hay," Orla warned. "You know he says it's only for the cow."

Caitríona looked around to make sure her father wasn't near. "You won't tell, will you?" she pleaded. "Connor works harder than that old cow."

"That old cow gives us milk and butter," Orla reminded her sister. "Come. Let's get this lot in the house."

Gathering up the paper-wrapped parcels of fish and salt, along with the tins of tea and flour, the girls ran through the rain to the house. The small cottage was also built of stone whose whitewash had long ago faded, beaten away by the relentless pounding of the storms blown in by the westerly winds. Rounding the corner, they skidded to a halt. A carriage was there, pulled by two fine bay hackney ponies covered with blankets against the weather. The coachman sat like a statue on the high seat, his heavily embroidered uniform getting wetter by the minute. The footman, dressed in a similar livery, stood miserably at the heads of the horses.

Ducking under the rocks anchoring the cottage's thatched roof, the girls peered through the low door to see a strange gentleman sitting in their father's chair by the fire. Niall O'Faolain jumped up from the bench at the table when he saw them.

"Come in, girls, come in," he said anxiously, gesturing them inside when they still hesitated. "Lord Playfair has been waitin' to see you."

The girls kicked off their muddy shoes as they entered and stood silently, still clutching their parcels. Lord Playfair's cold, indifferent gaze swept over them, passing quickly over Caitríona, but pausing on Orla for several seconds before he turned to Niall. Caitríona glanced quickly at her mother who sat with the baby and five other children on the bench along the far wall. The sight of her mother's ashen face frightened her.

"They both know how to read and write?" Lord Playfair asked.

"Yes, your Lordship," Niall answered, his head bowed, staring at Lord Playfair's shiny black boots. "English and Latin, and a little Irish."

Lord Playfair's eyebrows rose slightly in haughty acknowledgement of his surprise.

"Very well, then. We have an agreement," he said as he stood. "Five extra acres. Have them ready in two weeks. I'll send a wagon. They sail from Cobh." He pulled his oilskin cloak around his shoulders and, ducking through the cottage door, climbed into the waiting carriage and departed.

Niall collapsed into the vacated chair and stared into the low flames slowly consuming the blocks of peat. Orla dropped her packages on the wooden table and knelt beside her father as he rubbed the red stubble on his chin.

"Da?" She laid a white hand on his arm. "Da, what did he mean?"

Refusing to meet her gaze, Niall said, "Lord Playfair is sending his son to oversee his plantation in America. They need servants. You and your sister are to go."

Orla's hand flew to her mouth in disbelief, but Caitríona cried defiantly, "I won't! He can't force us!"

Niall shoved himself abruptly to his feet. "You'll do as you're told for a change!" he roared. He swept his arm toward the door. "All I've got is ten acres to feed this family. Look at them," he gestured with his other hand toward the other children watching wide-eyed. "Skin and bones. Orla's fifteen. She should be married, and you, not two years behind, should be following. But since the famine... all the young men have gone." His voice faltered. "There's not enough land to feed us all." His jaw worked from side to side. "It's time you were gone," he said.

His wife, Eilish, looked out the window at the three small crosses silhouetted on the hill behind the cottage, and said, "You would do well to remember, Niall O'Faolain, that we'd have lost more than three children to the famine if it weren't for the girls helping me make lace to sell in town."

She handed the baby to the boy next to her and stood, clearly pregnant again. Her smooth white skin and long black hair marked her as Orla's mother. She was still beautiful, despite the ravages of years of hunger and the hardships of bearing and burying too many children, the same beauty that now made men stop and look longingly at Orla.

"You're telling me I'm not man enough to work this land and feed my family?" Niall growled, his cheeks turning a blotchy red that matched his hair.

"I'm saying it's taken more than farming to feed this family these past seven years, and you've no cause to make the girls believe they've been a burden," Eilish insisted, refusing to back down despite his menacing tone.

His eyes flickered briefly in the direction of his two eldest daughters. "With five extra acres, I could get back on me feet."

"So you sold us like a pair of cattle!" accused Caitríona.

So fast she didn't have time to duck, Niall lashed out, backhanding her and knocking her to the floor. She stayed down, her unruly red curls falling over her face as Niall stomped out into the rain.

Eilish rushed over and brushed Caitríona's hair back to reveal a bloody lip. Angry tears spilled from her daughter's eyes.

"Will you never learn to hold your tongue?" she asked, shaking her head. "Come." She led Caitríona to the table. There, she dabbed at the blood with the corner of her apron. "Only, if you go, Lord Playfair will let your father keep five extra acres of crops, but if you don't, he'll take five away. We can't live on five acres and he knows it," Eilish explained gently.

"But he farms over fifty acres for that English bastard now!" Caitríona sputtered through her swollen lips. "We're not his property," she insisted bitterly.

"To himself, that's all we are." Eilish sighed in resignation. "I blame myself. If I hadn't taught you to read and write and make lace..." She looked over at Orla, still kneeling by her father's chair. "If I could, I'd send you to the nuns who raised me. You'd be safe there."

Orla turned to her mother. "Mam? For how long must we go? Will we ever come home again to Ireland?"

Eilish looked at her sadly. "I don't know, child."

CHAPTER 1

Green.

Later, when Conn tried to recall her first memories of the farm, green was what she remembered. So many different greens. The dark blue-green of West Virginia mountain ridges covered in pines; the soft, dappled green of sunlight filtering through the leaves of the trees that lined the rural highways and roads they traveled; the rich, cool green of the grass around the farmhouse, grass that tickled her bare feet — the first time she could remember being allowed to go barefoot outside. But it was all mixed up with the greens in the dreams — the soft green fields dotted with stone cairns and criss-crossed with low rock walls; the deepening purple-green of the undersides of the grasses and heathers when a storm blew in from the sea. Except Conn had never been to the sea.

The station wagon's tires crunched on the gravel of the dirt drive that wound uphill to the house. It took a couple of minutes for the dust cloud raised by the car to drift away and give them their first glimpse of the house.

"Oh no," groaned Elizabeth.

The house looked haunted. The grass was knee-high. Several windows were broken, and the white paint was peeling, exposing the weathered gray clapboards underneath. Extending from one side of the house was a portion made of log with a squat stone chimney. At the other end of the house, a larger stone chimney was almost completely covered by ivy so thick it looked solid in the deep shade of the enormous trees growing around the house — elms and maples and oaks and hemlocks with sad, droopy branches.

Ten-year-old Conn looked worriedly at her mother and said, "It's not so bad. We can fix it up, Mom. And look at the beautiful trees. We didn't have trees like this in New Mexico."

The brown desert landscape around Sandia Base in Albuquerque seemed a world away from this place. So did the day the Marines came to the door....

"Are we here?" Conn's brother, Will, who was seven, stirred in the back seat, unsticking his face from the vinyl where he'd been sleeping, scrunched between a stack of boxes and the side of the car.

They all climbed stiffly from their 1958 Chevy Nomad, "the same age as me," Conn reminded Will frequently. "Daddy bought it the day I was born. He didn't buy anything the day you were born," she also added frequently.

"Well, let's take a closer look," Elizabeth sighed, tossing her thick auburn hair over her shoulder and letting her car door close.

They climbed the wooden steps to the deep front porch where a lonely-looking porch swing hung at one end. Elizabeth dug the house key from her purse and tried to work it into the lock. It finally slid in, but wouldn't turn. She sighed in frustration as she tried to wiggle the key in the lock. Giving up, she said, "Let's go around back."

Conn led the way around to the screened porch on the back of the house. The screen door hung by one hinge, and inside the porch, the kitchen door was ajar.

"Hello?" Elizabeth called out, pushing the door open cautiously. All three humans jumped when two squirrels came racing through their legs.

Peering into the kitchen, it looked as if it had been ransacked. Cupboard doors stood open and drawers lay upside down on the floor. A huge wood-burning cookstove occupied one wall of the kitchen, while on an adjacent wall stood a cast-iron sink with an old-fashioned hand pump standing over it. A small electric icebox stood unplugged with its doors open. Cans of food were scattered everywhere. A bag of flour on the slate countertop had been chewed open and spilled onto the gray linoleum floor, the perpetrators leaving white telltale footprints all over the kitchen. "This is raccoon," Conn pointed. She had recently studied animal tracks in Girl Scouts. "And this one is rabbit, I think."

"Raccoon?" Will asked, moving closer to his mother and looking around uncertainly.

"It's okay," Conn said. "They only have rabies sometimes."

"Connemara," Elizabeth said warningly.

Grinning, Conn peered into the log room and saw a wide stone fireplace with a swiveling iron hook.

"Let's check out the rest of the house," Elizabeth said, pushing open the swinging door that separated the kitchen from the dining room.

All the furniture in the dining room and sitting room beyond had been covered by white sheets. A broad oak staircase brought them to the second floor where there were three bedrooms with similar sheets covering the beds and dressers.

"I guess nobody's been here since Nana died," Elizabeth sighed.

Will couldn't remember Nana at all, but Conn could, even though it had been five years. They had stopped to visit her on their way from Norfolk to New Mexico. Conn could recall sitting next to Nana on the front porch swing, holding her hand. Nana's skin was soft and dry and wrinkly, but what Conn remembered most was that Nana chewed her nails, something Conn did also. Since then, whenever Elizabeth scolded Conn for biting her nails so short, Conn stubbornly declared it couldn't be so bad if Nana did it.

"This used to be my room," Elizabeth smiled as she pushed open the door of the room at the end of the hall.

Conn looked around. Outside one window was a large branch from one of the elm trees, so close she could have reached out and plucked some of its leaves. "Can this be my room now?" she asked.

"Sure," Elizabeth answered, tousling her daughter's short red hair. "Let's take all the sheets off and clean everything before we unload the car."

"Hey!" said Will a few minutes later from behind the large pile of sheets in his arms. "Where's the bathroom?"

Elizabeth laughed. "I'll show you." She led the way back downstairs, gathering more sheets as she went through the sitting room. Outside, they all dropped their sheets on the grass. "There it is," she said, pointing to an outhouse a short distance from the house.

"For real?" Conn asked, her eyes wide.

"For real," Elizabeth replied. "And that's the first thing we're going to change. Come on. Let's get cracking."

Several hours later, the bedrooms were cleaned and beds made up with fresh sheets. The station wagon had been unloaded, the bikes untied from the roof and stored on the back porch. Elizabeth had found screens in the attic so they could open as many windows as possible to let fresh air into the musty rooms.

"Anybody want another sandwich?" Elizabeth asked, peering into the cooler serving as their makeshift ice box as the electric one wasn't yet cold, though so far, it seemed to be working.

"No," Will answered with a big yawn.

"Bed time, then. It's been a long day."

They made one last trip to the outhouse by the light of a flashlight. Elizabeth supervised the brushing of their teeth in the kitchen, pumping water for them at the sink, murmuring a prayer of thanks as it drew water after only a few dry pumps. Upstairs, she listened to each of the children as they knelt beside their beds and said their prayers, then kissed them both goodnight.

Will was asleep almost immediately, but Conn waited awhile then quietly stole out of bed and crept down the hall to her mother's door. She sank to the floor, her back resting against the wainscoting, and hugged her knees to her chest as she listened to the soft sounds of her mother crying.

As she sat there in the dark, Conn tried to remember how things used to be when Daddy was home with them. He was a Marine helicopter pilot at Sandia and mostly flew high-ranking officers to other bases. She remembered hearing his car pull up, and running to leap into his arms, his bristly Marine haircut tickling her cheek. Then, last summer, just before Conn was to start the fifth grade and Will the second, they got the news that their father was being deployed to Vietnam. Most of their school friends already had a parent serving in Vietnam — mostly fathers, but a few mothers who were nurses. Sandia Base was shared by the Navy, the Marines and the Army, and was so big that it had its own schools for the children of the military personnel stationed there.

After their father deployed, she and Will would sometimes come home to find a letter from him waiting there. "My little leprechauns," he called them. They would snuggle up on either side of their mother on the couch and ask her to read the letter over and over. Usually, there came a point when Conn could hear a shift in the sound of Elizabeth's voice, and she knew her mother was close to tears. Conn would take Will to the kitchen table then, and help him write a reply to Daddy.

As hard as those months were, spending Thanksgiving and Christmas without him, it all got harder in April. Conn remembered precisely when. It was April 5th, the day after Martin Luther King was shot. She remembered because they didn't have school that day, so she was home when the doorbell rang. Will was still in bed, but Conn crouched at the top of the stairs and peeked down at the two Marines in their dress blues. They removed their white hats respectfully when Elizabeth opened the door, and one of them read from a letter in his hand, "It is with regret that we must inform you that Lieutenant Colonel Mark Mitchell has been shot down and is reported missing in action." They spoke words of regret and condolence, handed Elizabeth the letter and left. As Elizabeth closed the door, she looked up and saw Conn. They stared at each other for several seconds before Elizabeth walked to the kitchen.

Conn went back to her room and waited. She tried to read the Nancy Drew mystery she had started, but she found herself listening for the sound of her mother's footsteps on the stairs. When Elizabeth knocked softly and opened the door, Conn put her book down.

"You heard?" Elizabeth asked as she sat on the side of the bed.

Conn nodded. "What do we do now?"

Elizabeth laid her hand on Conn's knee, still scabbed from a crash on her bicycle last week. "If anything happened to him, Daddy wanted us to go to Nana's. We'll wait for him there," she said.

Conn nodded again, staring hard at Nancy Drew's blond hair and blinking back tears. Elizabeth kissed Conn's forehead and went to Will's room to tell him.

That night, Conn had tiptoed to her mother's bedroom door where she could hear her mother crying. She slid to the floor and sat there until the sounds quieted, and then went back to bed.

She had done this nearly every night since, standing guard as she was doing now in Nana's house on this cool May night. She listened to the unfamiliar sound of crickets chirping as she waited. At length, her mother's room was quiet. She padded back down the hall and crawled into bed.

CHAPTER 2

The next morning, after a breakfast of cold cereal, Elizabeth and the children got back into the Nomad and drove to town. Like many small towns, Largo, West Virginia had a few houses lined up on a grid of dirt streets that surrounded a few prominent structures: a white clapboard Baptist church, a brick funeral home and a General Store, painted a dark, barn red. Elizabeth parked in front of the store and led the way up the wooden steps to a covered porch with several rocking chairs. Three old men sat there, gathered around a checker board on a barrel. They tipped their caps to Elizabeth and went on with their conversation.

Will climbed into one of the chairs, rocking madly, while Conn followed Elizabeth inside. Ceiling fans moved the air in the dark interior of the store. It took a moment for Conn's eyes to adjust after the bright sunlight outside. Everywhere she looked, there were shelves packed with goods — groceries, hardware, books. From the ceiling hung plows, chairs and rakes. It seemed that every available space was crammed with things for sale. She paused in front of large wooden barrels filled with nails of different sizes.

"Can I help you?" asked a man behind the tall glass-fronted counter. He peered at them through thick glasses, beads of sweat glistening on his forehead despite the ceiling fans. He had a heavy walrus moustache that obscured his mouth.

"Mr. Walsh? Do you remember me?" Elizabeth asked. "Elizabeth Cuthbert. Fiona Cook's granddaughter."

"Elizabeth!" Mr. Walsh exclaimed. "My goodness, girl, it's been an age since we seen you 'round here!" He turned to the doorway behind him, pulled aside the curtain and bellowed, "Betty? Betty! Come on out front and see who's here!"

A large woman emerged, her gray hair pulled back into a loose bun from which several strands of hair had escaped. She was drying her hands on a white apron that covered her front, stretched tightly across her ample bosom. She looked curiously at Elizabeth for a moment before exclaiming, "Land sakes! Elizabeth, I don't believe it! What brings you back to Largo?"

"We came here to wait for Daddy," piped up Will, who had come unnoticed to his mother's side.

"Are these your children?" Mrs. Walsh asked, noticing Will and Conn for the first time.

"I'm Will," Will announced, standing on his tiptoes and pulling himself up with his fingertips to see over the tall counter.

"Pleased to meet you, Will," Mr. Walsh smiled. At least Conn thought it was a smile. All she could actually see was his moustache moving. His bespectacled gaze shifted to Conn as he asked, "And what is your name, young lady?"

Conn looked at him for a couple of seconds before answering, "Connemara Faolain Mitchell."

"Good gracious," said Mrs. Walsh, her eyebrows lifting, "That's quite a name for such a little thing."

Not wanting to be left out of the conversation, Will quickly added, "My whole name is William Joseph Mitchell."

"Well, well," Mr. Walsh chuckled, "welcome to Largo, William Joseph and Connemara — ?"

"Faolain," said Elizabeth. "It's a family name. Anyway, we've come to live at Nana's house while my husband is overseas. We need these groceries and cleaning things," she said, handing Mrs. Walsh a list. "And I wondered if you could recommend someone who could do some work around the house."

Mr. Walsh frowned as he thought. "Probably the best handyman 'round here is Abraham Lincoln Greene. He don't have a telephone, but tomorrow is Saturday. He always comes to town on Saturday. I'll tell him to come by your place," he paused, glancing around to make sure no one else had come into the store, "if you don't mind that he's a Nigra," he whispered loudly.

Elizabeth blinked two or three times before replying, "No, I don't mind. Ask him to come by the house whenever he has time, please."

She turned back to Mrs. Walsh who was boxing the items on the list. "Are you still postmistress here, Mrs. Walsh?"

"Yes, indeed," Mrs. Walsh smiled, looking up as she put a sack of potatoes into the box. "I'll get you set up with a postbox when I'm through here."

Conn wandered off, exploring the mysteries of this store. It was so unlike the military exchange on base. She sniffed, and followed the scent of leather to a series of hooks anchored to the wall in a back corner, hung with bridles, halters and lead ropes. Longingly, she ran the smooth leather of a bridle through her fingers. Conn's dearest wish was to have a horse of her own, but being in a military family made that impossible. They'd never even been allowed a dog. The closest she ever got to her dream of having a horse was in her detailed and vivid games of make believe. She heard her mother call her name, and reluctantly put the bridle back, enjoying the lingering scent of leather on her hands.

When they got home, the children helped Elizabeth with a more thorough cleaning of the kitchen. They gathered up and sorted all the food that had been left, throwing away anything that looked too old or showed signs of animals having gotten into it, and wiped the pantry shelves clean before putting any of the new groceries away.

"Let's see about this stove," Elizabeth said. She opened one of the enameled doors and placed a few small pieces of kindling inside on top of some crinkled newspaper. When she lit the paper, the dry wood quickly caught, but smoke soon began backing out of the open door into the kitchen.

"Conn," she called, still squatting in front of the stove, "turn that handle," pointing to the coiled metal flue handle on the stove pipe.

Conn did as she was told, and almost immediately, the stove belched a thick cloud of black smoke and ash into Elizabeth's face.

Startled, Elizabeth fell back onto the kitchen floor and blinked, everything except her scrunched eyes blackened by the smoke. Sputtering and coughing, she got to her feet, waving her arms to fan the smoke away.

"Well, I don't remember Nana doing it that way," she said ruefully as Conn and Will giggled.

The children pumped water for her so she could wash her face.

"Let's have lunch," she said as she toweled off. "Then you can go play."

After a quick lunch of sandwiches and milk, Conn and Will hurried outside to explore. The barn near the house immediately drew their attention. Built into a hillside, the stone foundation opened onto the low side of the hill by means of a huge wooden sliding door that was too heavy for them to open. They climbed up the hill and around the other side of the barn where there was a smaller sliding door they were able to push aside enough to slip through. Taking a moment to let her eyes adjust to the dim light, Conn saw an old tractor sitting there, its green paint chipped away in places. There were old gas and oil cans and a mower meant to be pulled along behind the tractor. Up above them was a loft accessible by a wooden ladder. Over at one end of the barn was a set of wooden steps leading down to the stone level below.

"Wait for me!" Will cried as Conn disappeared down the stairs.

It was much darker in the lower level, and Will clung to the back of his sister's shirt. This level had a packed dirt floor and several stalls. A few bits of harness hung from nails, the leather cracked and brittle.

"Let's go," Will whispered. "I don't like it down here."

"Okay." Conn agreed grudgingly, deciding to come back later with a flashlight and explore more on her own.

Will started back up the steps, and as Conn reached for the handrail, she thought she detected movement out of the corner of her eye. She stopped and stared into the darkness, but could see nothing. She was aware of a sudden chill and realized she had goosebumps.

"C'mon," Will urged her.

"I'm coming," she said, with one more glance around.

Orla and Eilish sat outside the cottage, a freshening breeze tickling their faces as they sewed new undergarments for the girls to take on their voyage to America. Eilish had looked sadly at the few things they had to pack in their small bags — an extra dress for each of them, Orla's handed down from her mother, and Caitríona's from Orla; an extra pair of shoes, bought used with some of Eilish's precious lace money.

"At least you shall have something new to take with you," Eilish had insisted, using a bit more of her lace money to buy the softest, finest linen she could afford.

Caitríona sat in the grass, keeping an eye on the baby, who was beginning to crawl. She watched her mother worriedly; her face looked wasted and ill.

"You're not strong enough to have another baby," Brónach had pronounced, laying her knowing hands on Eilish's swelling belly. She was known to all as the *seanmhair*, though she wasn't actually anyone's grandmother. She was the mid-wife and knew much of the old ways. "'Tis not moving enough. You need to eat more."

"I'll be fine," Eilish had insisted, but Caitríona could see that this baby, her twelfth, was sapping her strength. She knew her mother's heart was as broken as hers and Orla's, though she would never show it. She had seen her mother slipping food from her own plate onto theirs, trying to make sure they were strong enough for the journey ahead of them.

"All because that bastard won't keep his hands off her," Caitríona thought angrily as she watched her mother sewing. In a one-room cottage separated only by a drape, she heard things in the night. "No man will ever do that to me."

Eilish glanced up and caught Caitríona's eye. "Daughter," she said, "go to my bed and fetch the parcel under my pallet."

Caitríona did as she was bidden, returning a moment later with a cloth-wrapped parcel which she handed to her mother. Eilish set her sewing aside and unfolded the cloth to reveal a small leather-bound book and a smaller leather pouch. She handed the pouch to Orla, who opened it and pulled out a wooden rosary.

"Oh, Mam," Orla breathed, "it's beautiful."

"It's been blessed with holy water," said Eilish, her voice cracking just a wee bit. "To keep you safe in your travels."

She turned to her younger daughter and held out the book. "I know you write things." Caitríona flushed. She hadn't thought anyone knew about her small collection of "scribbles," as she called them. Paper was hard to come by, and she hoarded every scrap she could get her hands on. "Now, you can write your thoughts properly. And show them to me someday."

Caitríona's face hardened as she tried not to cry.

"It's not a wake, child," Eilish said.

"'Tis!" Caitríona cried. "We'll never see you again!" She couldn't stop her tears, and ran from the cottage. She ran through the neighboring fields where sheep and cattle grazed until, clambering over a stone wall, she topped a hill at the bottom of which was the *seanmhair's* cottage, surrounded by old trees which sheltered it from the winds. The old woman was outside, tending to her plants. She spotted Caitríona with her red curls blowing in the breeze and waved to her, beckoning her down the hill. Wiping her tears from her cheeks, Caitríona descended the slope, crossing a small rocky stream at the bottom before climbing the gentle rise to the neat white cottage. This cottage had always seemed mysterious to Caitríona, with its bundles of flowers and herbs hung to dry from the rafters and little urns filled with roots and leaves.

"Come in, lass," said Brónach, leading the way inside. "Sit with me by the fire," she said, her black eyes peering up at Caitríona. Caitríona took the other stool near the fire, watching the *seanmhair* as she pulled the steaming kettle toward her and began dropping crushed leaves from some of her pots into the hot water. It was impossible to tell how old she was, with her white hair contrasted against her smooth skin. Caitríona knew that Father Cormac, the local priest, disliked Brónach, disparaging her as "unholy." Eilish said that was rubbish. She said it was only because the *seanmhair* knew how to brew teas and medicines for ailments that Father Cormac could only pray over, big lot of help that was.

Brónach put another block of peat on the fire and swung the kettle back over the flames to heat. Caitríona watched as she took yet more leaves from other pots and crumbled them into two earthen cups. Within a few minutes, she poured the hot water from the kettle into the cups, allowing the leaves to steep.

All of this took place in silence. Brónach put the kettle back on the fire and turned to Caitríona. "I hear," she said at last, "that you and Orla are to go to America."

Caitríona nodded as Brónach handed her one of the cups, and took the other herself. Caitríona sniffed at the aromatic steam rising off the hot liquid. It smelled of heather and lavender, and it smelled like the wind blowing in off the sea. It made Caitríona's heart ache for all the things she would never know again.

"Drink, child."

Caitríona had the feeling Brónach could read her thoughts as she raised the cup to her lips. She could feel the brew warming her as it went down her gullet, spreading out to her limbs with a tingle and making her face feel as if it glowed.

"What is this?" she gasped, a little frightened.

"'Twill help us see what is in store for you," said Brónach.

"You can do that?" Caitríona whispered.

"Aye, if the Dagda will show us," Brónach said, her eyes narrowing a bit.

"The Dagda?" Caitríona repeated, her mouth gaping. She made a quick sign of the cross.

"Do not insult the old ones with Christian nonsense," the *seanmhair* snapped. "The Dagda, his daughter Brighid — they cannot kill the old ones, so they turn them into something they can understand, into saints. Phah!" she said, spitting into the fire where her spittle sizzled and steamed.

Caitríona was frightened now. Brónach reached over and took her cup and, muttering a few words in the Irish, an older form than Caitríona could understand, she threw the remaining liquid into the flames. Peering intently, she watched the shapes assumed by the steam and smoke as it rose. She then turned her attention to the sodden leaves remaining in the cup. Still muttering, she drank deeply from her own cup and looked at the wet leaves there as well.

Caitríona was feeling strange. It seemed to her that the cottage was all in darkness, though it must surely still be day. The fire was the only light, and she found herself unable to look away from the flames. Brónach closed her eyes, swaying on her stool, and from her mouth issued a voice not her own.

> "Ill-fated shall your progeny be;
> From each generation after thee
> Only one girl child shall survive
> To carry on and keep alive
> The hope to right a grievous wrong,
> Until the one comes along
> Who may set the past to rights.
>
> None may help her in her quest, or
> Ease the burden laid by her ancestor
> On shoulders much too young to bear such sorrow.
> Not since barren fields stole all hope for tomorrow
> Has such a one been needed,

When father sold daughter for land he was deeded,
And plunged his soul into endless night.

Hatred is poison, like blood on the fields,
Father to daughter, a blackened soul yields
Naught but mem'ries of what once was good.
A child, ne'er soiled by hate or greed could
Bring forgiveness and healing to those long gone.
With the dead laid to rest, the living move on,
Freed at last by a soul blessed with light."

Caitríona stared aghast at Brónach's face, lit from one side by the fire as she slowly came out of her trance. Tears fell from the old woman's eyes as she stared at Caitríona. "Gods be with you, lass."

CHAPTER 3

"Can we help?"

Abraham Lincoln Greene straightened his wiry six-foot-three frame and looked down at Conn and Will. He had the peculiar habit of turning his head to the left when speaking to people so that only the right side of his face could be seen. Only when viewed full on was his scar visible, a jagged white line in his smooth, dark skin, running from his left temple to his chin. It had tightened as it healed so that it pulled his features to the side, half closing his eyelid.

"Well," he responded, his deep soft voice an unexpected contrast to his appearance, "I suppose I could use a couple of assistants."

The week previous, Elizabeth had answered a knock on the back porch door to find Abraham already stepping back to get a better view of how high the ivy climbed up the chimney. He seemed unsure of how to respond when she came out to introduce herself, extending a hand to him. He shook it tentatively, and followed her into the kitchen where she showed him the original log portion of the house.

"I want to convert this into a bathroom," she said.

After working out the details for what was to go where, he had started to work the very next day, roughing out the indoor portion of the plumbing and electrical wires. He had contacted a man who was putting in a septic system. Abraham was in the process of rebuilding the floor which had had to be raised to accommodate the new pipes.

He led the children to a pair of sawhorses where he had marked several pieces of lumber for new floor joists. He picked up his old cross-cut saw and started the cuts for them, teaching them how to cut on the push stroke. With Will holding a joist steady by sitting on it, Conn began cutting, standing on an old upside-down apple crate. When she got tired, they switched. Abraham went back to nailing, calling out when he was ready for a new board.

Elizabeth came out with three icy glasses of lemonade.

"We're helping Abraham!" Will bragged, his dark hair sticking to his sweaty forehead. "I mean, Mr. Greene," he corrected at the stern look on his mother's face.

"I don't mind if they call me Abraham," he said as he accepted a frosty glass.

"Thank you, Mr. Greene," Elizabeth smiled, "but I would prefer the children address adults by their proper names."

"Yes, ma'am," he nodded, wiping the sweat from his forehead with his sleeve, a move both children immediately mimicked. "I should have floorboards down by Friday. And then we can get the tub hooked up for you."

"It'll be heaven to be able to take a real bath," said Elizabeth wistfully.

"And use a real toilet," Conn added. Both she and Will had been chased out of the outhouse by hornets which had territorially nested in the eaves.

Slowly, the house was looking lived in. Abraham had shown Elizabeth how to operate the tractor and drag the mower through the grass. What the gang mower couldn't reach, the children mowed with a push mower, its spiral blades whirring through the wispy strands. He showed Elizabeth how to fix the cords of the sash windows and replace the broken panes of glass. Once the bathroom was done, he planned to begin pulling the ivy off the chimney stones.

They ate lunch outside in the shade where they could catch any hint of breeze there might be. It was only early May, but it was warm in the sunshine. Abraham initially ate by himself, reading a thick book he pulled out of his knapsack.

He looked up one day at Elizabeth who was offering him a glass of iced tea. Puzzled, he said, "You are most unusual, Mrs. Mitchell."

Elizabeth smiled, noticing his book was a volume of Shakespeare. "You're a bit unusual yourself, Mr. Greene. And I don't mean to intrude if you would prefer to eat by yourself, but you are most welcome to join the children and me."

A few days later, he did just that. He peered over Conn's shoulder as she lay on her stomach reading while eating her peanut butter and jelly sandwich.

"Tom Sawyer, Connemara?" he asked in surprise. "That's a pretty big book for someone your age."

"I reckon," Conn said as she sat up. "May I see your book?" He handed it to her. She carefully turned the pages. "What are these?" she asked, indicating tiny penciled notes in the margins.

"Those were my notes from my literature class," he replied.

"From when you were a student?" she squinted, trying to read the miniscule writing.

"No." He paused. "From when I taught."

"You taught English literature?" Elizabeth asked, her eyebrows raised in surprise. "Surely not around here."

"No, not around here. At a boys' school up north."

Conn looked up. "If you were a teacher, how did you learn to fix houses?"

Abraham chuckled. "This," he said, holding up his hammer, "I got from my father. And this," he held up his book, "I got from my mother."

"But… you got away," Elizabeth said, puzzled. "And you came back here? To this? Why?" she asked in disbelief.

Abraham's gaze went to the farmhouse and back to Elizabeth. "Why did you come back?"

Elizabeth's eyes fell. "I didn't plan to. I thought once I got out of here…" She sighed. "My husband is MIA," she explained. "We came here to wait for him."

"I'm sorry," Abraham said in his soft voice.

Will tilted his head to one side. "If you both grew up here, did you go to the same school?"

Abraham laughed, his scar pulling his mouth sideways. "No, William. Whites and coloreds went to separate schools, separate churches, separate everything."

"But that's wrong," Conn said, looking upset.

"Yes, it is wrong," Elizabeth agreed. "But it's changing." She glanced at Abraham. "Isn't it?"

He absent-mindedly traced a finger along his scar. "Some places, maybe. But there are still a lot of people who think all black folks should have stayed slaves."

"Your family came here as slaves?" Conn asked. "Ours, too."

Abraham frowned, puzzled. "You've got slave blood in your family?"

"Yes," Conn nodded. "My great-great-great grandmother. Right?" she asked her mother. Elizabeth nodded.

"Came from Africa?" Abraham asked skeptically.

"No, from Ireland," Elizabeth replied. "She and her sister were sold by their father for five acres of land and sent to work on a plantation in America."

"Her name was Caitríona Ní Faolain," Conn said.

"How do you know so much about her?" Abraham asked curiously.

"Mommy has been telling me about her since I was little," Conn responded.

Elizabeth smiled. "Her story has been passed down to each new generation," she explained.

"Every girl in our family has Faolain as a middle name so we don't forget," Conn said proudly.

"Why didn't I get Faolain, too?" Will asked, clearly feeling left out.

Conn's expression darkened as Elizabeth tousled his hair. "Because you're the first boy on this side of the family and you'll get to keep the name Mitchell. Conn's name will change when she gets married."

"Oh, no it won't," Conn said resentfully. Will always got attention for being the only boy, for being the one who would carry on the family name, even though she was braver and stronger than he would ever be. "I'm not getting married. And I'm not changing my name for anybody."

CHAPTER 4

Conn woke early and quietly dressed in shorts and t-shirt. Carrying her Keds, she tiptoed down the stairs. She opened the kitchen door silently and sat on the porch steps to put her shoes on. She'd been trying to talk Will into playing Huck Finn to her Tom Sawyer, but it was hard to have adventures with someone who was afraid of the dark and scared of climbing too high. She and her brother had explored much of the land around Nana's house. Most of it was overgrown pastureland, but there were large tracts of undisturbed woodland, and a few streams nearby. And streams had fish.

She ran to the barn, the cold dew on the grass tickling her bare ankles. She pushed against the door on the upper level and retrieved the pole she had hidden there, rigged with a long string and a safety pin for a hook. She remembered to grab the small coffee can she had stashed in the corner and stopped to dig up some worms. She made her way across a large, grassy pasture to one of the creeks they had discovered.

Following it upstream, she searched for a spot that looked fishy, and came upon a deeper pool nestled at the base of a small waterfall where the stream tumbled over some boulders. Reaching into her can, she pulled out a worm and, grimacing only a little, put the worm on the safety pin. Squatting on a rock above the pool, she dropped her line in and watched the worm sink out of sight.

She waited patiently, not sure what was supposed to happen. When she felt a tug on the line, she jerked the pole up so excitedly that the tiny fish on the safety pin flew in a wet arc over her head, landing on the grass behind her. She ran to scoop up her prize, admiring the blue and green and gold shimmers of the little fish's scales. Quickly, she dumped the worms and dirt out of her coffee can and dipped it in the creek to fill it. Releasing the tiny fish into the water, she watched it swim round and round. Out of the corner of her eye, a movement caught her attention. She thought she saw a flash of blue denim and bare feet disappearing behind a boulder on the other side of the stream. She watched intently for a few seconds, but saw nothing else.

Carefully, she made her way home, trying not to slosh the water out of the can. Her mother was in the kitchen by the time she got home. She had a fire lit in the stove and was adding more wood.

"Where have you been?" Elizabeth asked, startled at Conn's entrance into the kitchen. "I didn't know you were up."

"Look!" Conn exclaimed proudly, holding the can out.

Elizabeth peered into the can and jumped a little. "Where did that come from?" she asked.

"I caught it!" Conn crowed.

"What did you use for a pole?"

Conn explained how she'd made one, and suddenly realized she'd left it lying by the creek.

"Well, Jonah, set your whale out on the porch while you eat your breakfast, and then you can take it back and let it go," Elizabeth smiled.

Conn did as her mother asked and came back inside to wash her hands at the new faucet Abraham had installed in place of the kitchen pump.

Will came into the kitchen, yawning and rubbing sleep from his eyes.

"I caught a fish!" Conn announced.

Will woke up properly at that and followed his sister out to the porch to see. They were soon lured back into the kitchen by the smell of bacon. Elizabeth, who was getting the hang of cooking on the ancient woodstove, fried up some eggs in the leftover bacon grease.

The children hurried through their breakfasts and Will ran upstairs to get dressed.

"Be careful, and be home by lunchtime," Elizabeth called after them.

Conn let Will carry the can back to the creek where they released the fish back into the water. She looked around for her fishing pole. It wasn't where she'd left it. Will helped her look through the grass and bushes near the creek.

"Lookin' for somethin'?"

Conn and Will both jumped at the sound of the voice. Perched high on the rocks overhanging the stream was a boy. He had blond, untidy hair and patched denim overalls which he wore shirtless. In his hands was Conn's fishing pole.

"That's mine," Conn said.

"Prove it," the boy challenged.

Conn put her hands on her hips as she looked up at him. "It has a safety pin for a hook."

The boy seemed to consider this for a moment, then tossed the pole down. "Who wants it, anyway? It ain't even a real pole," he said disparagingly.

"It was good enough to catch a fish," Will declared. "Let's see yours."

The boy shifted positions so he was sitting with his feet dangling over the edge of the rock. "Don't wanna fish today," he said.

Conn laughed. "That means he doesn't have a pole," she said to Will.

"Do so," he countered. "I'm catchin' crawdads today."

"Come on," Conn said. "Just ignore him." She led Will over to the small pile of dirt and worms she had dumped out of her can earlier. Picking a worm out, she speared it on the safety pin, trying not to make a face with the boy watching. She showed Will how to drop the worm into the pool, and they waited. When they saw a tug on the string, Conn and the boy yelled together, "Pull!"

Will jerked up on the pole much as Conn had done, with another gleaming sunfish flopping at the end of the line.

"Okay," said Conn, "take it off the hook and let it go."

But Will was afraid to touch the fish. Every time he tried to hold it, it flopped and scared him.

At last, Conn grasped the little fish and unhooked it.

"You're pretty brave, for a girl," said the boy grudgingly as Conn dropped the fish back into the pool.

"Gee, thanks," said Conn sarcastically. "What's your name anyway?"

"Jed Pancake," the boy replied.

"Pancake?" Will laughed.

"Yeah, Pancake," Jed said defiantly. "I know who you are. You're the folks lives in the haunted house, where old lady Cook died."

Will's eyes got big. "It is not haunted," he said, but he didn't sound so sure.

"He's just saying that," Conn reassured him.

"Ain't," Jed insisted. "Everyone 'round here knows it. There's strange lights at night, in and outside the house. And folks've heard moanin'."

"Well, we haven't seen any lights or heard any moaning," Conn informed him. "Here's a new worm," she said, handing the pole back to Will.

Will dropped his line back in the water.

"Why ain't you in school?" Jed asked.

"Our school was almost done in New Mexico," Conn told him. "Mom says we'll start next year. Why aren't you?"

Jed shrugged. "Don't go 'cept when I wanna."

Conn turned to Will who had another fish. Without asking, Will swung the pole toward his sister. Embarrassed, Conn snuck a look over her shoulder to see if Jed was laughing at them, but to her relief he was gone.

"Huck would never ask Tom to unhook his fish for him," she grumbled.

ↀↀ

Orla and Caitríona trudged along behind the wagons, the sodden woolen blankets draped over their heads doing little to keep them dry, but at least keeping them warm. The wagons were loaded with trunks and crates carrying furniture, china and provisions. Besides the girls, there were two boys about Caitríona's age who were to be stable hands, and a woman, Fiona O'Hearn, who would be cook. The wagons rattled along the rutted lanes leading them ever farther from home. The girls had quickly discovered that walking was easier than being tossed about, and the boys followed suit. The lead driver was a taciturn man who spoke only when barking orders. Fiona rode with the second driver, keeping a tight hold on the edge of her seat to keep from being bucked off. When they stopped for the night, the wagons offered some shelter from the rain, though the ground was soaking wet.

For three days, they traveled thus.

What had felt like a prison sentence to Caitríona after Lord Playfair's visit now felt like a death sentence. Though she had heard the words of Brónach's prophecy only once, they were burned into her memory forevermore.

"What is it, daughter?" Eilish had asked as Caitríona isolated herself from the rest of the family those last few days before departing.

Caitríona could only shake her head wordlessly and let her mother assume it was just her sadness at having to leave. She couldn't express to her mother the hatred and loathing she felt — toward her father and toward herself. Her father was the cause of all this, but the curse indicated that she was somehow culpable as well.

Niall had only been home a few times since that afternoon. When he was home, he bellowed angrily at all of them, swaying drunkenly until he collapsed into his chair by the fire. Caitríona had watched him warily, and had seen him leering at Orla with a drunken lust that sickened her. She began to feel almost glad that she and Orla would be getting away from him.

"He's only drinking because he feels bad," said Orla.

Caitríona stared at her in disbelief. "He should feel bad," she retorted. "I hate him!"

"You don't mean that," Eilish said sharply.

"I do mean it," Caitríona replied emphatically. "I hate him. I will never forgive him and nothing you say will change that."

The day the wagons came for them, Niall wasn't there. Eilish, thinner than ever, held her girls to her, whispering to them in the Irish. Orla and Caitríona both clung to her tightly.

"I want you to take this," Eilish said, pressing a small book into Orla's hands. "It's not a full Bible, only the Gospels and Psalms, but I want you to read from it every Sunday. I've no idea if there'll be a church where you're going."

"But Mam," Caitríona protested, "the nuns gave you this."

"And I'm giving it to you," Eilish insisted.

Perched on top of crates in one of the wagons, the girls watched their brothers and sisters huddled together in the doorway waving to them, but Eilish stood off to one side, one hand clutching her dress over her heart as if trying to hold the broken pieces together.

After three days of slow travel, the bedraggled group neared Cobh.

The traffic on the road increased and the drivers insisted that everyone ride to avoid getting separated. Orla grabbed tightly to Caitríona's arm as the wagon rattled noisily over the cobblestones toward Cobh's wharves. None of the Irish bound for Lord Playfair's plantation had ever been to such a large city. They were overwhelmed by the noise. There were shops and vendors, people shouting, children running and laughing. The streets were littered with piles of manure and puddles of urine, animal and human. As they got closer to the wharves, there were corrals holding horses, cattle, sheep and pigs as well as wire cages containing chickens and geese — all waiting to be loaded onto one ship or another. The drivers guided the wagons to the pier where was anchored the ship that would take them to America. The lead driver barked at them to get out, and remain next to the wagon until it was time to board ship. Clutching their small bags to their chests, the girls watched the wagons being unloaded, the heavy crates and trunks hoisted in huge nets onto the ship where they were carried below deck to the cargo hold. Nearby, the horses and livestock added their terrified cries to the general din of the docks as they were walked up a wide gangplank directly into a lower hold of the ship. A short while later, as the Irish were ordered to board, Caitríona paused on the gangplank to look back, hoping for one last glimpse of the hills and colors of her beloved home, but all she could see was the confusion and filth of Cobh.

CHAPTER 5

"I won!" Will yelled as his back tire skidded, sending a spray of gravel and dirt flying.

Conn skidded up behind him and started to point out that the only reason he'd beaten her to the general store was because their mother had called her back to the porch to give her some letters to mail, but at the look on Will's face, she just shook her head. Back in New Mexico, back before Daddy was MIA… she would have argued that it wasn't a fair race, but now, "You won," she agreed. She leaned her bike against the store's front porch and followed Will inside.

He went straight to the glass case to decide what candy to purchase with his allowance. Conn deposited her letters at the small window that opened into the post boxes, and went to look at fishing poles — cane rods with reels. Her heart sank when she saw the price.

"Can I help you, young lady?" Mr. Walsh asked, mopping his forehead with a large, checkered handkerchief.

Looking at the coins in her hand, she asked, "How much are fishing hooks?"

A few minutes later, she and Will were rocking on the front porch. Conn admired the sharp points on her three new fishing hooks, trying to ignore Will as he gnawed on a licorice stick.

A familiar truck pulled up to the store. "Good morning, Connemara, William," said Abraham as he climbed out of his vehicle.

"Hi, Mr. Greene," Will grinned, revealing black teeth.

Abraham leaned over to peer at what Conn was holding. "I didn't know you fished, Connemara," he said, sitting in the next rocker.

"I do," she said. "Do you?"

"I do indeed," he replied. "If your mother gives her permission, I'll take you one day soon."

"Me, too," Will said eagerly, not wanting to be left out.

"Mom might say you aren't old enough to go," Conn said quickly. Sometimes, she got tired of Will always horning in on her adventures, and then getting too scared to have adventures.

"When are you coming back to our house?" she asked.

Abraham rocked and said, "After I finish fixing Mrs. Whitney's roof, I'll come and fix your chimney so you can use your fireplace this winter."

Mrs. Walsh came out onto the porch. "Oh, Abraham, I got your usual grocery order all boxed up."

"Thank you, Mrs. Walsh," Abraham replied. When he didn't get up immediately, she went back inside.

"Mr. Greene?" Conn began. "Do you know anything about our house being haunted?"

"Who told you that?" he asked, frowning.

"A boy, Jed Pancake," she said. "He was in the woods when we were fishing."

Abraham nodded a little. "Jedediah is a good boy at heart, but..." he paused. Conn could tell he was trying to decide how much to say. "He's left on his own a great deal," he said at last. "He could use a friend like you.

"Well," he said, getting to his feet, "I must be on my way."

He went inside to collect his groceries and came back out a moment later. "I'll see you both soon," he said as he put the box into the bed of his pickup and drove away.

Mrs. Walsh came back outside and said, "I've got your mail bundled up to take back to your mother," as she wiped down the rocker Abraham had been sitting in. Conn noticed she didn't wipe any of the others.

As she put the mail in her bike's basket, Conn also realized that Abraham hadn't answered her question about the house being haunted.

"Come on," she said to Will. They got on their bikes and began pedaling home, a much harder task since they were now going mostly uphill. No cars or trucks passed them on the dry, dusty road.

They stopped to rest in a shady section of the road, and were both startled when a large brown horse with black mane and tail walked out of the woods onto the road not twenty feet from them. Sitting astride the horse, riding bareback, was Jed, wearing the same patched overalls.

Conn's jaw dropped. "You have a horse?" she asked enviously.

Jed nodded. "This is Jack," he said, patting the bay's neck.

Conn lowered her bike's kickstand and walked over to Jack, holding a hand out. Jack lowered his large head, his gentle brown eyes blinking at Conn as he sniffed.

"His muzzle is so soft," she said.

Jack snorted, startling her. She jerked her hand away, and then blushed, embarrassed at her reaction. Jed surveyed her from his vantage point on Jack's back. "You wanna ride him?" he offered.

Conn's eyes got big. "Could I?" She was almost as scared as she was excited. She'd ridden ponies, but never a full-grown horse.

Jed slid down and led Jack to a nearby log so Conn could scramble up. Once atop Jack's back, the ground looked very far away. Jed handed her the reins, but kept hold of the bridle as he walked Jack up the road a way and back again.

Conn's heart was pounding, but she would have died rather than admit she was frightened. She slid down off the horse's back. "Thanks," she said breathlessly.

Jed grinned. Up close, she could see he had a few freckles sprinkled across his nose and a small scar on his lower lip.

"You want a ride?" he asked, turning to Will.

Will shook his head vigorously.

"I got real fishing hooks today," Conn said brightly. "Mr. Greene said he'd take us fishing sometime."

"Abraham? The nigger?" Jed asked.

Conn's fists balled up and her face turned red. "Don't you dare call him that!" she said angrily.

Jed stepped back hastily as if he were afraid Conn might hit him. "I didn't mean nothin' by it. It's just the way folks talk," he sputtered, confused as what he had done wrong.

"Well, it's a nasty word," Conn said, still fuming. "Nobody should be called that. Our parents say it doesn't matter what color someone's skin is, even if it's polka-dot."

Jed chortled. "Polka-dot? Who ever heard of a polka-dot person?"

Conn held out a vividly freckled arm. "I'm polka-dot. So if you're going to call Mr. Greene a bad name, you might as well call me one, too."

Jed blinked at her. "I didn't mean nothin'," he repeated.

Conn calmed down a bit. "Okay, then." She walked back to her bicycle. "Mr. Greene is one of the smartest people I know."

"Well, I know he can fix just about anything," Jed said, eager to stay on Conn's good side now that she wasn't yelling anymore. He led Jack alongside Conn and Will as they walked their bicycles.

"It's not just that," Conn said. "He reads Shakespeare."

"What's that?" Jed asked.

Conn looked at him as if she thought he was smarting off, but she could see he was serious. "Shakespeare was one of the greatest writers ever. He lived in England, about a thousand years ago. Mr. Greene taught about him when he taught school."

Jed's eyebrows raised. "That nig —" he stopped abruptly as he remembered. "I mean, Mr. Greene used to be a school teacher?" he asked incredulously.

Conn nodded. "He's very smart."

Jed thought about this. "Could I... could I come when y'all go fishin'?"

"Me, too, right?" Will reminded his sister.

"Maybe," Conn teased. She looked back over at Jed. "Yes. I suppose you can come, if you mind your manners."

Jed stared at her as if he had never seen anything quite like her. "Yes'm."

Conn giggled at being addressed like a grown-up. "Here's our road," she said as they came to their lane. "Thanks for letting me ride Jack," she said, giving the horse another pat.

"You're... you're welcome," Jed said, hesitantly, as if he wasn't certain he'd come up with the appropriate response.

Conn and Will climbed back on their bikes and pedaled away toward the house. Conn turned and gave one last wave before Jed disappeared from sight around a curve. By the time they got home, Elizabeth had lunch ready. She sent them to wash up. As Will chattered about their encounters with Abraham and Jed, Conn pretended to wash her hands so she wouldn't wash away the horsey smell on them.

"Pancake?" Elizabeth was saying as Conn came back into the kitchen. "There are a lot of Pancakes around here. I went to school with some of them. How old is Jed?"

Conn and Will looked at each other. "We forgot to ask," Conn said. "Mr. Greene said he could use a friend. Why would he say that?"

Elizabeth looked up. "I don't know. But if Mr. Greene said it, there must be a reason."

"Jed said our house is haunted," Will suddenly remembered. "It's not, is it?"

Elizabeth stared at Will for a few seconds before saying, "Of course not."

But Conn couldn't help noticing her mother had the same expression she'd worn last Christmas when Will came running home crying because one of the kids at school had laughed at him for believing in Santa Claus.

"He's real, isn't he?" Will had wailed.

"Of course he is," Elizabeth said, a little color rising in her cheeks.

Conn stared at her mother now as Elizabeth's cheeks burned scarlet and she quickly got up to clear the table.

❧

It was dark most of the time. Thirty-five Irish had been crammed into a hold fitted with thirty narrow bunks, fifteen on each side. There were two small wooden portholes on each side of the hold which could be opened in calm seas, but most of the time, the only light came from guttering wicks set in a few small dishes of rancid whale oil, producing a pungent smoke that intensified the other foul odors filling the hold: urine, vomit and feces, some it contained in overflowing buckets, but mostly swilling about on the floor of the dank hold.

The bunks were packed in so tightly that, when lying in one, it felt like a coffin, Caitríona thought. She and Orla and a few others shared bunks at the start of the ten week voyage, but soon, that wasn't necessary anymore. Seven died in the first two weeks. Still weak from years of near-starvation, many of them weren't strong enough to survive the inhuman conditions.

"I'll bet the horses and cattle have better," Caitríona complained bitterly one day as the hatch was opened and a basket of moldy bread and smoked sardines was lowered down to them.

Every few days, they were made to go above decks, at least those who could stand, so that they could carry up the waste buckets to be emptied over the side of the ship and the floor of the hold could be sluiced with clean salt water. The revulsion etched on the faces of the crew and the English passengers made Caitríona's face burn with shame. Keeping her eyes lowered didn't shut out the disgusted whispers. Sometimes the passengers didn't bother to quiet their voices. One young lady, wearing an elegant silk dress and sitting under a parasol, said loudly to her companions, "My father says the Irish should be exterminated, like rats. What their potato famine started, we should have finished. They breed like vermin; they spread disease like vermin. Really, I don't know why they're even on board."

Caitríona blinked back hot, angry tears as she felt Orla squeeze her arm, silently begging her not to say anything. She knew that if she made trouble, her ration and Orla's would be withheld, but her heart burned with a hatred such as she had never known.

One day, before they were ordered back down below decks, one of the sailors climbed out of the hold with another blanket-wrapped body draped over his shoulder. Without so much as a prayer or a reading of the poor soul's name, the body was dumped into the sea.

Caitríona and Orla both made the sign of the cross and whispered, *"Pater noster, qui est in caelis, sanctificetur nomen tuum; adveniat regnum tuum; fiat voluntas tua, sicut in caelo et in terra…"*

"His name was Cían O'Rourke," she wrote in her journal later. "He was to be one of the stable boys at Lord Playfair's plantation. I fear no one will ever know what became of him, or any of us. It will be as if we never existed."

ॐ

Conn's eyes opened. Groggily, she looked around and only slowly realized she was lying on the floor in her room. She wasn't on a ship; she wasn't surrounded by death. Picking herself up, she saw the scattered drawings of horses she had been working on before she fell asleep. Except it hadn't felt like regular sleep or like a regular dream. It had felt so real, she could almost smell the stench of the hold in her nostrils.

Downstairs, she heard her mother call her for supper. She rubbed her eyes, trying to get rid of the feel of the dream. "Coming," she called, but at her door, she paused, looking back at her bedroom as if… "Don't be daft," she whispered.

CHAPTER 6

"My goodness, Mrs. Mitchell," said Abraham in wonder as he looked the house over, "you've worked miracles here. And it's only been a few weeks."

Elizabeth had been steadily painting the house, one room at a time, so that gradually, the house was losing its musty, unlived-in smell.

"Thank you, Mr. Greene," she said, smiling proudly. "With a little more help from you, I think we'll make it through the winter." Her expression clouded at the realization that as May was coming to an end, she was planning — having to plan — to be here long-term. Maybe permanently.

"Anyway," she said brusquely, "there are a few things I still need your assistance with."

Conn and Will were delighted to have Abraham back with them. They helped him mix the mortar as he re-pointed the chimney stones where the ivy had worked its tendrils in between the stones, loosening some of them. He would not allow them to climb the ladder.

"It's too high," he said. But he did talk to them while he worked. The children lay on their backs in the grass, watching him high above them as they talked about books and stories they had been reading.

"Did your family read this much in New Mexico?" Abraham asked curiously.

"No," said Will. "We had television. But we don't get any channels here. Just radio."

Abraham laughed. "That is true, William. Our mountains block the television signals, I guess. And we're too far away from any large cities with television stations."

"Well, I always read a lot," Conn said with a superior air.

Abraham smiled. As he moved higher, it became more difficult to talk. He asked, "Are you sure there's nothing your mother could use some help with?"

Guiltily, Conn sat up and looked around. She wasn't sure why, but it wasn't as much fun helping Mom as Mr. Greene. They went to find her. She was on her hands and knees, her hair tied back with a bandana, scrubbing the wainscoting in the dining room. A thick layer of dust and grime had built up on the mouldings, and it all needed to be wiped down before it could receive a fresh coat of paint.

"Can we help?" Will asked.

Elizabeth looked up in surprise. "Wow," she said, dabbing some sweat off her brow with her forearm, "that's the nicest offer I've had in weeks."

She helped them fill buckets with clean soapy water. Will stayed downstairs with her while Conn went up to the second-floor hallway. She began working on the wainscot next to her mother's room, the spot she leaned against each night. Her mother had cried less frequently the last few nights. She never cried during the day, Conn realized as she scrubbed. Last night, Conn had stayed for only a few minutes and then crept back to bed.

She moved to the opposite bit of wall adjacent to the stairs. As she rubbed her wet rag along one vertical moulding, she heard a soft metallic click, and she realized that the inner panel of the wainscot had popped out toward her just a bit.

Glancing quickly down the stairs to make sure no one was coming up, she gently prized the door open and was startled to see, not a cupboard as she had expected, but a very narrow staircase built alongside the regular stairs, except it was hidden inside the walls. She crawled to her mother's room and looked. She had never realized that the wall in that room was inset more than the wall of the stairwell. She pushed the panel closed and heard it click shut. She clicked it again just to make sure the mechanism wasn't a fluke.

Her heart was pounding with excitement as she continued to clean her way down the hall. She kept pressing the mouldings, on the lookout for any other secret passages and wondering if her mother knew about the one she'd found.

She heard her mother moving around downstairs. "How are you doing up there?" Elizabeth called.

"Almost done," Conn called back. She finished cleaning the last few feet of wainscoting with no further discoveries, and carried her bucket downstairs.

Elizabeth frowned. "Are you okay? Your face is all red."

"I'm fine," Conn protested as her mother laid a hand on her forehead to see if she was running a temperature.

"Hmmm," said Elizabeth. "You don't feel warm."

"It's just the scrubbing," Conn insisted.

"Well, thank you both so much," Elizabeth said appreciatively. "That would have taken me the rest of today and tomorrow by myself."

"That's okay," Conn said, resolving to try and help her mother more often.

"Mrs. Mitchell?" came Abraham's voice through the back screen door.

"Come in, Mr. Greene," Elizabeth called. "Please, you don't ever have to knock or wait to be invited in."

He nodded deferentially as he entered the kitchen. "There's a storm blowing up, so I'm going to stop for today. The new mortar I already put in should set up before the weather gets here. I'll be back tomorrow if the storm passes."

❋ ❋ ❋

The storm did indeed blow in with so much thunder and lightning that they couldn't get a clear radio signal. The air became close and damp with the increased humidity.

"Just in case," Elizabeth said as she gathered candles and flashlights, along with a couple of old oil lamps.

"I'm sure glad we have a bathroom now," Will said as he and Conn brushed their teeth, listening to the downpour outside.

Lying in bed a little while later, Conn tossed restlessly, trying to find a cool spot on her sheets. She could smell the damp metallic air coming in through the screens as a steady rain fell, punctuated by continued intermittent flashes of lightning and low, long rumbles of thunder.

Elizabeth came in to kiss her goodnight. "Nana always told me it's cooler down here," she said, moving Conn's pillow to the foot of the bed. She laughed as Conn frowned at her skeptically. "Just try it."

Conn couldn't say it was any cooler with her head at the foot of the bed, but at last she fell asleep. She didn't know what time it was when she was startled awake. At least she thought she was awake. Someone had called her name. She lay quietly, listening in the dark for any sounds other than the rain and thunder. Just as she started to drift off again, she heard it.

"Connemara."

It was scarcely more than a whisper in the dark. Conn couldn't tell where it came from.

"Mom?" she whispered, her heart pounding a little faster. There was no answer. "Who's there?"

For a long moment, there was only the sound of the falling rain, then, "You must speak my name," came the whisper.

"But who are you?" Conn's heart was beating a more rapid tattoo in her chest now.

"You know me."

Conn frowned.

"You must speak my name," the whisper insisted again.

Conn thought. "Nana?" Silence. "Fiona?" she tried again, using her great-grandmother's name this time.

"Fiona knew me," said the voice. "And Méav. Elizabeth knew me as a girl, but not now."

Conn held her breath and then whispered, "Caitríona Ní Faolain." This time it wasn't a question. She knew.

A figure, misty and shapeless at first, appeared near the bed. Slowly, its form became more defined, more solid. As it did, the room's air became chilled.

"I know you! I've seen you in my dreams," Conn said as she recognized the wild curls, only faintly reddish now as if Conn were seeing her through fog.

"Yes," said Caitríona. "I've been coming to you in your dreams."

"Are you really Caitríona Ní Faolain?" Conn asked in awe.

"I am, child."

"Are you a ghost, then?"

"I am… a shadow," said Caitríona sadly.

Conn stared transfixed at Caitríona's image. "Why do you come to me?" she asked.

"I need your help," Caitríona responded.

Conn drew back a little. "What kind of help?"

Caitríona sighed and said, "Ah, Connemara, 'tis a terrible shame my father and I brought upon our family, and a curse as well."

"A curse?" Conn gasped. "What kind of curse?"

"A curse of deepest sorrow," said Caitríona. "Punishment for our sins." She closed her eyes and began, "Ill-fated shall your progeny be..."

Conn joined in, the words coming of their own accord, her mind filled with flashes of memory: an angry row in a little stone cottage, a feeling of terrible despair, an old woman's face, lit by a peat fire....

"... A child, ne'er soiled by hate or greed could
Bring forgiveness and healing to those long gone.
With the dead laid to rest, the living move on,
Freed at last by a soul blessed with light."

Conn looked at Caitríona as silence fell again. Caitríona opened her eyes and stared back.

"You are the one we have been waiting for, Connemara Ní Faolain."

※ ※ ※

Conn awakened to a crystal clear morning, washed clean of all heat and humidity. She sat up and looked around her room, confused. That... that dream, if that's what it was, had felt so real, as real as the other dreams she'd been having, as if she'd really had that conversation with Caitríona Ní Faolain. She dressed slowly and went downstairs to the kitchen where her mother was already making coffee.

"How about cereal this morning?" Elizabeth asked. "I don't feel like heating the kitchen up with the stove, it's such a lovely, cool morning."

Conn sat, unanswering, as if she hadn't heard.

"Connemara?"

Conn looked up. "Oh, um, cereal is fine. I can get it."

"Are you all right?" Elizabeth asked. "Are you coming down with something?"

Conn shook her head. "I'm fine." Instinctively, she felt she should not tell her mother about the previous night. She went to get a cereal bowl from the cupboard. As she poured milk over her cornflakes, she asked, "What ever happened to Caitríona Ní Faolain?"

"Why would you ask that?" Elizabeth asked.

Conn looked around. "This used to be her house. I know parts of her story, but what happened after she got here?" she asked, trying to sound no more than curious.

Elizabeth's gaze lost focus as she tried to remember. "She disappeared," she recalled.

Conn sat up straighter. "What do you mean she disappeared?" she demanded.

"Well, she came here with her daughter and a few freed slaves from the plantation. But a few years after they got here, she disappeared. No one knows what happened to her."

Conn gaped. "But what happened to her daughter, then?"

"Deirdre? She was raised by the colored people who came with Caitríona. And then when she got older, she married a man named McEwan. They stayed here and farmed this land."

"And they had Nana?" Conn asked.

Elizabeth nodded. "Yes, Nana — Fiona — was the only child who lived. I'm not sure how many other children they had. There's a cemetery somewhere nearby." She stirred her coffee absently. "Nana was born in 1893."

"And then Nana had your mother?"

"Yes," Elizabeth said, now frowning a little at Conn. "And my mother, Méav, was again the only one who lived to grow up. I think there were a couple of children who died as babies, but I know Mom had an older brother who died in a farm accident when he was thirteen. Then it was just Mom."

"Only one girl child shall survive," Conn breathed.

"What?" Elizabeth asked distractedly.

"And you never knew your father?" Conn asked.

"No," said Elizabeth. "Edward Cuthbert. My mother married him just before he was shipped overseas during the second World War. He was killed in action before I was born."

"And your mother?" Conn asked, though she knew this part of the story.

Elizabeth took a sip from her coffee cup. "She died of polio when I was five. And I came here to live with Nana."

"And then you met Daddy when you were in college?" Conn asked, never tiring of hearing this story.

"Yes," Elizabeth remembered with a misty smile. "I went to a women's college, Longwood, in Virginia. And my roommate had a boyfriend at the Naval Academy — one of many boyfriends, it turned out. Anyway, she talked me into going with her to a dance at the Academy to meet her boyfriend's roommate."

"And that was Daddy?"

Elizabeth nodded. "And that was Daddy. I think I fell in love with him before the first dance was over."

"And now..." Conn began, but stopped. "Our family has had a lot of sadness, hasn't it?" she asked quietly, the weight of her family's history settling around her like a mantle, linking her to all the previous generations who had lived in this house. If her conversation with Caitríona was real, all the sadness was down to this curse, whatever it was — the curse she was supposed to break somehow.

Elizabeth looked into her daughter's clear blue eyes. "Yes," she said, "I guess we have."

They stared at each other mutely for a long time, until Will made a sleepy entrance. Elizabeth took the opportunity to change the subject.

"What kind of birthday cake would you like?" she asked.

Conn's eyes lit up. She'd almost forgotten she would be eleven in, she counted quickly, ten days' time. June sixth. "Does it have to be a cake?"

"No," Elizabeth laughed. "Whatever you want. It's your birthday."

Will looked up from his cereal. "We could have chocolate pudding," he suggested.

Conn rolled her eyes. "You can have pudding on your birthday. I want cherry pie!"

"Cherry pie you shall have," Elizabeth said, getting a pencil and pad to make a list. "What about for dinner? Anything special you would like?"

Conn thought for a minute. "Barbequed chicken and corn on the cob?"

Elizabeth wrote. "It may be too early for corn, but I'll see."

"Can we invite Mr. Greene?" Conn asked.

Elizabeth looked up in surprise. "I think that would be very nice, but —" she said firmly, "you must tell him no present. We just want the pleasure of his company for dinner."

When Abraham returned later that morning to resume work on the chimney, Conn invited him to dinner.

"I would be honored, Connemara," he said, looking pleased. He mixed up a fresh bucket of mortar and was setting up his ladder when he asked, "Have you been fishing recently?"

"Yes," Conn said. "Fishing hooks work much better than a safety pin."

He chuckled. "Yes, I imagine they do. I haven't forgotten my promise to take you and William fishing one day, but it will have to wait until I have a little time off."

CHAPTER 7

After nearly twelve weeks, the ship finally reached America. A hurricane had blown it off-course to the north. Caitríona, Orla and the others took it in turns to look out their small portholes at the approaching coastline of Virginia. Caitríona was disappointed in the flat, sandy shores covered in scrubby pine trees as they entered the mouth of the James River. Once safely anchored at Newport News Point, the English passengers disembarked first. Then, the twenty-two surviving Irish were allowed above decks. They were made to stay on board while the remainder of the cargo was unloaded. After so many weeks in the dark, dank hold, the heat and humidity of Virginia in July were too much for Orla. She became faint. Caitríona half-carried her to a bit of shade against the wall of the pilot house and propped her up against the varnished wood.

Though the smell of fish and brackish water was not pleasant, anything was better than the putrid air they had been breathing. Leaving Orla to rest with some fresh water, Caitríona went to the rail to watch the activity below. This harbor was not as busy as Cobh, but there was a great deal of commotion nonetheless.

The trunks and crates were hoisted up from the cargo hold and transferred to waiting barges. Next, the horses and livestock were taken off the ship, some to waiting corrals, others taken directly to the barges on which they would travel the next leg of their journey. Only then were the Irish ordered off the ship and also dispersed to the various barges that would take them to their destinations and their new lives.

Clutching their small bags, Orla and Caitríona crossed the gang-plank to their assigned barge along with Ewan, the surviving stable boy, and Fiona. Seeing one another in daylight, Caitríona thought they all looked like the living dead — *like during the famine,* she thought. They had all lost a frightening amount of weight, their eyes sunken deep in their sockets, their cheeks hollowed, hair lank and lifeless. None of them had been able to bathe since before their voyage began. Orla clutched at the rosary hanging around her neck and whispered a prayer.

Patrick Doolan, the captain of the barge, looked upon them with a mixture of pity and revulsion. Shouting orders to his crew, he waited until the barge was safely underway up the river before ordering fresh water and bread for his passengers. He himself retrieved a smoked ham from his personal stores and cut slices off for them, the first meat they had had in nearly three months.

"Take it slow," he cautioned. "You'll be needing to give your bellies time to get used to real food again."

As they traveled along the river, Captain Doolan checked on them as often as he could. He arranged for a small tub to be filled with water and shielded behind a blanket so the women could bathe and wash their filthy clothing. Ewan was thrown into the river by the crew, mostly Irish themselves, as they put in at Williamsburg to take on some cargo. One of the men tossed him a bar of lye soap and shouted, "You'll not be comin' back on board till you smell human again!" When he was pronounced fit to climb back on board, the crew good-naturedly gave him a set of clothes, declaring his own beyond salvaging.

The effect Orla had on the crew was dramatic. Clean for the first time in weeks, her black hair rippling in the breeze blowing upriver, when her beautiful face broke into a smile, the men stopped what they were doing, watching her with their caps doffed until Captain Doolan roared at them to tend to business.

Caitríona scowled as she watched all this from where she sat curled up in a large coil of rope on the deck. She felt like a foreigner as they traveled up this river so broad she could barely see the opposite bank at times. The sky felt crushingly huge above them. She missed the sounds and smells and sights of Ireland so that she thought she would never feel whole again. Her loneliness was intensified as Fiona began helping the barge's cook, and Ewan was taken in by the crew and put to work. Orla, as often as not, was in the pilot house, keeping the captain company.

As the barge moved slowly upriver, it put in at Jamestown and other ports along the way, sometimes taking cargo on, other times off-loading some of what they carried, but the Irish bound for the plantation remained the only passengers.

Caitríona took to staying at the rear of the barge with the horses and cattle. Animals and humans alike were being besieged by hordes of mosquitoes and biting flies. It was enough to drive them all mad as they swatted and bit and stamped at the biting insects. Caitríona was soon given the job of keeping the animals calm, as she was the only one they would allow in their enclosure when the bugs were biting. She gently talked to them, patting the cattle and rubbing the horses' necks and faces, brushing them all with switches to keep the bugs off.

"You smell like a horse," Orla said, wrinkling her nose as Caitríona lay down beside her under the stretched tarp that served as a sort of tent. The barge had no actual sleeping quarters for passengers as it so rarely carried any. There was a small area in the cargo hold where the crew hung hammocks each night. Ewan slept there with the men, while Fiona shared the tarp with the girls.

"Good," Caitríona shot back as she smacked at a mosquito. "I'd rather smell like something honest and good from home than be prancing about making the men go all stupid."

Orla's fair cheeks flushed. "I don't prance… I can't help… Don't be mad at me, Caitie," she said, using the childhood nickname that never failed to cool Caitríona's quick temper.

"I'm not mad at you," Caitríona said grudgingly. "Only, I hate this cursed country."

Orla laid a calming hand on her arm. "Don't hate so. We're here now, like it or no. We may as well make the best of it. 'Tis no use constantly wishing to be somewhere we're not."

But Caitríona did wish. She wished so hard she thought her heart must burst from the strain of it — she wished for the cool sea breezes of Ireland, for the earthy smell of a warm peat fire, for the cleansing rains that fell soft on the fields leaving the hills and rocks glistening like jewels in the sun that would come out as the clouds scudded away. But all her wishing couldn't take her from this ugly land where she felt she was wrapped in a hot, wet blanket so that she never stopped sweating, where the river went on and on, the boredom broken only occasionally by the towns and ports they passed.

It wasn't until their eighth day on the river that they approached Richmond. The river traffic had been building steadily as the barges were diverted to the canal to get past waterfalls. Traffic slowed to the pace of the mules pulling the barges along the towpath, with regular stops at locks to raise or lower water levels. Captain Doolan told Orla that Richmond would be the biggest city the girls had ever seen. Even before they got to the actual outskirts, they could see mansions so grand they could never have imagined them before. Amidst the shouting of men on other boats and barges, the wharves of Richmond came into view. Looming over the river were huge brick warehouses and factories with black smoke churning from tall brick chimneys.

The barge eased up to one of the wharves where it was moored by enormously thick ropes. Caitríona went to the livestock to soothe them as they grew agitated with all the commotion. Standing in between two of the horses, she looked up to see Orla being helped off the barge by Captain Doolan. Taking his offered arm, she accompanied him down the dock, and was soon obscured from view by the dockworkers.

Caitríona was fuming by the time they returned to the barge a few hours later. Orla came to find her as the captain began shouting orders for them to shove off and get underway again, now carrying the last new cargo they would take on as they continued upriver to Scottsville, which was the closest the barge could take them to Lord Playfair's plantation.

"Caitríona —," Orla began excitedly, but her sister turned her back. "What's the matter with you?" she demanded.

Caitríona whipped around, glaring at her. "You're a traitor! That's what's the matter," she said waspishly.

"A traitor! And just how do you figure that?" Orla asked, getting angry herself.

Caitríona pointed accusingly. "You went off, with him!"

"The captain? He's old enough to be our Da," Orla sputtered. "He was a gentleman."

Caitríona knew she should stop — how many times had Mam told her she let her temper run away with her tongue? — but she heard herself saying, "Well, he wasn't looking at you like a daughter! And you… going off with him pretty as you please."

Orla's face reflected her anger as two vivid patches of scarlet rose in her cheeks, making her look as if she had been slapped. "That's a horrible thing to say!" she retorted as her eyes filled with angry tears.

Caitríona said nothing further, turning back to the horses and cattle as the barge resumed its slow way up the canal. Orla dropped a small paper-wrapped parcel on top of the water barrel kept near the enclosure. "Here's the chocolate the captain bought for you."

When Caitríona turned around, Orla was gone.

☙

"This is fun," Will said as he dipped his paint brush back in the can.

Abraham smiled. "You think so?"

Now that the chimney was repaired, the exterior of the house was receiving a much-needed coat or two of paint. After conferring with Elizabeth, it was decided that the children could help with the exterior painting while she continued working inside.

Abraham glanced down at Conn who was absent-mindedly running her brush over the same area repeatedly, apparently unaware that she was now wiping off more paint than she was applying. Squatting next to her, Abraham asked, "Connemara? Is there anything wrong?"

Startled, Conn looked at him. For an instant, her eyes were troubled and he had the feeling there was something she wanted to say, but then the moment passed and she smiled. "I'm fine. Just daydreaming. Mom always says I could get lost in my daydreams."

Abraham nudged the paint can closer to her, and said, "Then you could probably use some paint on that brush."

Conn laughed and burned red.

Abraham turned and paused. "I think you have a visitor."

She followed his gaze and saw Jed standing at the curve of the drive where it emerged from the woods.

"Hi," she called out.

"Hi," Jed said uncertainly.

"Come on up," she invited.

"We're helping Mr. Greene paint," Will said, stating the obvious as he had nearly as much paint on his elbows and hands as he did on his brush.

"Good morning, Jedediah," Abraham said congenially.

"Mornin', Ab —, I mean Mr. Greene," Jed said shyly.

Elizabeth appeared at the screen door, her auburn hair tied back in a ponytail, wiping her hands on a rag. "I thought I heard an unfamiliar voice," she said, smiling. "You must be Jed."

"Yes'm," Jed said, bobbing his head a little.

"We're about to break for lunch," she said. "Can you join us?"

Jed's eyes registered his surprise. "Yes'm."

"All right, then. Everybody wash up and we'll eat," Elizabeth commanded.

Jed followed Conn and Will into the bathroom, where they washed their faces and hands. In Jed's case, this effected a rather more dramatic change than it did in either Conn or Will, as several layers of dirt were washed down the drain as Jed rinsed the soap off.

He followed the others to the table where Elizabeth was pouring a glass of milk for each of them.

Jed looked around hesitantly as he waited for some signal as to what to do. He remained standing, mimicking Abraham, until Elizabeth was seated. Jed stared at her as if he had never seen a woman before.

"I hope you like egg salad, Jed," Elizabeth said as they all reached for the sandwiches piled high on a plate in the middle of the table.

He picked up his sandwich and took a tentative bite. His eyes widened in delight at the taste. "Yes'm," he said again as he tore off a huge bite. He glanced quickly at Abraham who gave a minute shake of his head, took a small bite of his sandwich and wiped his mouth with his napkin. Jed copied him and was therefore able to speak when Elizabeth asked him how old he was.

"I'm near twelve," he said. "In September."

"And who are your parents?" she asked.

"My ma's dead," he said, pausing in his attack on the sandwich. "When I was five. It's just me and my pa now. Sam, Samuel Pancake."

"I knew a Samuel Pancake," Elizabeth mused. "He's the right age to be your father."

"Connemara," said Abraham, "what are you reading now?"

"*Robin Hood*," Conn answered brightly. She turned to Jed. "Have you ever read it?"

Jed turned red and mumbled something indistinct.

"What an excellent adventure," Abraham said. "I think that was the first long book I ever read. Living in Sherwood Forest, archery contests, outsmarting the Sheriff of Nottingham — it certainly was exciting."

Will's eyes got big. "Can you read it out loud?" he asked his sister. "I want to hear the story."

"Me, too," Jed said before he could stop himself.

Elizabeth hid a smile as Conn said, "Sure. We can read a little every day if you want."

After lunch, Jed stayed to help as they resumed painting. By the end of the afternoon, all the clapboards under the front porch had a glistening new coat of white paint, while Abraham put the finishing touches on the dark green paint on the shutters.

"You three did an excellent job," Elizabeth pronounced when she came out to the porch to inspect their work. "Don't you agree, Mr. Greene?"

"I do, indeed, Mrs. Mitchell," said Abraham, as he began washing brushes in a bucket of turpentine.

"Can you stay to dinner, Jed?" Elizabeth invited.

"No, ma'am," Jed said politely. "I gotta get home." He hesitated as he descended the porch steps. "Can I come back tomorrow? To help paint?"

"Course you can," Conn said.

"All right," Jed grinned. "See y'all tomorrow."

Abraham watched him run down the drive and said, "That boy would thrive under a little kindness."

"What do you mean?" Conn asked.

"Well, after his mother died, his father began drinking," Abraham explained. "Jedediah just hasn't had contact with many people. Especially good people." He glanced at Conn and added, "That's what I meant when I said he could use a friend like you, Connemara. And you, William."

Will beamed.

"Well," Abraham said, straightening up as he wiped the clean brushes dry on a rag, "I shall see you all on the morrow."

"'Parting is such sweet sorrow,'" Conn quoted.

Abraham laughed, his face twisting grotesquely as his scar pulled. "Exactly."

CHAPTER 8

Conn woke early. She lay in bed listening to the plaintive call of a mourning dove perched in the elm tree outside her open window. Finally, a night with no dreams. Sleepily, she lay there enjoying the snuggly warmth of her covers despite the cool breeze coming through the screen when, suddenly, she remembered. She was eleven today! She stretched, shivering in anticipation. Slipping quietly out of bed, she dressed and crept out of the house before anyone else was up.

She headed past the barn, and through the pasture beyond to a knoll where she had discovered the most marvelous tree. It was an oak that, early in its life, had somehow split into three divisions sprouting from the main trunk so that there was now a flattened area nearly large enough to lie down in. It was the perfect place to read or think. This morning, she settled with her back against one of the smaller trunks. She could just see the roof of the house from here.

With the ivy gone and fresh paint going up and no more broken windows, the house didn't look haunted and neglected any longer. She giggled to herself, remembering that it was haunted, or at least she thought maybe it was. She still wasn't sure if her conversation with Caitríona had been real or not. If there was a ghost in the house, she hadn't reappeared since that night.

Sighing, she looked around and thought about how much she loved it here, and immediately felt guilty. It had been nearly a year since Daddy was deployed, but now... with him being MIA... Sometimes, when she was laughing or having fun, she would stop suddenly and remember. It felt wrong somehow to be enjoying herself, to be happy here, when he was out there....

She wasn't sure how long she'd been sitting in her tree, thinking about this when she noticed smoke coming from the kitchen stovepipe.

Mom was up, getting breakfast. Conn climbed down from the tree and ambled back to the house. As she entered the kitchen from the back porch, her mother was standing stock still in the middle of the room, her face as white as the towel hanging over her shoulder.

"Mom?" Conn asked, scared. "What's the matter?"

"Shhh."

Conn realized the radio was on and listened, too. The announcer was very somber, speaking of someone who'd been shot.

"Who?" she asked.

Elizabeth looked at her. "Robert Kennedy was shot last night. He died early this morning."

Conn's eyes got big. "President Kennedy's brother? But he's the one—"

She left the kitchen and went up to her room where she pulled an old shoebox out of the bottom drawer of her dresser. Elizabeth followed her upstairs and sat beside her on the bed, watching as Conn pulled her treasures out of the box: a feather from her parakeet who had died two years ago, a tarnished ring Mark had won at a shooting gallery at a county fair and given to Conn, school photos of each of her classes at Sandia. Folded at the bottom of the box were some newspaper clippings. Conn unfolded them.

"The day before Daddy — the day Martin Luther King was killed, Robert Kennedy was supposed to give a speech in a colored section of Indianapolis. When he heard about what happened, he gave a different speech to tell the people the news because most of them didn't know yet, and he asked them not to be filled with hate because he knew what it felt like to lose a family member. The papers said there were riots almost everywhere that night, but not in Indianapolis." She handed the clippings to her mother.

Elizabeth blinked back tears as she read. Turning to Conn, she looked at her daughter as if she had never seen her clearly before.

Conn's eyes searched her mother's. "I don't understand," she murmured. "How can people hate so much? How can they do things like this?"

"I don't know, honey," Elizabeth said, folding Conn in her arms and rocking her.

"I don't think we should do my birthday today," Conn said, her voice muffled against her mother's chest.

"Nonsense." Elizabeth held Conn by the shoulders and looked at her. "Especially today, we need to celebrate something good, and you are the best reason I can think of."

The rest of the day passed quietly, the atmosphere heavy with a sense of grief and foreboding. When Abraham arrived, they listened to the radio a bit longer as he hadn't heard the news. Elizabeth turned the radio off when Jed arrived. He could see that they were distressed, but he didn't know who Robert Kennedy was. Conn tried to explain, but, "He can't understand," she said to her mother and Abraham after lunch when Jed took his leave. "How do you make someone understand when he doesn't know who the Kennedys or Martin Luther King were?" she asked in frustration.

Abraham glanced at Elizabeth as Conn went back to her painting. "Has she always been like this, Mrs. Mitchell? I mean," he added hastily as if he feared his question sounded insulting, "I don't know too many children her age who would even know who King and Kennedy were, much less grasp the impact of their assassinations."

"I don't know many adults who feel things as deeply as she does," Elizabeth said thoughtfully, remembering the newspaper clippings Conn had cut out and saved. "And yes," she sighed, "she has always been like this."

It was mid-afternoon when Elizabeth announced, "We've worked enough today. Time to celebrate. Let's clean up."

She soon had Abraham firing up and tending the grill while Conn and Will were put to work shucking the early corn she'd been able to find.

"It's such a nice day," she said, "how about we move the kitchen table and chairs outside and make it a picnic?"

Before long, they were seated around the table under one of the elms, enjoying Conn's birthday dinner. Conn had to grin when her mother lit the eleven candles stuck in the crust of a cherry pie while everyone sang.

The sun dipped below the mountain ridge to the west as they finished their pie and ice cream. Elizabeth said, "Time for presents. Close your eyes."

Conn obeyed, and a moment later, she heard, "Okay, open them."

She opened her eyes to see her mother and Will holding a cane fishing rod with a reel and actual fishing line instead of string.

"We couldn't wrap it," Will said, bouncing in his excitement.

"Wow," Conn breathed, taking the rod in her hands. "It's beautiful."

She admired it for a few minutes, and then Elizabeth placed a small wrapped box on the table. "This is from Daddy," she said as Conn took her seat again. "He left it for you… in case he couldn't be here for your birthday."

Conn's throat got tight and her eyes burned as she blinked fast. Her hands trembled a bit as she fumbled with the wrapping. Inside the box was a folded note lying on top of a smaller velvet box. She opened the note and, in her father's handwriting, read, "For my favorite leprechaun. Love you forever and a day, Daddy." She lifted out the little velvet box and opened the hinged lid to reveal a gold Celtic cross suspended on a fine gold chain.

When Conn just sat there looking at it, Elizabeth asked, "Don't you like it?"

All Conn could do was nod. She closed the box gently without taking the cross out.

Abraham broke the silence by clearing his throat softly as he slid a package wrapped in plain, brown paper across the table to Conn.

"I thought we said no gifts," Elizabeth said sternly.

"Connemara did tell me that, Mrs. Mitchell," Abraham hastened to explain. "But this is an old book I had as a student, and I thought she might enjoy reading it."

Conn waited for her mother to nod her consent before carefully pulling the crinkled brown paper away from a small leather-bound edition of Longfellow's *The Song of Hiawatha*.

"Gosh," Conn murmured, leafing through the beautiful little book.

"You read that, and we can discuss it," Abraham said to her.

"I will," Conn said solemnly.

Inside the house, the telephone rang.

"You'd better answer it," Elizabeth smiled. "It's probably your grandparents."

Conn ran into the kitchen and answered. It was Grandma and Grandpa Mitchell who lived in Indiana, near Indianapolis. Conn talked to them for a few minutes, and then covered the receiver, calling out, "Mom, they want to talk to you."

Elizabeth closed her eyes for a moment, and muttered, "Better get it over with."

Conn helped Will and Abraham carry the remainder of the dishes in from the table, and then the chairs while they could hear Elizabeth saying, "We're fine here, Mother… No, we have people nearby to help out… We miss you, too…"

"We stopped by to see them on our way here from Sandia," Conn explained to Abraham. "They wanted us to stay with them."

Abraham's eyebrows raised a little. "Didn't you want to stay with them?"

Conn shrugged. "They're really nice, but I think they would have driven Mom crazy."

Abraham smiled. "I think your mother likes her independence."

Conn grinned. "I think you're right."

Elizabeth sighed as she hung up. "I think I talked them out of coming for a visit, but I'm not sure."

"I'd better be going," said Abraham as he and Elizabeth carried the table back into the kitchen. "I can't remember a nicer evening."

Outside, they could hear the sound of tires crunching on the drive. Mr. Walsh climbed out of his truck and was on the back porch, walking uninvited into the kitchen before he saw Abraham.

"Well, Elizabeth, Abraham," he said genially enough, but there was no amusement in his eyes as he spoke. "What are you doing here this time of the evening?"

Elizabeth stepped forward. "Mr. Greene was our guest for dinner. What brings you out here, Mr. Walsh?"

Mr. Walsh tore his gaze away from Abraham and held an envelope out to Elizabeth. "This come special delivery. From the gov'ment," he said. "Thought I ought to bring it out to you straight away. Didn't know when you might be comin' into town next."

"Thank you," said Elizabeth, taking the envelope from him.

Mr. Walsh stood there, clearly hoping she would open it in front of him, but she set the envelope on the kitchen counter. "Thank you, Mr. Walsh, and be sure to say hello to Mrs. Walsh for me."

With another curious glance at Abraham, Mr. Walsh nodded and left, letting the screen door bang shut behind him.

"Oh dear," Elizabeth said, turning to Abraham. "I hope this won't make trouble for you."

Conn looked up at him. His scar was a vivid red.

"No more than I'm used to," he said, but his words were clipped.

Looking down at Will and Conn, he smiled crookedly. "Good night, William, and happy birthday to you, Connemara." He bowed his head slightly in Elizabeth's direction. "Thank you again for dinner, Mrs. Mitchell."

As his pickup truck rumbled away, Elizabeth picked up the envelope. She pried the flap open as she sat at the table, and shook out the folded sheet of paper within. Her hand flew to her mouth as she read the typewritten page.

"Mommy?" Will leaned against her. "What does it say?"

Elizabeth's voice shook as she said, "Daddy's a POW in Vietnam." Her hands dropped to her lap as the letter fluttered to the floor. "He's alive."

CHAPTER 9

A few hours later, Conn sat on the floor outside her mother's room. She'd known, after the letter, that this would be a crying night. She listened to the soft sounds of her mother's sobs, feeling as if the past twenty-four hours had aged her so that she felt much older than eleven. She felt weary with the weight of all that had occurred — the world had changed and she had changed. She realized how childish she'd been to have never questioned that Daddy was alive as her mother clearly had. She ran her fingers over the Celtic cross now hanging around her neck and whispered a prayer for him.

She thought, too, about her visions and dreams of Caitríona Ní Faolain. She wasn't sure she had actually talked to a ghost, but the words of that awful curse had played over and over in her head. Everything her mother had told her of their family history supported the curse as being real. For some reason, it had not occurred to her previously that, if it were indeed true, then she would live, but Will would not. It made her feel guilty about all the times she'd wished she didn't have a little brother. And it wasn't just Will. All the husbands and fathers had died young as well. This realization drove home to her the urgency of ending the curse, but how? She was at a loss to think of what she could do that could change anything.

She sat with her elbows braced on her knees, staring at the wall with her forehead pressed into her hands as she thought. Suddenly, she remembered — the hidden staircase. Caitríona's appearance that night had driven it from her mind. She tiptoed to her room and retrieved a pair of sneakers and a flashlight. As quietly as she could, she pressed on the moulding and popped the panel open. She clicked her flashlight on and shone it down the narrow stairwell. It looked sturdy enough. She descended a couple of steps and turned back to the panel where she could see a handle on this side of the door for pulling it shut to engage the locking mechanism. She decided tonight was not the night to test whether it worked from this side. She pulled the door most of the way shut, but didn't latch it.

Sitting on a stair, she quickly laced up her Keds, and then, step by step, she descended. Pausing every now and again to brush cobwebs off her face, she got to a point where the hidden stairwell turned back on itself and continued descending in the opposite direction. It continued this pattern every eight to ten steps so that she soon guessed she was well below the level of the house, but almost directly under the point where she had started.

The stairs ended at a dirt floor and what looked like a rocky tunnel. The air down here was old-smelling and a little musty. The darkness seemed to swallow the meager light from her flashlight so that only a few feet at a time were illuminated. She could see timbers reinforcing portions of the tunnel roof. As she began walking along the tunnel, she realized she'd lost track of the twists of the staircase so that she had no idea which direction she was going. The tunnel twisted to the left and went downhill for a bit, then leveled off. She walked for a few minutes before coming to an intersection where the tunnel forked and a wooden ladder led up into blackness that her flashlight couldn't penetrate.

She stood for a moment, undecided, and then started climbing. The ladder ended at a trapdoor. She turned her flashlight off, her heart pounding, and pushed cautiously on the wooden trapdoor. Poking her head up a few inches to see over the edge, she couldn't see anything at first in the darkness, but just as she was getting ready to turn the flashlight back on, she realized there was dim light coming in through grimy windows. She was in one of the stalls in the lower level of the barn. Why in the world would someone have built a tunnel connecting the house to the barn?

Conn carefully lowered the trapdoor and climbed back down the ladder. She considered exploring one of the forks of the tunnel, but realized her flashlight was getting dim. She decided to go back, and was soon glad she had, as her flashlight was nearly dead by the time she got back to the narrow, twisting staircase. She listened at the top to make sure her mother and Will were still asleep, and then crept back to her room.

She lay awake for a long time, staring at the ceiling. She was beginning to realize that her dreams of Caitríona were not like regular dreams. She could remember every detail, more like a story she had read than a dream which faded upon waking. And they seemed to be unfolding like a story, sequentially. What would they reveal about this house and the purpose of that tunnel? She felt again that sense of urgency, as if the sooner she got through the dreams, the sooner a solution to the curse might present itself.

ᑤ

Within a few days of leaving the barge, Caitríona thought she might rather be on the river again. They had been met in Scottsville by Burley Pratt, a fat, jovial man who had been sent to collect them and the cargo bound for Fair View. The girls and Ewan drove the horses and cattle along behind the heavily-laden wagon while Fiona rode with Burley. Occasionally, they passed large fields of tobacco being worked by slaves, the first Africans any of them had ever seen. The blacks stood to watch them pass, their dark faces impassive under broad straw hats.

The Irish soon wished they had such hats as they trudged along, their fair skin burning and blistering under the Virginia sun. Orla fashioned a bonnet of sorts out of a shawl; it was hot, but it kept the worst of the sun off her head and shoulders. Caitríona stubbornly refused to follow suit. She had barely spoken to her sister since Richmond. Orla, ordinarily not as proud or mulish as her sister, was holding her ground this time, as Caitríona's words had stung deeply.

"The mosquitoes here are almost as bad as they were on the river," Caitríona complained as she swatted miserably at the bloodsuckers attacking any bit of exposed skin they could find.

"It's all them freckles," laughed Burley from the wagon. "The skeeters sees 'em and thinks it's a party."

He was an older, affable man who liked to laugh and joke. He told them that Hugh Playfair, Lord Playfair's son, had sent a message that he was in America, but would be staying in Richmond indefinitely, and didn't know when he would arrive at the plantation.

"How much longer till we get to the bloody plantation?" Ewan grumbled on the afternoon of the second day marching through the hilly country of what they'd been told was Buckingham County.

"Good Lord, boy," chuckled Burley, "we've been on Fair View land since yesterday noon. Five thousand acres, give or take. Mostly bright tobacco, with some corn and wheat and cattle."

"Five thousand acres?" gasped Caitríona. She couldn't conceive of so much land being owned by one man. "And we were sold for five." Her expression darkened as her anger and resentment were ignited anew.

"We'll be at the house afore supper," Burley told them. "I bet you ain't never seen nothin' like it."

Sure enough, late in the afternoon, an imposing three story stone house loomed into view. It was sheltered by enormous sycamore trees, their aged trunks a stark white under their thick leafy canopies. As the wagon approached, other servants, both black and white, emerged from the house and the barns to greet the newcomers.

One tall, gangly African opened the corral gate. The cattle and horses rushed in, eagerly crowding the water trough.

Burley climbed down off his wagon, surprisingly agile for such a large man. "Welcome to your new home," he said proudly, sweeping an arm around at the house and grounds. "Ever'body," he said to the other staff, "these folks are just over from Ireland, and they've had a rough time of it. This," he clapped Ewan on the shoulder, "is young master Ewan, what works with horses. You'll be workin' with Nate, there," he said, pointing to the tall black man still standing near the corral.

"And the ladies are come to work in the house," he said leading Fiona, Orla and Caitríona over to a plump woman. "This is Ellie, my wife," he said, kissing her cheek. She swatted at him good-naturedly. He introduced Fiona and the girls.

"Land sakes," said Ellie, "they're just girls, Burley. What was he thinkin', takin' such young things so far from their home?"

She clucked and fussed like an old hen, looking the girls up and down and said, "They're so thin. They need fattenin' up."

"Well," laughed Burley, "we brought some help for that, too. Fiona," he said, pulling her forward, "is the master's new cook. This is Dolly, our old cook," he said, indicating an older Negro woman standing behind Ellie.

From the dour expression on her face, Dolly was not happy about having a new cook on the place. Fiona, shrewd enough to realize the value of having allies rather than enemies in the kitchen said, "Sure, and I was afraid there'd be nobody here to show me how to cook the strange things I've heard you eat in America."

"Oh, not so strange," Burley laughed. "But maybe not fancy enough for Lord Playfair or his son."

Caitríona caught a glimpse of movement at a window. She saw a pale-faced man standing there a moment before he moved away. Burley followed her gaze, and said in a low voice, "That's Mr. Batterston, the overseer. You'd best stay clear o' him."

Turning back to the wagon, he called out, "Come on, all. Let's get things unloaded and get these folks a decent meal."

They quickly unloaded the wagon, and Orla, Caitríona and Fiona were shown to the servants' quarters on the third floor. The house, having been modeled after Lord Playfair's country house in Ireland, had not taken Virginia's weather into consideration, as the upper floor was sweltering. Forcing open the small window in the room she would share with her sister, Caitríona gasped, "How is anyone supposed to sleep in this?"

"Maybe it gets cooler at night," Orla said without much conviction. She sat on one of the narrow beds. "At least we each have our own bed. We won't have to share anymore."

Caitríona blinked back sudden tears as a wave of homesickness overwhelmed her. "I never minded sharing," she said softly.

CHAPTER 10

Conn pushed her way through some brambles, grimacing a little as tiny thorns tore at her arms and bare legs. She had spent the last couple of days wandering much of Nana's property, searching for the family cemetery. She carried a small notebook and pencil, making a rough map and taking notes on the birds and animals she saw. Will had accompanied her one time, but he got tired quickly and wanted to go back home. Emerging from the tangle of brambles, she found herself on what looked like an old road through the woods, now little more than two dirt tracks meandering among the trees.

She began following the old road and, as she rounded a bend, was startled to see Jed coming toward her, mounted on Jack.

"Hi," Conn said brightly.

"Hi," he returned, looking around as if hoping to escape.

"Where've you been?" Conn asked. "We haven't seen you for a couple of days. Hey…"

Jed tried to turn his face away as Conn drew near, but she had already spotted his black eye. "What happened?" she asked, laying a hand on Jack's shoulder. "Your father?" she guessed when Jed didn't answer.

"It's nothin'," he said with a shrug. "He was drunk. He didn't mean it."

Conn looked up at him, not sure what to say.

"What are you doin' out this way?" Jed asked.

"I'm hunting for our family cemetery," Conn said.

Jed pointed. "It's just down the road a piece," he said. He edged Jack over to a tree stump and said, "Climb up."

Conn scrambled up behind Jed, and they ambled down the lane, dappled sunlight and green shadows rippling over them. Within a few minutes, they came to a small clearing on the left side of the lane. Conn slid down off Jack's back and climbed over a low rock wall forming an uneven boundary around the tiny graveyard. She walked among the gravemarkers there, mostly stone, though a few were made of wood. Jed followed her in, looking as if he couldn't leave fast enough.

There was one newer grave, with long, unmown grass growing patchily over it. The stone marker read, "Fiona Faolain Cook, born 12-1-1893, died 1-23-1967." She took out her notebook and began making notes as she wandered among the graves.

"What're you doin'?" Jed asked.

"I want to know more about my family," Conn answered absently as she wrote. "Does your family have its own graveyard?"

"Yeah, but we don't go there," Jed said.

"Why not?"

Jed looked at her as if this should be obvious. "'Cause they're dead. That would be as crazy as goin' to the witch's house."

Conn stared at him. "What witch's house?"

Jed stared back to see if she was serious. "The witch. The Peregorn witch. Nobody in their right mind goes to that old lady's house."

Conn frowned skeptically. "You're crazy. There's no such thing as witches," she said as she resumed her wanderings.

"So," Jed said, deciding to let the subject of witches go, "what do you think you're gonna learn here?"

"I'm not sure," Conn said. "Maybe what things were like for them." She thought about the curse. "We can learn why they came here, or how they struggled, or why bad things happened to them. They worked hard to make a life here, to make it better for us. Seems we should get to know them."

Jed seemed to think about this as he followed her around. Most of the names could still be read, though not all the dates could. She found an older section where the headstones were so weathered that she had a hard time making out the names carved in the pitted limestone.

Off to one side were three stones. She realized these stones were carved more crudely, different from the others. She knelt before them, running her fingers over the irregular depth of the gouges in the stones, trying to read them. Each had a single name. "Henry," she read. The next one was "Ruth." She moved to the last grave. "Hannah," she whispered. Suddenly, she felt a familiar chill and the hairs on her arms and

neck stood on end. She was overcome with an onslaught of emotions —
overwhelming sadness and terrible anger. The feelings passed as quickly
as they had come, leaving her woozy and disoriented for a moment. She
stood weakly.

"What's the matter?" Jed asked from a little distance away. "You
look like you saw a ghost." As soon as he said it, he looked around fearfully. "Let's get out of here," he said nervously.

Conn followed him back over the stone wall. He helped her climb
back up on Jack's back, and he shimmied up behind her. Nudging Jack
into motion with his heels, he turned the horse's head into the woods
along a path Conn had never been on.

Presently, they emerged from the woods into a field that Conn recognized. Within a few minutes, they were in her backyard.

"Hello, Jedediah," Elizabeth said, carrying a basket of wet sheets
out to hang on the line. "What have you two been up to?"

"Jed helped me find our cemetery," Conn said. "I found Nana's
grave."

"Really? I never went there often when I was a girl. I doubt I could
even find it again," Elizabeth said. "How about we go after lunch?"

Conn slid down off Jack's back and Jed reined him toward the lane.

"And where do you think you're going, young man?" Elizabeth
asked with mock sternness as she fastened the sheets to the line with
clothespins.

"Ma'am?"

"You can turn your horse out to graze in the barn pasture, and
come get cleaned up for lunch," she said. "And be sure to pump some
water for him."

"Yes'm," Jed grinned.

Conn opened the gate for him as he slipped Jack's bridle off and
hung it on a fence post. It took their combined weight to pump water
into the trough, and then they hurried inside.

"Whoa!"

Elizabeth had just noticed Jed's black eye. His face flushed pink as
she held him gently by the chin to get a better look. Her expression was
angry, and he looked at her as though he were afraid she was angry with
him. She released him and said quietly, "Go wash up."

When Conn and Jed came back into the kitchen, Will was already seated at the table, propping his GI Joe against his milk glass. "Hi, Jed!" he said.

"Hey," Jed smiled, taking the chair next to him.

"William," said Elizabeth.

Will immediately moved his GI Joe to the floor next to his chair.

After a quick lunch, they all set out by foot for the cemetery. As Jed led them into the woods, Elizabeth pointed off to their right. There, deep in the shadows and so covered by undergrowth that Conn hadn't even noticed it when she and Jed passed by earlier, was a small log cabin.

"This is the house the slaves used," Elizabeth said. "Well, I guess they weren't slaves anymore. I should say the black people who came with Caitríona."

Next to the cabin was a towering ash tree which had been splintered at one time by a lightning strike. Both tree and cabin were being slowly consumed by an expansive trumpet vine, just beginning to show its red blooms. The little house stood near a large outcropping of rock jutting up out of the ground with a small, clear spring trickling out of a crevice and splashing along a shallow streambed into the woods.

"The black people didn't live in our house?" Conn asked.

"Well, back then, our house was only the log part where our bathroom is now," Elizabeth explained. "All the rest was added later. And it wasn't considered proper for white people and black people to live together."

"So, only Caitríona and Deirdre lived in our house?" Conn asked. "What happened to Deirdre after Caitríona disappeared?"

Elizabeth thought about this. "I'm not sure. Nana told me the colored people who came with Caitríona raised Deidre, but I never really thought about where they lived. Come on, let's get to the cemetery," she said.

They picked their way through the undergrowth back to the path and within a few minutes were in the small graveyard.

Elizabeth stood in front of Nana's grave, her hand pressed to her chest. "She was a wonderful person," she said softly.

She wandered and found her mother's grave. She called Conn and Will to her and they read, "Méav Faolain Cuthbert." She knelt for a moment, pulling a few weeds. "We need to take better care of this place," Elizabeth said. "Plant some flowers, mow the grass. Once the house is done."

They walked on and found a headstone carved with "Deirdre Faolain McEwan."

"This was Caitríona's daughter," said Conn.

"Yes," Elizabeth said. "Nana's mother." Near them were seven small headstones bearing names and dates of children aged four days to thirteen years. "Oh." She put her hand to her mouth. "I didn't realize so many had died. It's so sad."

Conn thought again of the curse, and turned to watch Will who was following Jed as he climbed a nearby tree. She thought what it would be like to be standing here staring at Will's name on one of these stones....

⌘

Caitríona looked up as she heard a small moan from the corner of the parlour where Orla was scrubbing the floor on her hands and knees.

"Haven't you ever cleaned before?" Ellie had asked, trying to mask her exasperation when neither of the girls seemed to know how to do anything needed in the large house.

"Of course we cleaned," said Caitríona indignantly, but how to explain that their entire house in Ireland could have fit inside the plantation house's dining room, and that their floor had been flagstone that needed only daily sweeping, not polished wood planks that needed scrubbing and waxing and buffing.

Caitríona hurried over to Orla now. "Stop," she commanded. "I've got the parlour rug rolled up. I'll take it outside and hang it. You do the beating and I'll do the floor."

Orla nodded, wiping sweat from her pale brow. She was not regaining her strength as Caitríona was. She barely ate, stating she wasn't hungry, but Caitríona, for the first time since she was little, had as much to eat as she wished. She left Orla in the deep shade of a large chestnut tree, beating the dust out of the rug while she went back inside and took up the scrub brush. She was glad her appetite was good, for the work was neverending. Though the master was not there, the house was kept in constant readiness for him. Ellie had a carefully arranged schedule of rooms to be cleaned from ceiling to floor. Each room had soaring windows that had to be cleaned, curtains and rugs to be beaten, walls to be wiped down, furniture dusted, fireplaces swept and floors scrubbed. And the silver and the china and the paintings and the sculptures — it all had to be wiped down regularly. The only break in the routine came on Sundays, when they only worked a half-day. Orla and Caitríona kept the Sabbath faithfully by reading a bit from their mother's prayer book each week as there was no church anywhere near.

Caitríona took her bucket of dirty water outside to dump and refill at the pumphouse. As hard as their work was, the slaves' work was harder. The house slaves had to do the laundry, empty and clean chamber pots, cut and carry firewood, kill and clean the chickens or whatever was needed for meals that day. They hauled water and tended to the large vegetable garden near the house. The rest of the slaves, nearly a hundred of them Burley said, worked the fields. Mostly they were weeding now as they waited for the tobacco to mature to the point where the large aromatic leaves were ready to be cut and hung to dry.

The girls and Fiona had been surprised to find themselves the only occupants of the third floor, though there were ten rooms in each of the four halls forming the house's square contour. Burley and Ellie shared a small set of rooms off the kitchen, while Mr. Batterston had his own small house nearby.

The slaves occupied a small colony of cabins built under a copse of willow trees. Other than Dolly, only a handful of them were assigned to work in the house. A woman named Ruth was in charge of them. She was also the plantation's healer, and knew how to make poultices and salves as there were no doctors nearby. Ruth's husband, Henry, was the plantation's blacksmith and woodworker. He had his own shop not far from the stables.

"Dolly says it was their grandparents who came from Africa, most of them," Fiona told the girls. "She's been here for ten years. Her last master sold her husband and son to someone else."

"They split a family?" Caitríona asked in disbelief. "Could they do that to us?" she asked Orla.

"I don't know," Orla replied fearfully.

"She also said," Fiona whispered dramatically, "that Batterston has sold slaves. She says he lords it over all of them when the master ain't here, and nobody dares say a word."

Though the girls had heeded Burley's advice and avoided contact with Batterston as much as possible, he had the disconcerting habit of silently appearing in unexpected places, so that the staff never knew how long he had been watching them. His eyes were such a pale gray that they sometimes appeared to be colorless, giving the illusion of pupils staring from the eyes of a predator.

Despite the girls' efforts to steer clear of him, inevitably, "I was told you both read and write," he said one day.

They both jumped at the sound of Batterston's cold voice behind them as they cleaned and dusted the china in the hutch.

"Yes," said Orla.

"Tomorrow, you will assist me with the plantation's accounts," he said, looking at Orla.

After that, Orla was tasked once a week to spend the morning in the house's study, helping him to update the plantation ledgers.

"He's cheating on the accounts," she whispered to Caitríona one night in their room.

"How do you know?"

"Ellie told me they got five sacks of flour and four tons of coal two days ago, but he had me enter four sacks and three tons in the book. I'm guessing he sells the extra and pockets the money." Orla's eyes were big and scared.

"Does he know that you know?" Caitríona asked.

Orla shook her head. "No. I didn't let on that I knew anything."

"Well, don't," Caitríona urged. "And don't say anything to Burley or Ellie or anyone."

"But he's stealing!" Orla protested.

"I don't care," Caitríona said emphatically. "He's dangerous. And if Lord Playfair or his son cared, they'd be here, wouldn't they?"

As if in response to that criticism, a courier brought word the next day that Hugh Playfair and his party would be arriving within the week. The entire household went into a frenzy of activity.

Ellie came to check on Orla and Caitríona as they cleaned and aired the bedrooms. Their sleeves were rolled back as they wiped down windows and woodwork. "Don't forget to change the linens," she said to them.

"But no one's slept in these," Caitríona protested.

"Don't matter," Ellie said. "The bed needs clean sheets."

A moment later there was a timid knock on the door. "Excuse me, Miss."

Caitríona looked up to see a Negro girl about her own age standing in the doorway. Her skin was a beautiful chocolate brown, but her eyes were blue.

"I was sent for the sheets," said the girl, pointing to the pile of linens they had just stripped off the massive four-poster bed.

Caitríona nodded dumbly and the girl scurried in to gather the sheets. She had difficulty getting everything gathered into her arms — one piece or another kept falling back to the floor. Caitríona rushed forward to help.

"What's your name?" she asked as she helped tuck the loose ends into the girl's arms.

"I'm Hannah, Miss."

℘

"Conn!"

Conn blinked and looked around. She was kneeling in front of Hannah's grave marker, though she couldn't remember walking over here.

"Connemara Faolain!"

She turned to her mother, who was standing with her hands on her hips.

"Are you deaf? Or just ignoring me?" Elizabeth asked with mild frustration.

Conn got to her feet, feeling a little giddy. "Sorry, Mom. I'm coming."

They all walked back to the house, Conn barely aware of what the others were saying. She'd never had one of these dreams without being asleep before, and it left her feeling disoriented. She didn't know who Hannah was, but somehow, she was the key to everything.

CHAPTER 11

Conn woke, blinking in the early morning light of her room. It took her a moment to realize where she was. She felt as if she had barely slept. Her mind was still filled with the vision from the cemetery yesterday. She pressed her hands to her eyes. These glimpses into Caitríona's life were starting to feel more real than her own.

She kicked off the covers and got dressed. Downstairs, she stumbled into the kitchen where her mother was pouring herself a cup of coffee and Will was already eating breakfast.

"Well, good morning, sleepy head," said Elizabeth. "I was getting worried. You never sleep this late." She looked more closely at Conn and frowned. "Do you feel all right?" she asked, noting the dark circles under Conn's eyes.

Conn shrugged wordlessly. The truth was, she didn't feel all right, but it wasn't anything physical.

"Sit down," Elizabeth commanded as she poured Conn a large glass of orange juice. "Drink this while I make you some breakfast."

A few minutes later, as Conn ate her eggs and toast, Elizabeth said, "I need to go into town for groceries and a few other things. Do you want to go, or would you rather stay home?"

Conn looked up in surprise. "Could I stay here?"

"Sure," Elizabeth said, looking over her grocery list. "We might be a couple of hours, though. You'll be okay?"

"Verily, I say to thee, fair lady, I shall take me to my room and my books," said Conn dramatically.

"All right, Robin Hood," Elizabeth laughed, "but no arrows in the house."

Conn laid her hand over her heart. "Upon my honor."

From her bedroom, Conn watched the Nomad drive away in a cloud of dust. She quickly went down to the pantry and retrieved one of Nana's old oil lamps. It took her a minute to figure out how to pry up the glass chimney so she could light the wick.

She went back upstairs and clicked open the hidden panel. From inside the stairs, she pulled the panel shut, and heard it click. She gave it another tug and saw it pop back open. Reassured, she closed it and descended the steps to the tunnel. Walking more quickly than she had the last time, she came to the ladder that led up to the barn, and the place where the tunnel forked. Undecided for a moment, she finally chose the left-hand fork.

This tunnel went on much longer than the distance from the house to the barn, and began sloping downward as the floor and walls became more rock than dirt. Small rivulets of water could be seen dampening the walls here and there, and small puddles sat in depressions in the rocky floor. The tunnel gradually grew in height and width until, suddenly, it opened into an immense cavern.

Holding her lantern high, Conn realized she could not see the top of the cavern. She began following the wall to her right, passing fissures in the rock face that looked as if they could be openings to other tunnels, but she refrained from exploring them. She suddenly wondered if she would recognize the entrance to her own tunnel, and hurried back to it. Thinking she needed to mark this tunnel somehow, she pulled off one of her socks and laid it at the entrance.

She resumed her exploration of the cavern, following the perimeter wall. She had no idea how far she had gone when she came to a shaft of sunlight shining deep within a fissure set high in the wall. Climbing up, slightly off-balance because she still held the oil lamp in one hand, Conn ventured into the cleft and saw that the sunlight was creeping in through a tall vertical slit in the rock. She stepped through the slit and found herself standing on an outcropping of rock overlooking a small house being overgrown by a red flowering vine. It took her a moment to realize that she was staring down at the old slave cabin.

Clambering carefully down the rocks, descending with the spring water as it tumbled down to the streambed, Conn looked up and realized that the fissure opened at such an angle that no one would ever guess at the hidden entrance she had just come through.

Turning back to the cabin, she tried to imagine why Caitríona and the others would have needed this network of tunnels. She picked her way through the undergrowth blocking the path to the cabin, some of the trumpet vine tendrils looping themselves around her legs as if trying to pull her in. It took her a few minutes to locate the door of the cabin. Pushing down on the rusty iron latch, she shoved hard. The door shuddered open on noisy hinges, allowing her in at last.

The cabin was only one room. In one corner was a framed-in bed with a thin straw-filled mat. A stone fireplace took most of one wall, and there was a roughly made table with a few rustic stools gathered around it. Pewter plates and cups still sat on the table, almost as if the last inhabitants had been interrupted at a meal and had never returned.

"What happened to all of you?" Conn whispered as she sat down on one of the stools and looked around.

Deciding not to return home via the tunnel, she blew out her oil lamp and left the cabin, pulling the door shut behind her. Meandering through the woods, as she came within view of the house, she could see both the Nomad and Mr. Greene's pickup. She quickly hid the oil lamp in the barn and ran to the house.

"Halloo!" she called out as she entered the kitchen.

Abraham's expression reflected his amusement as he carried a box of groceries into the pantry, replying as he did so, "Halloo, thyself."

"Mr. Greene was wondering if you would like to go fishing with him this afternoon," Elizabeth said as she laid out bread for sandwiches.

"I get to go, too!" Will said excitedly.

Elizabeth, immediately reading the jealous expression on Conn's face, said, "Do you want to go or not?"

"Yes!" Conn said, echoing Will's excitement despite her irritation that he'd been invited before she was. "What about Jed?"

"Well," said Abraham, "I'm not sure where Jedediah is today. We'll take him next time. Go get your fishing rod and we'll leave as soon as you're ready."

"I shall return forthwith."

Abraham turned to Elizabeth. "Forthwith?"

He laughed as she replied only with a raised eyebrow that spoke volumes.

✳ ✳ ✳

A short while later, as they all munched on their sandwiches, Abraham drove them to a river the children had never been to.

"Where have you been working, Mr. Greene?" Will asked as they bounced along the dirt tracks.

"I've been over at the Peregorn place," he said, "rebuilding some of their calving sheds."

"Peregorn," Conn said, trying to remember where she had heard that name. "Jed! He said something about a Peregorn witch."

Abraham glanced over at her. "Connemara, I know you are too intelligent to believe the local superstitions."

Conn looked up at him. "But why would people say that? And who is this person?"

"Miss Molly Peregorn lives by herself, and likes it that way. People always like talking about anyone different, but Miss Peregorn is a good woman."

Conn mulled this over, but her thoughts were interrupted when Abraham stopped the truck.

"Here we are."

Conn waited with her new fishing rod, trying to be patient as Abraham got Will set up on the bank with an artificial lure tied to his fishing line.

"This," he said as he tied a buggy-looking fly to her line, "looks to the fish like a grasshopper that has fallen into the water."

They waded out into shallow water, and he showed her how to cast the hopper, mending her line when the current dragged it so that the hopper floated along naturally. Conn was not prepared for the excitement of a trout rising to snatch the fly. She could feel the tension on the line as the fish swam into deeper water.

"Don't jerk," said Abraham calmly, standing beside her. "Just keep the line tight and let him go a bit."

The line felt like a live wire as the cane rod bowed under its tension. Conn felt connected to the fish.

"Now, slowly, try reeling him in," Abraham instructed.

It took a few minutes, but soon, the fish was swimming around Conn's legs as she stood knee-deep in the river. Abraham bent to hold the trout by its belly just under the surface of the water.

"It's a brook trout," he said, turning it so she could see the beautiful slash of brilliant red behind the gills.

"It's the biggest fish I ever caught!" Conn said as Abraham dislodged the hopper from the corner of its mouth.

"Do you want to keep it?" he asked.

She nodded excitedly and turned back to the river while Abraham strung the trout on a line and went to check on Will.

✳ ✳ ✳

It was nearing dinner time when Elizabeth heard Abraham's truck rumble up to the house. The screen door slammed and Conn ran through the kitchen and up to her room.

"What happened?" Elizabeth asked in alarm as Will and Abraham came in.

"I'm afraid it's my fault," said Abraham gravely. "Connemara wanted to keep a fish she caught. I assumed she knew that meant we would be cleaning and eating it."

"Oh," said Elizabeth, comprehending. "I'll talk to her. She'll be okay."

Abraham nodded with an apology and took his leave as Will thanked him.

Elizabeth went upstairs and found Conn curled up on her side, facing the wall. "Hey," she said, sitting on the bed and rubbing Conn's back. "Mr. Greene told me about your fish."

Conn sniffed and said nothing, trying to forget the sight of the once-beautiful fish lying in her hands, limp, lifeless, its cloudy eye staring up at her.

"Around here, most people go fishing or hunting so they can eat what they catch," Elizabeth said. "Sometimes we have to kill to stay alive."

"Like Daddy?"

"What?" Elizabeth asked, startled.

Conn rolled over, wiping her eyes. "Isn't that what Daddy was doing in Vietnam?"

Elizabeth steadied herself with a deep breath. "For some people, that is their mission. To kill the enemy. Your father was flying rescue missions. But… he would kill if he had to."

Conn's blue eyes bored into her mother's soft brown ones. "Would you?"

"How did we go from a fish to this?" Elizabeth joked uncomfortably.

"Would you?" Conn repeated.

Elizabeth returned Conn's gaze for a long moment. "If I had to, yes. To protect you or Will, then I think I could kill."

Conn blinked and looked away. "I don't know if I could," she said softly. "I don't want to kill anything, ever again."

"Why have you been thinking about this?"

Conn shrugged, but said nothing.

Elizabeth gave her a shake. "Come on. Your brother is being way too quiet downstairs. He's probably eating everything he can get his hands on."

CHAPTER 12

"Aren't they beautiful?" Will whispered, his face illuminated only by the yellow glow of the fireflies in his jar.

He hadn't always thought so. A few nights after Conn's birthday, they were outside as dusk fell and they noticed the first tiny flickers of light out in the yard.

"They're ghosts," Will said fearfully when they first appeared. "Jed said our house is haunted and has strange lights."

"They're not ghosts," Elizabeth laughed. She caught one and showed them. "See? They don't bite. They just want to fly around and light up the night."

She got two old jars and showed the children how to punch air holes in the lids. She sat and watched as they ran around collecting fireflies.

"Maybe they're really faeries," Conn whispered dramatically as they held their jars up, entranced by the glowing insects within. "And they can do magic and transform after we're asleep."

"Faerieflies," Will breathed, and ran off to collect some more.

After a while, Conn came and sat beside her mother in the grass.

"Got enough lightning bugs?"

Conn nodded, leaning against her mother. "I wish Daddy was here with us."

Elizabeth kissed the top of her daughter's head. "Me, too."

She held up her jar. "They won't live very long in here, will they?"

"No," Elizabeth said, ruffling Conn's hair. "We'll let them go after Will's asleep, okay?"

✳ ✳ ✳

The day after Abraham took them fishing, Will came to his mother. "I don't feel good."

When Elizabeth took his temperature, it was a hundred two. She made him go back up to bed and brought him some hot soup for lunch. He didn't feel like eating and by late afternoon, his fever had climbed two more degrees.

Alarmed, she called the general store. "Mrs. Walsh? This is Elizabeth Mitchell. Who is the local doctor? Jenkins…" she repeated as she jotted the name down. "Do you have his number? It's my son."

Conn watched anxiously as her mother wrote the number down. As she hung up, Elizabeth berated herself for not having made contact with the doctor sooner, but none of them had been sick since they came here. At Sandia, the base had its own clinic and doctors any time they got sick.

Within an hour, Dr. Jenkins had arrived at the house. He was short and round, with wire-rimmed glasses that he kept pushing up to rest on his forehead above his bushy eyebrows. Conn waited in the sitting room while he and her mother went upstairs. It seemed they were up there a very long time before she could hear them coming down the stairs, talking in low voices.

"You're sure he got all the boosters?" Dr. Jenkins was asking.

Conn came to the staircase and crouched there, listening.

"Yes," Elizabeth said firmly. "He got the last one when he was five. After my mother… both children got the vaccine."

"Well, I can't be sure of course, and it would be rare, but…"

"I thought polio was eradicated," Elizabeth said in a dazed voice.

"The vaccine did nearly eradicate the disease, but we haven't eradicated the virus. It's been years since I treated an active case around here," Dr. Jenkins said. "Just to be safe, I would keep your daughter away from him for a couple of weeks."

"What can we do?" Elizabeth asked as she and the doctor went through the swinging door into the kitchen.

Conn crept around the staircase to the swinging door and listened as the doctor sighed, "I wish there was something we could do. Just give him plenty to drink, children's aspirin to get his fever down. We'll have to wait it out. You have my number. Call me if his fever climbs, otherwise I'll be out tomorrow to check on him."

Conn came into the kitchen as the doctor drove away. Elizabeth sat heavily, her head in her hands. Conn came to the table and sat also.

"He's not… he's going to be all right, isn't he?" she asked.

"Of course he is," Elizabeth said sharply, tossing her hair back and wiping her cheeks. She pushed up from the table and went to the refrigerator. Pouring a large glass of orange juice and another of water, she said, "You'll get yourself something to eat?"

Conn nodded.

"I don't want you going near his room," Elizabeth said firmly. "Do you understand me?"

"Yes, ma'am," Conn said solemnly.

Elizabeth gave her a small smile before going upstairs.

Conn made herself some peanut butter crackers and went out to the front porch where she sat on Nana's swing and munched, feeling horrible, but not in a sick way. She kept thinking about all the times she'd been mean to Will, and made up her mind to be nicer to him. She was trying not to think of the curse, but found herself angrily wondering what Caitríona had done to call such wrath down upon the rest of the family.

Her mother was still upstairs with Will as dusk fell. The first fireflies of the evening glowed out in the yard, and a sudden thought came to Conn. She retrieved her jar and collected a couple dozen lightning bugs. She took them up to her room and climbed out her window onto the porch roof. Walking carefully to avoid the seams in the tin roof, she squatted low and placed the jar of fireflies on the sill of Will's window. Stealthily, she crept to her window and crawled back inside. Out in the hallway, she heard his excited gasp.

"Mom! Look! A jar of faerieflies!"

Conn heard the screen slide open and then shut again.

"You know," said Elizabeth, "I've heard it said that faerieflies can make wishes come true. Let's make a wish together for you to get better fast, shall we?"

Out in the hall, Conn closed her eyes and wished with them — wished with all her heart.

"And we thought there was a lot of work before these useless lumps got here," Caitríona grumbled in the dark as she and Orla dressed.

"Shhh," Orla hissed. "Someone will hear you."

"I don't care if they do," Caitríona replied, though she dropped her voice to a whisper. "We were up past midnight, waiting till they didn't need us anymore, and now we're up again at four while they won't get up until noon."

Hugh Playfair and his party had arrived at Fair View the week prior. He had come with his friend, John Willingham, and their wives, as well as a personal servant for each of them. Apparently, they had thought a trip to America would be a bit of a lark, but had obviously expected more of the comforts to which they were accustomed.

Playfair, mopping his handsome face with a scented handkerchief as he stepped from the carriage, had looked upon the house for the first time and declared, "At least Father had the sense to bring some civilization to this God-forsaken wilderness."

"I thought we would never get here," said Amelia, his wife, as the footman helped her from the carriage.

"But this is charming," said Willingham, looking with delight at the trees and grounds.

"Honestly, John," said his wife Ernestine, petulantly. She had already removed her bonnet and was fanning herself vigorously with a vividly-colored silken Chinese fan. "How you can find this delightful is beyond me."

Nearly as bad as the ladies and gentlemen were the servants who accompanied them, arriving in a second carriage loaded with trunks and cases. Addressed only by their surnames, the two men and two women clearly saw themselves as much higher-ranking than Burley and Ellie, whereas Orla and Caitríona were little more to them than the Negroes. Almost as soon as they arrived, they established that they were to be the intermediaries between their masters and mistresses and the plantation staff.

"If you need to speak at all," said Johnson, Hugh Playfair's valet, "you will speak to me. Under no circumstances are you to address the master or his lady or their guests." As he gazed disdainfully at the assembled household staff, he said, "I realize you may not be trained in the running of a proper English house, but we will maintain the standards to which his Lordship and Master Hugh are accustomed."

"How long d'you think it'll take 'em to realize they're in America, not England?" Burley asked under his breath when they were dismissed.

One of the first changes implemented upon their arrival was Mrs. Playfair's insistence that none of the Negroes was to come further into the house than the kitchen. "They're heathen," she had pronounced, not bothering to lower her voice the first time she had encountered one of the slaves coming into the bedchamber to collect the chamber pots. "For all we know, they could be cannibals waiting to attack us in our sleep. I won't have them near me. Let the others do their work," she said, pointing dismissively in Orla's direction.

And so, Orla and Caitríona were tasked with bringing the bed linens, clothing, chamber pots and other items downstairs so that the slaves could clean them. This, in addition to their normal cleaning of the house, and now having to ferry trays between the kitchen and the dining room added hours to their day as dinner often lasted late into the night.

The personal servants took rooms in other halls up on the third floor, segregating themselves from the girls and Fiona.

"Have you heard them talking about 'the Irish' the way they would talk about 'the hounds'?" Caitríona complained. "As if we can't hear or understand them."

"Aye," agreed Orla conspiratorially, "but it also means we can overhear things they don't think they need bother to keep quiet."

"Like what?"

"Like the fact that the master doesn't want to be here," Orla said. "He barely looks at the ledgers Batterston shows him. He'll never realize Batterston is stealing from him. His wife was trying to convince him over breakfast to go back to England, but he said his only chance of inheriting property, as the second son, is to stay here and do as his father wishes."

"Well, seeing as it is likely to be his inheritance, you'd think he would want to be taking better care of it."

The days passed, bringing, if possible, even more heat and humidity. Tempers flared, especially Caitríona's, as successive nights of three to four hours' sleep took their toll.

"Here," said Fiona in a harassed voice one morning as the bell rang yet again. "Would you be taking this breakfast tray up to Mrs. Playfair before they yank that bloody bellcord out of the wall?" She thrust the loaded tray into Caitríona's hands and shooed her from the kitchen.

Balancing the tray on one arm, Caitríona raised her other hand to knock on Mrs. Playfair's door. She listened to the voices within while she waited impatiently to be summoned inside. Finally, she heard, "Come."

Mrs. Playfair's maid, Feathers, was fluffing her mistress' pillows behind her as she sat up in bed. Feathers took the tray from Caitríona and positioned it over Mrs. Playfair's lap.

"Wait," Feathers commanded as Caitríona turned to leave. "Take this while you're here," she said, picking up the chamber pot and shoving it roughly into Caitríona's arms so that the contents slopped down her front. Feathers' mistake was to smirk, igniting Caitríona's already short fuse. Without thinking, Caitríona threw the remainder of the contents back at her, lid and all.

"You're no better than I am, you little squint," Caitríona said furiously.

Feathers let out an irate close-mouthed scream as she stood, holding her arms out, her face scrunched up against the disgusting mess dripping from her face and hair, covering her front. Mrs. Playfair leapt out of her bed. Her eyes narrowed maliciously as she approached. Caitríona lowered her eyes, though her face burned scarlet with her temper.

"You will be punished for that," said Mrs. Playfair, taking care to step around the mess on the floor. "But first, you will clean this up. And you will apologize to Feathers."

Caitríona's eyes blazed as she raised them defiantly to stare at her mistress. "I'll clean, as I've always done. But I'll not apologize to her, or to you or to anyone!"

By the time Caitríona had the bedroom floor cleaned up, it seemed the entire house knew of what had happened. Batterston himself volunteered to cane her. He took her out to the flagstoned area between the kitchen and the pumphouse while the household staff was assembled to witness her punishment. There, he ordered Orla to unbutton the back of Caitríona's dress and peel it away. Caitríona stood in her shift, proudly refusing to cover herself as she focused defiantly on some far point. Ten times, Batterston raised the cane, making it whistle through the air as he whipped the supple branch across her back so that it bit into the flesh, cutting as it hit. She refused to cry out. Only her trembling gave away the pain she was feeling. Not until she and Orla were alone did she cry.

"Will you never learn to control your temper?" Orla asked a short while later up in their room as she gently bathed the welts and cuts on her sister's back with cool water.

There was a timid knock on the door. Orla opened it and quickly pulled Hannah inside. "What are you doing up here?" Orla asked. "You know the mistress forbade any of you to come into the house."

"I know," said Hannah, "but..." her gaze lit on Caitríona's back, and Caitríona knew that Hannah understood first-hand the pain she was feeling, "we have a salve. Ruth makes it. It'll help the cuts heal."

Caitríona, wiping hastily at her tear-stained cheeks, murmured, "Thank you."

Hannah turned to leave, but stopped and said, "If you had cried down there, he would have stopped sooner. You made him mad."

Despite her pain, Caitríona's eyes flashed angrily. "I'll never cry in front of him."

Hannah looked at her with those curiously light-colored eyes. "I know." She cracked the bedroom door and checked that the hall was clear before slipping out.

Orla dipped her fingers into the pungent dark ointment and applied it gingerly to one of the deeper cuts on Caitríona's back. Bracing herself for it to sting or burn, Caitríona felt instead a gentle deadening of the pain. As Orla applied the salve to more of the lash marks, she felt Caitríona's body begin to shudder. "What is it? Am I hurting you?"

"I want to go home," Caitríona sobbed.

"Hey," Elizabeth said, shaking Conn gently.

Conn opened her eyes and realized she was still sitting in the hall.

"Come on," Elizabeth said, pulling Conn to her feet. "You need to get to bed." She walked Conn down the hall, helped her change into pajamas, and then tucked her into bed. "Good night, my love," she said, kissing Conn on the forehead.

"Night, Mom," Conn said sleepily.

But as soon as the door shut, Conn was wide awake, listening. Once she was sure the house was quiet, she sat up in bed. Concentrating with all her might, she whispered, "Caitríona Ní Faolain."

To her gratification and dread, Caitríona's shape appeared. Her reddish curls blew gently as if ruffled by a light breeze.

Conn stared at her for several seconds. "My brother is sick," she said at last.

Caitríona's eyes lowered. "I know."

"He may die."

"I know."

"This is your fault!" Conn said angrily.

Caitríona's misty outlined grew a little fainter as she said, "Yes."

"I need your help if I'm to put an end to this," Conn said beseechingly.

"'None may help her in her quest'," Caitríona quoted.

"But how am I to find the answer to this?" Conn asked in frustration. "I have no idea what to do."

"You will," said Caitríona. "You've already begun."

Conn thought hard. "The hidden stairs and the tunnel?"

Caitríona nodded.

"So you do know about them!"

"Yes."

"And who was Hannah?" Conn asked.

Caitríona faded almost completely at this.

"Don't go!" begged Conn. Caitríona's shape reformed. "Who was she?"

"She was everything."

CHAPTER 13

It was still dark out when Conn was awakened by the sound of car tires skidding on the gravel of the drive. She jumped out of bed and ran to her window. Dr. Jenkins was retrieving a large plastic bag from his trunk.

Cracking her bedroom door open as he came upstairs with her mother, she heard Elizabeth say something about "one o six" and the doctor saying he'd brought ice. She opened her door wider as they emerged from Will's room, Dr. Jenkins cradling Will in his arms.

"You stay there," Elizabeth ordered, her eyes red and puffy. "Close your door."

Conn obediently closed her door and went back to her bed. A few minutes later, unable to stand the suspense of not knowing, she got dressed and climbed out her window onto the porch roof. From there, she was able to grab an overhanging limb of the elm tree next to the house, and climb down to the ground. Once down, she crept around the house to the back porch where she could see through the kitchen door into the bathroom. Her mother and the doctor were both kneeling next to the tub; she guessed Will must be inside. The doctor was scooping ice from his bag into the tub. She couldn't hear what they were saying.

Suddenly, she heard more tires crunching, and headlight beams swept around the back of the house. Before Conn could escape off the back porch, an old-fashioned truck pulled up and parked. An older woman got out — at least Conn thought it was a woman. She had very short silver hair, and wore dungarees and a men's shirt. She was carrying a basket as she let herself onto the back porch. Conn crouched unnoticed in the dark as the woman knocked and let herself into the kitchen. Conn crept to the door and peered through the glass. She couldn't hear what was said, but Elizabeth looked up as if in shock for a moment and then got to her feet and hugged the older woman. Conn watched as the woman went to the stove and stirred the fire while Elizabeth returned to the tub with the doctor. The woman took a jar out of her basket and poured the contents into a pan, heating the mixture on the stove. A few minutes later, she ladled some of it into a cup and brought it to Elizabeth. The doctor propped Will up and they spooned some of the mixture into his mouth. His face was red and sweaty and his eyes were closed.

Conn watched as her mother mouthed her thanks to the woman, and turned her attention back to Will. The woman moved the pan to a back burner and headed toward the door, barely giving Conn time to back away. Closing the kitchen door behind her, the woman turned and looked at Conn, staring at her wordlessly for several seconds before letting herself through the screen door. Conn resumed her vigil at the kitchen door as the woman drove away.

Daylight slowly lit the porch and the yard beyond, and still Elizabeth and Dr. Jenkins crouched next to the bathtub, occasionally trying to get Will to take more of the brew Molly Peregorn had brought. For Conn knew now that that's who the old woman must have been. At one point, Elizabeth came out to the kitchen to make coffee. Dr. Jenkins came and sat heavily at the table, rubbing his tired eyes and sipping his coffee while Elizabeth kept vigil. Conn could see the clock on the wall creeping toward noon. Her stomach growled, but she did not dare go in to get something to eat. She was sitting on a box on the porch, dozing, when she was startled awake by an exclamation from inside.

Jumping up, she went to the kitchen door, and saw Dr. Jenkins holding a thermometer up for Elizabeth to see. Elizabeth covered her face with her hands and cried, her shoulders shaking. Dr. Jenkins lifted Will out of the tub and they carried him back upstairs.

Conn knew that sooner or later, her mother would realize she wasn't in her room anymore, but she didn't have the energy to climb back up the tree. A little while later, the kitchen door creaked open.

"You must be starving," Elizabeth said. "Come on in and eat."

Conn obeyed and said, "Sit down. I'll make us some eggs."

"You can do that?" Elizabeth asked.

"I think I can," Conn said. She poked the fire back to life, adding a few sticks of wood and put the big cast iron skillet on the burner. The eggs broke and weren't very pretty, but soon, there were three plates with eggs and toast sitting on the table. Dr. Jenkins joined them as they all ate ravenously.

"Is Will going to be okay now?" Conn asked hopefully.

Dr. Jenkins shrugged. "We won't know for a while yet. But his fever is down, and that's a good sign." He drained his coffee cup and yawned. "Keep an eye on his temperature. I'll be back later today to check on him."

※ ※ ※

It was nearly a week before Will's fever broke for good.

"Well, there is no paralysis," Dr. Jenkins pronounced on the third day. "I'm fairly certain it would be manifesting itself by now if there were going to be any."

Elizabeth spent nearly all her time in Will's room, still not allowing Conn to see him. She grudgingly allowed her to continue delivering a fresh jar of faerieflies to Will's windowsill each evening, after inspecting the porch roof herself to see that the pitch was very shallow.

"You'd better be careful, young lady," she warned with mock sternness. "If you fall, you're going to be grounded until you're old enough to vote."

For Conn, the focus on Will meant that she had hours and hours to herself. Once she knew Will was out of danger, she decided she needed to do some more exploring. She shook a few dollars of change out of her piggy bank and rode her bike down to Walsh's.

"How's your brother?" Mrs. Walsh asked, breaking away from a whispered conversation with a woman Conn didn't know as Conn entered the store.

"He's getting better, thank you," Conn replied politely.

"What can I get you?" Mrs. Walsh asked as she wiped her hands on her apron.

"Nothing," Conn said vaguely, noticing that the other woman was staring at her covertly. "I'll just look around."

"You help yourself, then," Mrs. Walsh said as she returned to restocking the candy in the glass case.

Conn wandered around the store, enjoying the breeze from the ceiling fans cooling her sweaty face. She could hear the soft hisses as the women resumed their whispered conversation, but she couldn't hear what was being said. In one of the back aisles, she found what she sought.

"Well, I've got to run now, Betty," said the strange woman in an unnaturally loud voice as Conn carried her finds up to the counter.

"What in the world are you going to do with all these?" Mrs. Walsh asked nosily as Conn deposited an armful of items on the counter. She had a box of colored chalk, a dozen candles, a small oil lamp and a bottle of oil.

"The chalk is for Will, and we needed extra candles and lamps in case we lose electricity," Conn fibbed. "Oh, and can I have two licorice sticks, please?" she added as she counted out her change.

As Conn wheeled home, steering carefully to avoid tipping the oil lamp balanced in her basket, a familiar-looking pickup rumbled into view.

"Hello, Connemara," said Abraham, braking to a stop and leaning out the window.

"Mr. Greene!"

"How is William?" he asked.

"How did you know he was sick?" Conn asked, tilting her head.

"Your mother called Mrs. Walsh to ask for the doctor," Abraham laughed. "That means the whole county knows."

"Well, the doctor says he's getting better, but he's still in bed."

"And your mother?"

"I think she's a wee bit tired," Conn said, "but she's all right."

"Please give them both my best," he said as he put the truck in gear.

"I will, Mr. Greene. Good day to you."

Conn pedaled on as the truck drove off. When she got home, she rode straight to the barn. Pushing hard against the lower level door, she was able to inch it open enough to squeeze through with her bag. She went into the second stall. She was fairly certain this was the one with the trap door and, sure enough, when she brushed the straw away, there was an iron ring set into the wood. She pried the ring up and tugged. The trap door came away and propped against the back wall of the stall. She started down the ladder, grabbing her bag as she descended.

Peering into the darkness, she saw a small chink in the wall. She wedged the bag inside and climbed back up the ladder to hear her mother calling her from the house. Quickly, she lowered the trap door, scattering straw over top of it, and squirmed back through the barn's sliding door.

"Coming!" she yelled as she ran around the corner of the barn.

"Where have you been?" Elizabeth asked as Conn ran to the back porch.

"I've been to Walsh's," Conn said. "Would you be needing something?"

"Would I be needing something?" Elizabeth laughed. "What are you reading now?" Conn blushed and laughed, too, but didn't answer. "I just wanted to have lunch with my daughter," Elizabeth said. "I've hardly seen you lately." She opened the refrigerator. "How about BLTs?"

"That sounds good," Conn said. "I'll make the toast. Oh, I almost forgot," she remembered, pulling a few crumpled envelopes from the back pocket of her cut-offs.

"Gee, thanks," Elizabeth said, flipping quickly through the slightly damp missives.

"I ran into Mr. Greene," Conn said as she put two slices of bread into the toaster. "He asked me to give you and Will his best."

"That's nice of him," Elizabeth said.

"Do we have any more jobs for him?"

Elizabeth shook her head as she laid bacon strips in the frying pan. "None that we can afford right now."

"Oh." Something occurred to Conn that she hadn't considered before. "Are we poor now?"

Elizabeth turned to look at her. "Noooo...," she said slowly. "But we have to be careful. We spent a lot of money getting the bathroom and chimney done, and... we have to be careful."

Conn thought about this as the bacon cooked. A few minutes later, they sat munching on their sandwiches. "Will is going to be all right, isn't he?"

Elizabeth nodded. "It looks like it."

"Do you —" Conn began, but paused, biting her lip as she tried to figure out how to phrase things. "From what you told me, only one girl has lived from each generation since Caitríona. Have you ever noticed that?"

She watched her mother closely to see if this triggered any sense of memory in her expression. Elizabeth frowned as she thought. "You know, I think you're right," she agreed, but with no telltale blushing or other sign that she was in any way familiar with the wording of the prophecy. "I never realized it before. Boy, if you believed in such things, you could think our family has some kind of curse or something, couldn't you?" she said with a small shake of her head as she cleared the table.

CHAPTER 14

By October, the tobacco was all harvested and the Playfair party had quit the plantation to return to Richmond.

"I must declare, I'm glad to see the backs of them," Ellie confided to Orla.

All the household staff seemed to breathe easier, for not only were the English gone, but Batterston as well. The tobacco leaves had been dried in the enormous drying sheds, and now wagon loads of the leaves were ready to be sold. He personally accompanied the wagons to the river to see the harvest loaded onto barges and brought to Richmond where he was tasked with getting the best prices at auction.

"But he won't be back for weeks," Burley told Caitríona. "So, until then, we can relax a bit."

One particularly fine autumn morning, after she had finished her morning chores, Caitríona went out to the stables. They had only had glimpses of Ewan since arriving at Fair View. She nearly didn't recognize him as he had grown three or four inches.

"Caitríona!" he said in welcome as she stepped into the stable's cool interior. Curious at the arrival of a stranger, the horses approached to stare at the newcomer, their graceful necks arching over stall doors. She patted their faces, tugging at forelocks as she murmured to them. She realized how much she missed being around animals.

"How are you, Ewan?" she asked, stopping to pat a gray Arabian mare.

"I'm good," he said, shrugging philosophically. "Life here is as good as it would have been back in Ireland, maybe better."

Caitríona's face darkened. "For you, maybe."

Ewan tilted his head as he considered her. "For you as well, I'm thinkin'."

"How so?" she asked, frowning.

"Well, back home, you would have been expected to marry and start having babies. And I'm thinkin' that's not what you would want."

Caitríona laughed bitterly. "Hell would freeze over first."

"So," he said, spreading his hands. "Me mam told me before I left Ireland, 'tis my lot to clean up horse shit, no matter where I am. 'Tis yours to clean a house. At least here, you're not cleanin' for a husband and a bunch of squallin' babies."

She smiled in spite of herself. "Do you always look at things so?"

He grinned. The mare nudged Caitríona, almost knocking her over. "Would you like to take her out?" he asked. "She's needin' to be worked."

Caitríona's eyes opened wide. "Could I? I haven't been on a horse since we left home."

"Sure, but don't you be tellin' anyone or it's both our necks." He turned toward the tack room. "Side saddle?"

She scowled at him, and he laughed. A few minutes later, she was astride the high-spirited mare, cantering across the fields. Topping a grassy knoll, she drew the mare up. For a moment, the rolling terrain stretching out before her could have been Ireland. The mare stamped impatiently, and Caitríona let her have her head, rising in the stirrups as the little mare gracefully jumped a gully without so much as a break in her stride. Cantering up the next hill, they neared an enormous oak tree with a wide, spreading canopy.

A figure lying in the grass under the tree leapt to its feet with a small scream. The mare shied sideways, unseating Caitríona who managed to hold onto the reins as she landed flat on her back. The impact knocked the wind out of her. All she could do was lie there, waiting until her lungs could pull air back in. A figure loomed over her.

"Are you all right, Miss?"

Caitríona could not answer immediately. When at last she could force air into her lungs, she sat up, wincing a little.

"Miss?"

It was Hannah, looking very frightened.

"I'm fine, Hannah," gasped Caitríona when she could talk. "And you don't have to call me Miss. My name is Caitríona."

"Yes, Miss."

Caitríona smiled. "What are you doing out here?" she asked as she got to her feet. She spotted a piece of parchment lying in the grass.

"Nothing," said Hannah, snatching it up and hiding it behind her back.

Caitríona looked at her in puzzlement. "You can trust me. I'm not going to tell anyone."

Shyly, Hannah held out the parchment. One side was covered in drawings, small sketches of flowers, faces, birds. Crammed into the spaces between the drawings were random letters. Caitríona squinted at them, but they didn't spell anything.

"The drawings are beautiful," she said, "but… were you trying to write something?"

Hannah lowered her eyes and said nothing.

"Do you know how to read and write?" Caitríona asked.

Hannah shook her head. "We're not allowed. It's against the law."

Caitríona looked back down at the parchment in her hand. "Would you like to learn? I could teach you."

Hannah raised her eyes and her face was transfigured. Caitríona had never seen her look so happy. She was beautiful.

"You would do that?" Hannah asked.

Caitríona blinked and looked back down at the parchment, nodding. "No one should be able to tell us we're not allowed to learn."

"Us?" Hannah repeated, puzzled.

"Slaves."

Hannah laughed. "You're not a slave, Miss."

Caitríona let the mare graze as she sat down in the grass. Hannah sat beside her. "Lord Playfair bought you," Caitríona said, "and he bought Orla and me as well. Our father sold us to him."

Hannah frowned, trying to grasp this. "I never heard of a white person who was a slave. What would happen to you if you ran away?"

Caitríona picked up the piece of charcoal Hannah had been using and began writing as she replied, "I don't know. But we work for no money. What would we do? Where would we go? And for us, Lord Playfair owns the land our family lives on and farms in Ireland, so if we displease him, he will punish them."

She looked over at Hannah. "How old are you?"

Hannah shrugged. "I don't know, Miss."

"Doesn't your mother celebrate your birthday?"

"I don't have a mother, Miss," Hannah said softly. "I was sold when she died having another baby. I've been here with Ruth as long as I can remember."

"I'm sorry, Hannah," Caitríona said, laying a hand on Hannah's shoulder.

Hannah stared down at Caitríona's hand. "You have very strange ideas, Miss," she said, shaking her head.

"Like teaching you to read and write?" Caitríona smiled. "This," she said, holding up the parchment, "is the alphabet."

❦

"Where do you think you're going?"

Startled, Conn almost fell over in the grass as she balanced on one foot, trying to put her Keds on. She turned to see her mother watching her through the screen door. "Uh…"

"Hi!"

Conn whirled around in the other direction to see Jed loping up the drive, his fishing pole in hand. Gritting her teeth in exasperation, she thought quickly. She turned to her mother and said, "Jed and I are going fishing."

"Aren't you forgetting something?" Elizabeth asked.

"Ummm…" Conn stalled, trying to think of what she'd forgotten.

"Your fishing rod?"

"Oh." Conn grinned sheepishly and came back onto the porch to retrieve her rod from the corner. "I guess that would help."

"Did you have breakfast?"

"Yes. Cereal and orange juice," Conn said. "Already washed my dishes."

"Thank you for everything you've done to help out lately," Elizabeth said. "I think I just might keep you."

Conn grinned again. "See you later, Mam."

"Have fun, and be careful," Elizabeth called to Conn's back as she ran, waving, toward Jed.

"Come with me," Conn said in an urgent whisper to Jed, and led the way past the barn, doubling back to it once they were out of sight of the house.

"What're you doin'?" Jed asked in confusion as he followed Conn.

"I —" Conn tilted her head as she looked at him properly for the first time. She reached up to pull a few pieces of straw from his hair which was sticking out at odd angles anyway. "You look like you slept in a barn."

"Well, that'd be 'cause I slept in the barn with Jack," he grinned.

"How come?"

"Pa was in a rage last night," he shrugged. "I haven't seen him that drunk in a long time."

"What was he in a rage about?"

"Nig —" He cut himself off abruptly. "Uh, colored folks. Old man Hardy hired him to fix some fence, but Pa... well, he got drunk and passed out under one of the trees, and some of the cattle got loose. So, old man Hardy fired my pa and gave the job to Abraham instead."

"Oh." Conn wasn't sure what to say.

Jed seemed to read her mind. "It's not Abraham's fault. He'll get the job done right. But... we coulda used the money," he finished, embarrassed.

"Oh," Conn said again.

"So, what are you doin'?" Jed repeated. "Aren't we goin' fishin'?"

"Not today. Can you keep a secret?"

Jed nodded, and Conn led him into the lower level of the barn. Standing in the dim early morning light there, she ordered him to raise his right hand.

"Swear you won't tell a soul what I'm about to show you, or..." She thought hard. "... or the ghost of this house will haunt you the rest of your days," she said dramatically.

Jed's eyes got big and he looked around, letting his hand lower. "There really is a ghost?" he whispered fearfully.

"Of course there is," Conn said. "Now swear."

His hand trembled a bit as he raised it again. "I swear," he croaked.

His mouth fell open as Conn opened the trapdoor.

"Climb down the ladder and wait for me at the bottom," she said. When he had descended, she started down, pausing to grasp the trapdoor and pull it shut over top of them.

When she reached the bottom of the ladder, she dug into the pocket of her shorts and pulled out a wooden match. She scraped it against the ladder and it flared with a hiss, lighting the absolute darkness of the tunnel. She handed the match to Jed and retrieved the bag she had hidden earlier. She quickly pulled out a candle and lit it before the match burnt down to Jed's fingertips.

"Here," she said, handing him the candle while she squatted down and carefully filled the oil lamp she had bought. After igniting it and adjusting the wick, she reached yet again into her bag and pulled out the box of chalk, handing Jed a piece and pocketing one herself.

"What is this place?" Jed asked in awe as he looked around.

"That's what we're going to find out," Conn said as she stood. "Come on."

She led the way down the right hand fork of the tunnel. With the oil lamp casting broader light, she could see other fissures that looked as if they might be additional tunnels. Seeing one that looked a little larger than the others, she paused. "Let's see where this goes."

She stepped into the fissure and could immediately tell that its walls and floor were more jagged and narrow than the tunnel they had just left. She took her chalk and drew an arrow on the wall, pointing back the way they had come. Inching forward, she could hear Jed's nervous breathing behind her. She held the oil lamp high, trying to see the roof of the fissure when Jed suddenly grabbed her by the shirt, pulling her backwards.

"What?" she asked, startled.

"Look," he said, pointing.

Just in front of Conn was blackness. Kneeling down and adjusting the position of the lamp, she saw that she had been about to step into a chasm about six feet wide, her light unable to penetrate its depths.

"Thanks," she said shakily.

"Let's go back," Jed suggested. "We can't get across that nohow."

They retraced their steps to the main tunnel and continued along it. This tunnel seemed to Conn to go on longer than the one that ended near the slave cabin. They noted other smaller tunnels branching off, but Jed said, "Let's stick with this one."

The tunnel veered sharply to the right and they suddenly came upon a wall of rock and dirt.

"It caved in," Conn said, holding the oil lamp high to examine the impasse. As far as she could tell, the rubble looked solid all the way to the roof of the tunnel, with no openings or pockets that they could squeeze through.

Jed reached out and pushed at some of the rocks and dirt. It all felt solid, compacted. "This happened a long time ago," he said.

Conn felt a sudden rage so strong it made her dizzy. Gasping, she reached out to the wall to support herself. The air around them became chilled enough that she could see her breath. She looked around, but didn't see anything.

"Are you all right?" Jed asked, looking around nervously.

Conn leaned against the wall, trying to slow her heart. "I'm fine."

"How did you know all this was down here?" Jed demanded.

She quickly considered how much to tell him. "I found the trap door in the barn," she said, deciding to tell part of the truth. "I haven't had a chance to really explore. I don't want to worry my mother. She's had enough to worry about lately." She turned to him. "Remember, you swore you wouldn't tell anyone."

"I know I did," he said defensively. "But why are these tunnels here?"

"I don't know," Conn admitted. She turned from the cave-in with a sigh. "Come on. Let's go back."

Their trip back to the ladder was uneventful.

"Where does that one go?" Jed asked, indicating the left-hand tunnel.

Making her mind up quickly, Conn said, "Meet me at the old slave cabin tomorrow morning at eight, okay?"

CHAPTER 15

Conn and Jed spent the following day exploring some of the other cracks and tunnels that branched off the cavern she'd discovered near the slave cabin. Jed was flabbergasted when she led him up the rocks and into the opening in the rock face.

"This is where that other tunnel under our barn comes out," she said, holding a candle aloft and finding her sock where she'd left it to mark that tunnel.

Jed let out a low whistle as he looked around. "Where do these others go?" he asked.

"That's what we're going to find out," Conn said, kneeling to light the oil lamp.

Most of the fissures were dead ends, or got too narrow to safely squeeze through. Those she marked with a big X on the cavern wall with her chalk. The seventh or eighth opening they explored unexpectedly opened up, becoming wide enough for them to walk side by side and high enough that Abraham could have walked in it without stooping. They followed it, Jed holding the oil lamp as Conn marked the walls every few yards to indicate the direction they'd come from. After they'd walked for what felt like fifteen or twenty minutes, they could hear a strange sound. The tunnel ended abruptly at a waterfall. They could see daylight on the other side of the cascading water. There was a narrow, slippery ledge of stone that allowed them to shuffle sideways behind the sheeting water.

They looked around as they emerged into sunlight, trying to get their bearings.

"This is where I first saw you fishin'," Jed exclaimed. "You and Will were over there," he said, pointing.

"You're right," Conn realized. She turned and looked at the rocks above them. "You were up there."

"If you knew about these tunnels," she said, looking around, "you could get all around this area without anyone seeing you." She began picking her way down the rocks. "We've done enough exploring for today. Let's go back to my house. I'm starving."

"Me, too," Jed said, rubbing his belly.

They ambled back to the house, speculating as to the purpose of the tunnels. "Remember," Conn said as they deposited the oil lamp in the barn and she retrieved her fishing rod, "my mom thinks we've been fishing."

As they rounded the barn, they were surprised to see Abraham's truck parked near the house. Hurrying into the kitchen, Conn stopped so abruptly that Jed ran into her.

"Will!" she said in surprise.

"Mom said I can come downstairs," he said happily. He looked very pale, and there were dark circles under his eyes.

"Hello, Connemara, Jedediah," said Abraham from where he was seated next to Will at the table.

"Hi, Mr. Greene," Conn said enthusiastically. Jed mumbled a hello, and followed Conn to the sink to wash.

"Did you two work up an appetite?" Elizabeth asked as she opened the refrigerator.

"We sure did," Conn said, grinning at Jed.

As they sat down to lunch, Conn asked Abraham, "Are you here to fix something?"

"No," Abraham smiled. "As a matter of fact, I was looking for Jedediah and thought I might find him here."

Jed's pale blue eyes narrowed warily. "What'd I do?"

Abraham chuckled. "You're not in trouble," he said, taking a bite of potato salad. "I've taken on a few jobs that are turning out to be bigger than I anticipated, and I wondered if you would be interested in becoming my helper?"

Jed stared at him, mouth hanging open. "Me, work for you?"

Conn's eyes flitted back and forth between the two of them as she chewed her sandwich. She knew Jed was wondering what his father would say about this.

Abraham nodded. "I could teach you and you would be helping me. I'll pay you a fair wage." He looked at Jed, weighing his next words. "I don't mean to tell you what to do, but if you accept, it might be best if you use your pay to bring home groceries or whatever you need, rather than bringing cash home."

Jed swallowed, looking at him shrewdly. "You mean my pa."

Abraham inclined his head a bit. "He's a proud man, but… he's got some problems."

Jed thought for a moment. "And this ain't charity?"

"Absolutely not," Abraham said emphatically. "This is business. I can get more done if I have some help, and you can learn a trade you'll be able to draw upon your whole life if you want to." He held out his hand. "Deal?"

Conn doubted Jed had ever shaken hands with a black man in his life, so she was a little surprised when Jed accepted his hand and said, "Deal."

"Very well," said Abraham. "I'll see you tomorrow morning at Mr. Hardy's east pasture at eight o'clock sharp."

Jed grinned. "See you tomorrow, Ab — I mean, Mr. Greene." He finished his sandwich and carried his dishes to the sink. "I better be goin'."

"And I as well," Abraham echoed as he also carried his dishes to the sink. "Thank you for lunch, Mrs. Mitchell. William, I hope you are up and around in no time." He looked down at Conn and said, "Connemara, would you walk me to my truck, please?"

Puzzled, Conn accompanied him outside.

"So, you and Jedediah spent the morning fishing, your mother said."

"Yes," Conn said uncomfortably.

Abraham nodded. "Interesting that when I passed Jedediah this morning, he didn't have a fishing rod with him and he wasn't headed toward the creek."

Conn's face turned red, but she didn't say anything.

"I trust," said Abraham quietly, "that you would not do anything to cause your mother more worry or heartache than she is already dealing with."

Conn looked up at him, wishing she could blurt out everything.

"Not if I could help it," she said cryptically.

Abraham frowned. "Are you all right? Are you in any kind of trouble?"

Conn opened and closed her mouth a couple of times before saying only, "I'm fine."

Abraham looked intently into her eyes for several seconds. "Very well. But if you need help — anytime — you can come to me."

Conn nodded and stepped back as he drove away.

※ ※ ※

Conn splashed in the tub, mounding up what remained of her bubbles. There was a knock on the door.

"Got your hair all washed?" Elizabeth said as she entered. "Ready to have your back scrubbed?"

"Yup," Conn said.

Elizabeth knelt next to the bathtub. "So, you and Jed seem to be getting along well," she said as she soaped up a washcloth.

"Yeah."

"He seems like a nice boy."

"He is, deep down," Conn agreed. "I feel sorry for him. His dad sounds pretty mean."

Elizabeth began rubbing the soapy cloth over Conn's back. "Well, when people drink, they —"

Elizabeth dropped the soap and quickly sluiced the suds off her daughter's back. "What happened to you?"

"What?" Conn asked, craning her head to try and see what her mother was referring to.

Elizabeth ran her hands over Conn's back. "You have welts all over. I can feel them; they're not red, they look old, but… where did you get these?"

"I don't know," Conn said, bewildered.

"It looks like someone whipped you," Elizabeth said angrily. "Look at me."

Conn looked up into her mother's eyes.

"How did you get these?"

"I really don't know," Conn said truthfully.

Elizabeth stared intently into Conn's eyes for several seconds.

"Maybe I got scratched by some sticker bushes in the woods," Conn suggested.

"Any sticker bushes that could leave marks like this would have torn your shirt to shreds," Elizabeth insisted.

Conn reached back, trying to run her own fingers over the welts she could now feel. They were vaguely tender, like a scar that's still healing. Suddenly, an image came to her of a supple branch being lashed repeatedly across her back — except it hadn't happened to her. It had happened to Caitríona.

Elizabeth's voice was strained as she asked, "Conn, has Mr. Greene ever —"

"No!" Conn swirled around in the tub so quickly that water sloshed over the sides. "Mom, no."

She couldn't have her mother thinking anything so terrible. "I really don't know what I got into, but you know me. You used to tell me I could get scabbed up just getting out of bed. I've been all through these woods. It could have been anything. But Mr. Greene has never laid a finger on me."

Elizabeth's brown eyes softened and she smiled a little sheepishly. "All right. But you would tell me if anyone was hurting you, right?"

"Yes," Conn said, her fingers crossed under the suds.

CHAPTER 16

"I'm bored."

Now that Will was feeling a little better, he was chafing more at being confined to the house.

"You were very, very sick," Elizabeth reminded him. "And you're not completely better yet."

Outside, the sky had let loose with a steady rain that was forecasted to last for a few days, bringing an unseasonable chill to the air for mid-June.

Elizabeth was opening cupboard doors and checking the pantry as the children ate breakfast. "I hadn't realized how low we are on everything," she said. "Tell you what, if you two will stay here and keep each other entertained, I'll bring you each back a surprise."

Will brightened at that. Conn nodded, understanding "keep each other entertained" to mean that she was to keep Will entertained.

"Under no circumstances are you to go out in this rain, young man," Elizabeth warned as she donned a raincoat and gathered her purse and car keys. "All we need is for you to get sick again."

As the Nomad splashed away through the muddy puddles in the drive, Conn turned to Will and said, "How about a ghost story?"

Will nodded, looking equal parts scared and excited. Conn collected a flashlight from a kitchen drawer, and together, she and Will spread a couple of sheets over the dining room table so that they hung down to the floor, enclosing them in a tent.

"Now," said Conn in a dramatic whisper, the flashlight illuminating them from below and casting spooky shadows over their features, "once upon a time, two sisters lived with their family in Ireland…"

By the time Elizabeth got home, Will was completely engrossed in Conn's story of Caitríona and Orla.

"Mom!" he shouted as they heard her enter the kitchen. He scrambled out from their tent.

"What in the world have you two been doing?" Elizabeth laughed as she saw what they had done to her dining room.

"Telling ghost stories!" Will said excitedly. "Conn's been telling me more about Caitríona Ní Faolain and her sister."

Elizabeth glanced curiously at her daughter as she set a box of groceries on the kitchen counter. "Like what?"

"Like how their dad sold them and how they almost died on the boat," blurted Will.

"And how do you know these things?" Elizabeth asked, turning back to her groceries.

Conn shrugged. "I guess I dreamed them," she said nonchalantly. "I'll get the rest of the groceries," she volunteered as Will launched into a recap of his sister's tale.

When she came back in, letting the screen door slap shut behind her, Elizabeth was still listening to Will. She turned and looked at Conn with a curious expression, and Conn knew that the stories were stirring something deep within her mother's memory.

"What's our surprise?" Will asked, interrupting the moment.

Elizabeth blinked. "Oh yes, your surprise." She pulled a new Hardy Boys mystery out of the box and handed it to Will. "Here you go," she said. "This might be a little hard for you to read, but I think you'll enjoy it." Then she turned to Conn and held out a book with a plain black cover. "I know you like to read," she said, "but I thought you might like to start keeping a journal."

"Hey," said Will, "just like Caitríona."

Conn had been thinking the exact same thing, remembering the journal Eilish had given to her younger daughter. As she accepted the journal from her mother, lifting it to smell the leather, she felt a sense of continuity and suddenly wondered if Caitríona's journal still existed.

They whiled away the remainder of the dreary, rainy day — Will lost in his Hardy Boys adventure, Conn up in her bedroom writing in her journal. At first, she had stared at the empty pages, not sure what to write, but then she thought about the day the Marines came to the house, and it seemed her pencil could not move fast enough to keep up with her thoughts.

She glanced up as her mother knocked on her bedroom door and peeked in. Conn quickly closed her journal and sat up on her bed.

Elizabeth smiled. "You don't have to worry. Journals are meant to be private. I would never read yours without your permission."

Conn nodded.

"You've been up here all day," Elizabeth said. "Hungry?"

Conn realized her stomach was rumbling. "I'm starving," she said. She hopped off her bed and accompanied her mother downstairs. "What have you been doing?"

"Oh, catching up on letters, reading a little. It seemed like a good day for that sort of thing."

Conn sniffed as she followed Elizabeth into the kitchen. "Boy, that smells good. What is it?"

"Johnny cake and beans," Elizabeth said, stirring a large pot of beans on the stove. "Nana used to make this. I'd forgotten, but I found an old cookbook with some of her recipes. It sounded good today."

A short while later, she laughed as Conn reached for a third piece of Johnny cake and spooned a generous helping of beans over it. Even Will had had seconds.

"Well, I guess we'll be having this for dinner more often. But I have a feeling," she said with a wry expression, "that within about twelve hours, you're going to be very glad we have an indoor bathroom."

❧

Winter came to the plantation with leaden skies and many days of cold, dreary rain. The upper floors of the house were kept clean and ready for the master, but no fires were lit in the bedrooms. Unfortunately, this meant that by the time Orla and Caitríona got up to their room at night, it was freezing. The tiny coal stove in their room eventually made it tolerable, but the girls learned quickly to heat water in the kitchen and fill glazed crocks to take upstairs at bedtime to use as bedwarmers.

"One good thing about having six of us in a bed," Caitríona said one night, her teeth chattering, "was we kept each other warm."

Orla sighed. "Oh, all right then. Come on over."

Caitríona quickly padded over to her sister's bed and slipped under the covers.

"Your feet are like ice!" Orla yelped.

Caitríona's shivers gradually calmed as she warmed up. She startled Orla with a sharp intake of breath. "Orla, do you know what day this is?"

"Of course I do. It's Monday," Orla said groggily.

"No, silly." Caitríona slipped back out of bed and lit a candle which she placed in the window. "It's Christmas Eve."

She crawled back under the covers. *"Nollaig Shona Duit,* Orla," she said softly.

"Nollaig Shona Duit, Caitríona."

Caitríona's candle was the plantation's only acknowledgement of Christmas. Work continued unceasingly through the short, dark days. Most afternoons, Caitríona slipped away for an hour to meet Hannah and continue her reading lessons. With the master and Batterston both gone, Caitríona had felt brazen enough to borrow books from the house's library.

"They'll never miss one book at a time," she insisted when Orla warned her not to do it.

The library's selections were somewhat limited, with mostly dry histories and accounts of military campaigns, but there were a few volumes of Milton, Chaucer and Shakespeare. Hannah could not yet read these by herself, but Caitríona read aloud to her, sitting up in one of the stable's lofts, huddled together with a horse blanket wrapped around their shoulders.

"If anyone finds out, we'll both be in trouble," Hannah reminded her often, but Caitríona didn't care. The hours she spent with Hannah were the happiest she'd been since leaving home.

One day, a wagon rattled toward the plantation in the midst of a fierce wind blowing from the north. The horses pulled with lowered heads while the driver sat shivering on his high seat, wrapped to his eyes with heavy wool throws. Burley rushed out to meet him and help unload the sugar, flour and salt he had brought.

The driver gratefully accepted Burley's invitation to unhitch the horses for the night and come into the kitchen for some hot food and drink.

"The river and canal are iced over," the driver told them as he shoveled some of Dolly's chicken and dumplings into his mouth. "Most like, won't be no more traffic till spring. Oh," he added, reaching toward his coat and pulling out an envelope from an inside pocket. "I near forgot."

Burley took the envelope, and then, in surprise, handed it to Orla. It was addressed simply, "Orla & Caitríona Ní Faolain, Lord Playfair Plantation, America," in rather scratchy handwriting.

As mail was such a rare thing, Orla was surrounded in the kitchen as she broke open the seal, which looked like plain candle wax.

"It's from Colm," she said, frowning. She read aloud, "Dear Orla and Caitríona, I hope and pray this letter gets to you. I am writing to tell you the sad news that Mam and the new baby died…" Orla's voice caught as her hand flew to her mouth.

Caitríona gently pulled the letter from her sister's shaking hand. "… died 3rd September. Da is drinking worse than ever. Mary and I have been trying to take care of the wee ones, but I may have to leave soon to find work as we have no money and no food." Her voice also faltered.

"Oh, my poor dears," Ellie said, near tears herself. Everyone else in the kitchen was silent. She wrapped a matronly arm around Orla's shoulders. "How old are the other children?"

Orla brushed tears from her cheeks. "Colm is twelve and Mary is eleven. And there are four younger," she said.

"Oh dear, oh dear," Ellie said.

Caitríona stood abruptly. "I'm going to cut more kindling for the fire."

"Leave that," Burley tried to object as she pulled a heavy wool cloak off a hook near the door, but as she yanked the door open, she heard Orla say to him, "Let her go."

Orla found her nearly an hour later, out in the bitterly cold wind, still trying to cut wood with hands so numb they could barely hold the axe.

Gently, Orla pulled the axe handle from her sister's frigid fingers and led her into the wood shed. Orla's eyes were red from weeping, but Caitríona's were dry. They sat on a stack of split wood, and Orla waited.

"He sold us for land he's not even working!" Caitríona exploded at last.

"Maybe he will, now," said Orla calmly. "He's just grieving for Mam."

"He's no time to grieve," Caitríona said angrily. "He's got six living children to feed."

They sat in silence for a while, until Caitríona moaned, "If they're going hungry, if they end up in the poorhouse after everything, what was the bloody point of it all?"

೨

Elizabeth rushed into Conn's dark bedroom, having been awakened by the sound of her daughter crying.

"Hey, hey," she said soothingly, brushing Conn's hair off her sweaty forehead and trying to wake her from her nightmare.

Conn sat up, sobbing, and clung to her mother, still crying.

"It's okay," Elizabeth murmured. "Whatever it was, it's not real. It was just a dream."

She held Conn, rocking her and humming until her crying stopped. She laid Conn back on her pillow, brushing her face again.

"What was it?"

Conn rubbed her red eyes, sniffing. "I dreamed… I dreamed someone told me you were dead," she said.

"Oh, honey," Elizabeth said, softly. She leaned forward and kissed Conn's forehead. "I'm right here. I'll always be here."

CHAPTER 17

The melancholy Conn felt after that vision hung on, like a cloud that wouldn't leave her. It felt like someone she'd known had died. She wandered the house listlessly, wishing she could go back to the tunnels, but after her conversation with Mr. Greene, she wasn't sure she should do any more exploring on her own. Jed hadn't been by, though she didn't know if it was because he was working with Mr. Greene or if it was because of the continued rain.

As soon as the rain let up, she slipped out of the house alone. Picking her way through the woods, she went to the cabin. Her legs were soon soaking wet from the drenched vegetation, water running in rivulets down to her socks, soaking them as well. Shoving the door open on its rusty hinges, she entered the cabin.

"What am I missing?" she asked the emptiness. "What happened to all of you?"

She sat down on the low hearthstones, looking around the room. She tried to picture the people who had lived in this cabin, but had a hard time imagining that Caitríona would have been content to live in the big house, even just the log portion, and leave her friends to live here. She shifted on the stones, and her heel caught the edge of one of the flat stones stacked up to build the hearth. It slid out of position a tiny bit. Reaching between her knees, she grasped the stone and wiggled it. With a scraping sound, it slid out into her hands.

Excitedly, she dropped down to sit on the floor, setting the stone beside her, and peered into the opening where the stone had been. Something was in there. Reaching in, she felt a piece of cloth. She pulled gently and disengaged an object wrapped in a piece of old oil cloth. Carefully, she unwrapped the cloth to reveal a stack of pages. Her heart was racing as she flipped through them. Most of the pages were covered by sketches done in charcoal and pencil. There were drawings of a house she recognized as the plantation house at Fair View. There were several drawings of Caitríona and Orla, and some other people Conn recognized from her dreams — Ruth and Henry, Burley and his wife Ellie. The drawings were very good — Conn knew from her visions what these people looked like and the sketches were accurate likenesses.

Scattered amongst the drawings were some short journal entries, beginning in 1856. The letters were crude and uneven, describing ordinary events of the day — chores, reading lessons. Conn realized this must have been Hannah's. Later entries in 1858, with better handwriting and grammar, indicated that Lord Playfair had come to the plantation for a few months, but after he left, his son was still there. Subsequent entries mentioned Deirdre, but no further mention of Orla. There were references to the war in 1861 and 1862, and one more detailed entry about Hannah's excitement over the Emancipation Proclamation. Conn flipped through the last pages which contained less frequent entries. The very last one was dated 8th August 1863.

> Tomorrow we leave here. Ruth, Henry and I will go with Caitríona and Deirdre to West Virginia. God help us.

Conn sat there. She felt as if she held a bit of Hannah's life in her hands. She had touched these papers. She had made these drawings. And she had hidden them away — to keep them private? Or to keep anyone else from knowing that she could read and write? Carefully, she wrapped the oil cloth back around the sheaf of papers and replaced the hearthstone. Tucking the precious package under her arm, she let herself back out the door of the cabin.

She picked her way through the tangles of trumpet vine and the brushy undergrowth beyond. Rounding a large tree, she was nearly bowled over by a man coming from the opposite direction. Startled, she looked up into a dirty, unshaven face. The man's bloodshot eyes peered at her blearily. There was an overpowering odor of stale sweat and alcohol about him. Conn knew immediately who this was.

"Yer the girl what lives in old lady Cook's house, ain'tcha?" he growled through the tangled beard obscuring his mouth.

Conn nodded.

"Where's m'boy?"

"I don't know," Conn answered.

"He ain't with you?" Mr. Pancake asked, squinting about as if Jed were here somewhere just out of sight.

"Obviously," Conn nearly retorted, but stopped herself in time, sensing that sarcasm might get her a smack across the face. Instead, she replied, "I haven't seen him for a few days."

Mr. Pancake swayed a little as he looked around. "Wait'll I git my hands on him," he mumbled as he lurched past Conn and crashed through the woods.

Conn stood there, her heart racing, trying to decide what to do. She ran home, pausing to stash Hannah's drawings in the barn, and then on to the house. She found her mother doing laundry in Nana's old-fashioned washing machine with wringers.

"This is going to be the next thing we replace," Elizabeth was grunting as she tried to wrest a pair of Will's pajamas from the jaws of the wringers which had eaten the legs of the pajama pants.

"Mom," Conn said breathlessly. "Where's Mr. Hardy's farm?"

"Why?" Elizabeth asked, still tugging on the pj's.

"I just ran into Jed's father, and he's looking for him," Conn explained. "He looked mad. We should warn Jed."

"Ohhh…" Elizabeth ceased tugging. "And Mr. Greene. Come on," she said, abandoning the pajamas and calling for Will.

They all climbed into the station wagon, Will sliding into the front seat between his mother and sister, and Elizabeth drove them out their lane, away from town in a direction Conn had never been.

"If he guesses where they are and heads across the fields," Elizabeth said worriedly as she drove, "he could get there before us."

After a mile or so, she turned onto a smaller dirt road that bordered a large pasture surrounded by four-board fencing. Across the field, they spied two figures. Elizabeth parked the car and the three of them climbed the fence and made their way through the tall grass to Abraham and Jed who were digging a new post hole.

"Mrs. Mitchell?" Abraham asked in surprise as he straightened.

"It's Jed's father," Elizabeth explained. "He's looking for you," she said to Jed, "and we wanted to warn you, both of you."

Jed, still wearing his patched overalls without a shirt, swiped a sweaty arm across his sweatier face, leaving a streak of grime smeared across his forehead.

"He don't know where I am, does he?" he asked in alarm.

"Not yet," Conn replied.

"Jedediah," said Abraham, "if you are — unsure — about going home, you may come stay with me."

Elizabeth cleared her throat pointedly. "Excuse me, Mr. Greene, but I can't think of a situation that would put you both at more risk." She turned to Jed. "Jed, you may come home with —"

They all turned as they heard a roar like a bull. Mr. Pancake was charging across the field toward them. Abraham laid a hand on Jed's shoulder and Elizabeth stepped forward as Jed's father drew near.

"What do you think yer doin'?" he bellowed. "Workin' with this nigger what took my job!"

"Stop right there," Elizabeth commanded, holding a hand up like a traffic cop.

"Who're you?" Mr. Pancake asked, peering into her face with his reddened eyes. "I know you," he mumbled.

"You should know me, Samuel Pancake," Elizabeth said boldly. "I slapped your face when we were fourteen because you were acting like a bully. And I'll do it again if I have to."

She actually stepped closer to him, forcing him to back up.

Samuel blinked down at her. "My boy, workin' for that..."

"Your boy is more of a man than you are," Elizabeth snapped. "Mr. Greene was good enough to take him on, and he's doing more work than you've done in years. He's working to put food on the table — something you should be doing, not him."

Conn could hear Jed's sharp intake of breath at anyone speaking to his father like that.

Elizabeth turned to Jed and asked, "Jed, do you want to come live with us?"

Jed looked from Elizabeth to his father and back again. "No, ma'am," he mumbled.

"Very well," said Elizabeth, turning to face Samuel again. She pressed a finger into his chest and said, "But if you lay a hand on him again, you will answer to me, Samuel Pancake, and Jed will be coming to live with us. Now, go home and clean yourself up while your son gets back to work."

Samuel Pancake blinked down at her a few times as her words slowly sank in. He glanced at Abraham and muttered, "Ever'body knows there's somethin' funny between you an' him anyhow," as he turned and lurched back across the field.

Frowning, Elizabeth turned back to Jed and Abraham. "And I meant what I said. If he beats you again, if he touches you, you will be coming to our house."

"Yes'm," Jed said, looking at her in awe.

"And unless you have other plans, you are both expected at our house for dinner this evening, cleaned up and hungry."

"Are you sure that's a good idea?" Abraham asked, pulling a checkered handkerchief from his back pocket to mop his face. "You heard what he —"

Elizabeth silenced him with the fierce expression on her face. Conn grinned as Abraham's crooked smile tugged his face to one side and he said, "Yes'm."

CHAPTER 18

"Well, young man," Dr. Jenkins pronounced as he listened to Will's lungs, "I think you are well enough to do anything you want to do." He folded his stethoscope and tucked it back inside his black bag. Turning to Elizabeth, he added, "He'll be a while building his energy back up. Make sure he gets to bed early and gets plenty of sleep, but other than that…"

"Thank you, Doctor," Elizabeth said.

"We were lucky," Dr. Jenkins said philosophically. "He was a very sick little boy, and there wasn't anything I or you or anyone else could do about it. If you want to thank anyone, thank God."

She saw him out, and turned to Will and Conn. "How about we go down to Walsh's?" she suggested. "We need to get the mail, and you haven't been out of the house for weeks," she said as she rumpled Will's hair.

A short while later, the Nomad pulled up to the general store and Will and Conn tumbled out, rushing up the porch steps. There were three women gathered around the counter as they entered, heads together, whispering. As one, they looked up when the bell on the screen door signaled the Mitchells' entrance into the store, and immediately broke off their whispered conversation.

"Good morning, ladies," Elizabeth said.

All three women turned their backs as if she had not spoken and scattered around the store, placing items in the baskets hanging from their arms.

Elizabeth's face burned scarlet as Mr. Walsh came out from the back. "Mornin' Elizabeth," he said a little coolly. "What can I get for you?"

"I need our mail and the things on the list," she said, handing a slip of paper to him.

"Right," he said. "Be just a few minutes."

Will pressed his face to the glass fronting the candy bins, but Conn, who had picked up on the interaction among the adults, went back outside to the rocking chairs, where she rocked agitatedly and waited.

Just as she could hear Mr. Walsh tallying the bill, Abraham pulled up in his truck. Conn hopped out of her chair and ran down the steps.

"Hello, Connemara," Abraham said genially as she jumped on the running board.

"Quick," she whispered, "before my mother comes out. I need to talk to you. May I come to your house today or tomorrow?"

"Well, yes," he replied in surprise. "Here," he said, pulling an old envelope and pencil from the glovebox and drawing a hasty map. "I'll be home by three today or anytime tomorrow."

"Thanks," Conn grinned, jumping down as Elizabeth and Will emerged, blinking in the bright sunshine after the darkness inside the store.

"How's Jed doing, Mr. Greene?" Elizabeth asked as she deposited her box of groceries in the back of the station wagon.

"Very well," he relied, unfolding his lanky frame from inside his truck. "It seems his father has been rather subdued since your... ah... talk with him. And I think it bolstered Jedediah's confidence considerably to know that other people would stand up for him."

He looked down at Will. "Well, young Mr. Mitchell, you are looking hale and hearty."

Will giggled, but couldn't talk as his jaw was glued shut with his teeth stuck in a large caramel.

"Have a good day, Mrs. Mitchell," Abraham said, giving Conn a small wink before he climbed the porch steps.

✳ ✳ ✳

Conn waited impatiently for an opportunity to slip away. Finally, after lunch, she took a book and said she was going to her tree to read. Once out of sight and shouting range of the house, she headed across the fields in the direction that would take her to the road Abraham had indicated on his map. Twenty minutes later, sweaty and out of breath, she came to his neatly painted small white clapboard house. Abraham wasn't home yet, so she sat on the front porch and waited.

He pulled up not long after.

"Come in, Connemara," he invited, holding the screen door for her.

Conn moaned enviously as she entered. There wasn't much furniture — only two cushioned chairs flanking the fireplace with low tables next to each, but nearly the entire space was filled with books. They filled bookcases lining every wall; there were random stacks of books tottering in piles on the floor.

"Wow," she breathed. "Look at them all."

Abraham grinned. "Yes, you and I share a love of books. Would you like a glass of cold water?"

"Yes, please."

"Have a seat, then. I'll be right back." He returned momentarily, handing her a glass of very cold water, and took the other chair. "Now, what can I do for you?" he asked.

Conn took a long drink. Now that she was here, she wasn't sure how to ask the questions she needed answers to. "I was hoping you could explain some things to me."

"Like what?" Abraham asked, puzzled.

"If... back in the old days, if a slave was caught reading or writing, what would have happened to them?"

Abraham frowned as he considered how to answer. "Well, I suppose it would have depended on the owner. From what I've read and what I remember of my grandparents' stories, some slave owners were actually tolerant of their slaves being literate, but most were afraid that if the slaves knew how to read and write, they might revolt. Any slave caught would have been punished severely."

"Punished how?"

"Most likely by being whipped in front of the others as a warning," he replied. "But it wasn't unheard of for slaves to be hung for that offense."

"Hung?" Conn asked in horror.

Abraham nodded. "Fear is a powerful deterrent to the others."

Conn chewed her lip as she thought about this, unconsciously reaching back to rub the tender welts on her back. "What would have happened if a black slave and white slave became friends?"

"I don't think that would have been tolerated," Abraham replied pensively. "By either side. Both whites and blacks would probably have viewed such a friendship as improper. The black person would have been thought to be getting above his station, and the white person would be sinking." His eyes focused on the distance as he said, more to himself than to Conn, "People are expected to stay in their place." A note of bitterness had crept into his voice.

"Did that happen to you?" Conn asked hesitantly.

Abraham blinked and looked at her as if he'd forgotten she was there. "Yes."

Conn waited, watching him expectantly.

"When I was teaching… there was a white woman, another teacher at the school. We fell in love. I was foolish enough, naïve enough to think that people up north, people who'd been willing to give me a job teaching white children, were progressive enough to accept us. They didn't. They fired me when they found out. We went out, Adrienne and I, to discuss our options, decide what to do next. Some men followed us, began shouting things. One of them picked up a broken bottle…" Abraham blinked and swallowed, waiting for the lump in his throat to lessen. "They didn't hurt Adrienne, thank God, but they could have."

Conn set her glass down and came to him. Gently, she touched a finger to his scar. Abraham flinched, but didn't pull away. Her blue eyes looked into his gentle brown ones. "Is that when you decided to come back here?" she asked softly as her hand dropped back to her side.

He nodded.

"What happened to Adrienne?"

"We wrote for a little while, but… I don't know what she's doing now."

Conn wished she could do something to ease his sadness. "Love seems like something that should be simple to understand," she said, shaking her head. "Why does it matter to people who someone else loves?"

To Conn's embarrassment, Abraham's eyes suddenly glistened with tears.

Blinking rapidly, he laughed and said, "You are wiser than your years, Connemara. Are you sure you're only eleven?"

Conn stepped back to her chair.

"So," said Abraham, clearing his throat, "what prompted all these questions?"

When Conn didn't answer immediately, he asked, "Has something happened? Have you found some old papers or something?"

Conn bit her lip. "Kind of."

Abraham frowned. "What does that mean?"

"I can't say."

"Why not?"

"I gave my word."

"To whom?" When Conn just stared at him, he said, "You can't say." She shook her head. "Connemara, I asked you the other day if you are all right. I'm going to ask you again, are you in any kind of trouble?"

Conn considered her answer carefully. "I don't think so."

Abraham puzzled over this for a moment. "Is there anything I can do to help you?"

Conn thought. "I don't see how you can."

"But you will not put yourself in any danger?"

"Not on purpose."

Abraham expelled a frustrated breath. "This is not helpful."

"Tell me about it," Conn said, with some frustration of her own. "Can I ask you another question?"

"Of course."

"Why are people talking about us?" Conn asked.

Whatever Abraham had expected to come next, this was not it. "Don't you think you should be asking your mother about this?"

Conn looked at him directly, and it did not escape her notice that he had not denied that people were indeed talking about them. "She's the one they're talking about, aren't they?"

He nodded. "I think so." He paused, choosing his words. "You remember how quickly word got around that William was sick?"

Conn nodded. "You said it was because Mom called Mrs. Walsh."

"Do you remember who came to your house the evening of your birthday?" he asked.

"Mr. Walsh?"

Abraham looked at her, clearly uncomfortable with where this conversation was going.

"You mean the Walshes have told people that you were at our house that night?" Conn asked, putting the pieces together.

"I think so," Abraham replied honestly.

"And they think that's wrong?" Conn asked in bewilderment, tilting her head to one side. Her eyes widened suddenly. "They think you and Mom...?" She'd heard things... on base, when the adults were playing cards and drinking and didn't know any children were near....

Abraham's face hardened. "People enjoy gossip more when it's malicious. I hope you and your mother are not too upset by this. Sometimes, all you can do is arm yourself with the knowledge of the truth and let it go. They will tire of it eventually."

They sat together in silence for a moment before Conn stood. "I should go. Thank you for talking with me."

"You can come to me anytime," he said, standing also. "And, uh... about my scar..."

"I won't say anything," Conn promised with a lop-sided grin. "I'm good at keeping secrets, remember?"

She gave him a wave as she trotted down the steps and headed home. The sun was warm on her head as she walked down the dirt road, and the shade of the woods was welcome. Sunlight and shadow rippled over her as she traipsed along....

ભ

Ewan galloped toward the plantation house, bent like a jockey over his horse's lathered neck.

"They're coming!" he yelled as the horse's hooves skidded to a halt.

Burley and Ellie rushed outside.

"They're coming," Ewan repeated breathlessly. "I was out in the south fields and I saw the carriage."

"How far?" came Batterston's cold voice from an open window.

"Three, maybe four miles," said Ewan, wiping his sleeve over his sweaty face.

The plantation had received word a few months previously that not only was Hugh Playfair returning, but his father, Lord Playfair, would be accompanying him, as he wished to personally inspect his holdings in America, in particular, the tobacco crop. The house had been readied early, just in case they arrived unannounced.

"Are the ladies with them?" Ellie asked.

Ewan shrugged. "Don't know. There was only one carriage and I couldn't see who was in it."

Amelia Playfair had not returned to Fair View since her first visit, and Hugh Playfair had been there only sporadically. It was rumored among the staff that she had returned to England, leaving him in Richmond, though, as none of them but Batterston had been to Richmond, and he rarely spoke to them, they did not know if this was true.

"Well," Batterston snapped at no one in particular, "what are you waiting for?"

Ellie asked Orla and Caitríona to double-check that the upstairs rooms were perfect in every detail.

"I wonder if he'll know anything of Da or the children," Orla wondered nervously.

"That's not likely," Caitríona said. "They'll be of less notice to him than the muck on his boots."

"Please hold your tongue," Orla begged. "Don't be shaming me by getting into trouble."

"When do I ever cause trouble?" Caitríona asked indignantly as she ran a rag along a windowsill. She and her sister both broke into laughter.

When the carriage pulled up, only Lord Playfair and his son emerged from its interior. Johnson, Hugh's valet, climbed down from a seat atop the carriage, and immediately began to oversee the unloading of the trunks, while Lord Playfair's valet, introduced to the staff as Pierce, went inside to inspect the masters' rooms.

The household staff were all lined up to receive the masters. Orla and Caitríona curtsied with the others as the two men walked past the staff toward the house, but stood stiffly as Lord Playfair paused in front of them.

"I know you," he said, frowning.

Orla kept her eyes lowered, but Caitríona raised hers to look at him directly.

"Niall O'Faolain's daughters," he recalled. "How long have you been here?"

"Five years, your Lordship," Orla replied softly.

At twenty, Orla's beauty had surpassed even her mother's in her youth. Lord Playfair's eyes lingered on her for an uncomfortable length of time before he made to continue toward the house.

"If you please, your Lordship," blurted Caitríona, ignoring the soft hiss of disapproval from Batterston. "We've had no word from our family these past four years. Would you be knowing what's become of them?"

Lord Playfair looked at her properly for the first time. She met his gaze unflinchingly.

"No," he said at last. "The farm was vacant the last I checked. I have a new tenant there now."

Prompted by Orla's discreet nudge, Caitríona curtsied again and said, "Thank you, your Lordship."

"I'll deal with you later," Batterston muttered under his breath as Lord Playfair and Hugh moved on into the house. Following them inside, he said, "I'm sure you would like to rest now —"

"No," Lord Playfair cut in. "I want to go over the plantation's accounts. We'll rest later."

The three of them remained shut in the study for the balance of the afternoon until the bell rang for tea. As the valets were still upstairs, unpacking the masters' clothes, Ellie took the tray Fiona had prepared and carried it in to them in the study. She came bustling back in a few minutes.

"They want you," she said in an awed whisper to Orla.

Caitríona, still reeling from the news that their family was no longer on their land, looked up. "Be careful," she warned.

Orla returned to the kitchen over an hour later. When Caitríona opened her mouth to ask what happened, Orla silenced her with a minute shake of her head. Not until they were alone, preparing salvers of food to be carried into the dining room for supper, did Caitríona have a chance to ask.

"He suspects," Orla whispered. "Lord Playfair knows there's something wrong with the books."

"What did you say?" Caitríona asked in alarm.

"I told the truth, of sorts," Orla replied. "I verified that the numbers in the ledgers were the numbers I'd been given."

"Did he believe you?"

Orla shrugged. "I don't know. I think he understood what I wasn't saying."

Later that evening, when Caitríona was sent to cut more kindling for the kitchen fire, Batterston cornered her in the wood shed.

"How dare you address his Lordship," he said in a threatening tone.

Caitríona stood up to face him, holding the axe defensively. "I had a question only he could answer," she said.

"Do you need another caning to remind you of your place?" he growled.

"If you try, Lord Playfair is going to see the real figures for the plantation," she said.

He stared at her and licked his lips. "What do you mean?"

"You know perfectly well what I mean," she said. "Ever since we realized what you were doing, we've kept a proper set of ledgers, hidden where you'll never find them. And if you so much as lift a finger against my sister or myself again, we'll turn them over."

He stared at her for long seconds more, but could not, it seemed, think of anything to say. Spinning on his heel, he walked away into the twilight.

Later that evening, supper was done and the servants could finally relax a bit. Caitríona carried the heavy pan of dishwater outside and dumped it. Checking that she was alone, she slipped away into the darkness. Across the expansive lawn, a small stream meandered through the property. A stone foot bridge traversed the stream and nearby, an ornate gazebo stood. She ran lightly over the bridge and cautiously climbed the gazebo steps.

"I'm here."

Hannah stepped out of the shadows and they sat together on one of the benches built into the sides of the gazebo. Hannah had long ago mastered her reading and writing lessons, but she and Caitríona still met whenever they could.

"What is it?" Hannah asked when Caitríona sat silently. She always seemed able to read Caitríona's moods.

Caitríona took a deep breath and told what she had learned of her family. "We've no way of knowing where they've been scattered," she said sadly.

Hannah wrapped an arm around Caitríona's shoulders, a liberty she would never dare take with anyone else, and said, "Maybe it's time you realize that we're your family now."

Caitríona looked at her. The moonlight spilling onto the side of Hannah's face accentuated the high cheekbones and smooth skin. A longing tingled inside her as Hannah met her gaze.

"I've heard rumors," came Lord Playfair's voice from an alarming proximity, startling both of the girls, "of a possible war."

Caitríona and Hannah dropped to the floor and squeezed under the benches, hidden in the deep shadows there as Hugh and his father climbed the gazebo steps.

"Just fearmongers, Father," said Hugh dismissively, "trying to jack up prices."

"Perhaps," said Lord Playfair doubtfully. He struck a match off the heel of his boot, Hannah's face momentarily illuminated as the match flared inches from her nose. He puffed on his cigar as he lit it. "But the anti-slave element is growing in the North."

Hugh filled a pipe and lit it. "Nothing more than sanctimonious hypocrites."

"Yes, well, those same sanctimonious hypocrites got slavery abolished in England," said Lord Playfair.

"But America is too vast," scoffed Hugh. "No matter what the abolitionists say, the people in power aren't foolish enough to risk losing what the South produces, and the South cannot produce without slaves. Trust me, America will never abolish slavery."

CHAPTER 19

The Mitchells were just sitting down to dinner when there was a knock on the back screen door.

"Jed!" Elizabeth said warmly. "Come in."

Jed bobbed his head politely as he entered the kitchen. His blond hair was plastered to his head with sweat, and his cheeks were flushed from the heat.

"Have you had supper yet?" she asked, getting up to pour him a cold glass of milk.

"No, ma'am," he replied, accepting the glass and drinking deeply. "But I'm too dirty and —"

"Nonsense," said Elizabeth. She got him a towel and said, "Go wash up, run some cold water on your head to cool down and come eat. We've got plenty."

A few minutes later, looking considerably cleaner and cooler, Jed took a seat at the table where Elizabeth filled a plate for him.

"What have you been working on?" Conn asked.

Jed's mouth was full of a large forkful of sweet potato. He swallowed painfully and said, "Peregorn's barn."

Conn opened her mouth to ask another question, but Elizabeth cut in, saying, "Let the poor boy eat, and then you can talk."

Jed grinned and dug into his food, eating ravenously. Conn and Will finished their own dinners and waited. A thought occurred to Conn and she asked, "That was Molly Peregorn who brought some medicine when Will was sick, wasn't it?"

"Yes," said Elizabeth, looking surprised. "How did you know who she was?"

Conn shrugged. "Just guessed."

Jed looked up. "She's a witch."

Elizabeth looked at him reprovingly. "There is no such thing as a witch, Jed. Miss Molly and the women who came before her got that reputation because people around here love to talk. And anything they don't understand, they're afraid of."

"Yes'm," Jed said politely, but he didn't look as if he believed one word of what she said. "Anyway, we're not working at her place. We're at the Peregorn home place, out the river road. I never seen such a big house or barns. I swear it feels like we're a hundred feet up when we're on the barn roof."

"You're working all the way up on the roof?" Elizabeth asked disapprovingly.

Jed grinned. "It's all right. Mr. Greene makes me tie on to a rope in case I slip."

"Wow," Will breathed, his eyes big, and Conn knew he was thinking how scary it would be to be that high up.

"He's teaching me how to repair some of the timbers where the roof had a leak," Jed was saying, proudly adding, "He says I'm a good helper."

Conn couldn't help feeling a little envious of all the things Jed must be learning, but she reminded herself that Jed and his father needed the money.

As if she were thinking the same thing, Elizabeth asked, "How are things with your father?"

"Better," Jed replied. He shook his head. "I never seen anyone stand up to my pa like that Miz Mitchell."

Elizabeth smiled ruefully. "Well, as I said, your father and I had a few run-ins in school. He always backed down if anyone had the nerve to speak up. I don't think he's a bad person at heart, but I think he gets mean when he's been drinking. I won't let him hurt you anymore."

To Conn's amusement, Jed blushed. He turned to Will and asked, "You feelin' better?"

Will nodded and said, "It was the faerieflies."

"That's what he calls lightning bugs," Conn explained at Jed's puzzled expression.

"You want to stay and catch some tonight?" Will invited.

"Can't. Got to get home," Jed replied. "I should get goin'. Thank you for supper, Miz Mitchell." He turned to Conn with a meaningful glance.

"I'll walk you down the drive," Conn said, jumping up from her seat. "And I'll be right back to help with the dishes," she said to her mother.

She and Jed walked down the twilit lane. "What's up?" she asked once they were out of earshot of the house.

"I got tomorrow off," Jed said. "And I wondered if you wanted to do some more explorin' in the tunnels?"

"Yes," Conn said eagerly. "But I'll have to sneak out of the house early to get away from Will. He wants to follow me everywhere lately."

Jed grinned. "Well, how 'bout we meet at the cabin at sun-up? We'll be in the dark anyways, so that won't matter."

"Okay," Conn nodded. "Sun-up. See you."

"See you," Jed said as he disappeared into the gloom.

⁂ ⁂ ⁂

The next morning, Conn arrived at the cabin before the sun was fully up. Jed was waiting.

"What's that for?" she asked, indicating the large coil of rope lying at his feet as she shrugged off a green canvas rucksack.

"We've had a couple of close calls," he said. "I thought we better have some rope handy in case one of us really does fall."

"Good idea," Conn said as she squatted down and undid the flap of her rucksack. "This was my dad's. I packed us some sandwiches and cookies and a jug of water. Did you have any breakfast?"

Jed shook his head.

"Here," she said, digging around in the rucksack and pulling out a slightly squashed peanut butter and jelly sandwich wrapped in wax paper. "I made extras, just in case."

"Thanks," said Jed gratefully, ripping open the wax paper and taking a huge bite.

When he was done, he slipped the coil of rope over his head so that it lay across his chest while Conn slid the rucksack's straps over her shoulders. Carefully, they climbed up the rocks to the crevice which led to the cavern.

"Wait," Conn said, "I'm stuck." The crevice was too narrow to get through wearing the rucksack. She pulled the straps off again and carried it through, passing it down to Jed once she was in the cavern. She quickly climbed down, knelt and rummaged in the pack, pulling out the oil lamp from one of the inside pockets. Lighting it, she handed it to Jed while she retrieved a piece of chalk. Holding the lamp high, they walked around the cavern, noting the marks they had previously made on the walls indicating the openings they had explored.

"Let's keep going in order," Conn suggested, "or we'll never keep track of which ones we've been down."

The first two fissures they tried were dead-ends, ending in solid rock after about fifty feet. The third crack in the cavern wall, like last time, opened unexpectedly into a wider tunnel. Conn estimated it was roughly opposite the original tunnel she had followed from her house and barn.

"Do you miss your pa?" Jed asked, his voice echoing a little as they walked.

"Yeah," Conn sighed. "But... it's more than just missing him. We don't know for sure if he's alive. I think that's the hard part for my mother."

They walked on for several minutes as the tunnel twisted right and left until Conn had lost all sense of direction. "Do you remember your mother?" she asked.

"A little," Jed said. "I was five when she died. Got sick. She used to make us go to church and she read the Bible after supper. Pa was better then..."

Conn could hear the wistful note in his voice. "He must miss her, too," she said.

"I guess he does."

Jed stopped abruptly. Squatting down, he held the lamp out in front of him. The floor had ended at the edge of a large pool of water. Off to their left, another tunnel opened onto this same pool. He set the lamp down and slipped the rope off his shoulder, tying one end tightly around his waist. He kicked off his shoes and rolled up the legs of his overalls. Tying the laces of his shoes together, he draped them around his neck.

"You keep hold of this end of the rope," he said. "I'm gonna see how deep it is."

"Are you sure?" Conn asked nervously.

"If it drops off, I can swim," Jed reassured her. "The rope is just in case."

"Okay." Conn reluctantly, wrapping the rope behind her waist and feeding it out little by little as Jed waded into the ice cold water.

"It's not even up to my knees," he said as he carefully probed the stone floor of the pool with each step. Nearing the other side, he said, "Come on. It's colder than a witch's — uh… it's not deep."

Conn kicked off her Keds and waded in, holding the oil lamp high. She had never felt such cold water. Within seconds, her feet and legs felt as if thousands of needles were pricking them. By the time she got across the pool, Jed had his shoes back on and was coiling the rope again. Conn brushed her feet dry and tied up her sneakers.

"Ready?" she asked, holding the lantern out in front of her and leading the way as the tunnel began to twist, with occasional drops in elevation.

"Do you have any idea where this is taking us?" Conn asked after what felt like a very long time.

"Nope."

Small rivulets of water chased along with them as they descended. Conn stopped so suddenly that Jed ran into her. The tunnel had forked, the left hand fork disappearing into blackness along with all the water, while the right hand fork angled upward in what looked like a crudely hewn staircase. They could hear water falling to their left.

"It sounds like a long way down," Jed whispered.

"Let's go up," Conn suggested.

They clambered up the rocks, some of the steps so steep that they had to set the lantern above them and use hands and feet to scramble up to the next level. A thin shaft of daylight appeared above them and became brighter the higher they climbed.

The tunnel flattened out without warning and they found themselves standing inside some type of shed. The sunlight they had seen was filtering in through cracks between the rock face and the rough board walls of the shed which seemed to have been built so that the rock formed the back wall. The shed was filled with rakes, pieces of broken plows, old wooden buckets and barrels and an assortment of old hand tools hanging from nails pounded randomly into the three wooden walls. Across the assorted junk, Conn and Jed could see the outline of a door.

"Be careful," Jed cautioned as they began climbing over the clutter filling the shed. "This stuff is rusty."

When they got to the door, he pushed down on the old-fashioned iron latch and shoved with his shoulder. It wouldn't budge.

"I think it's padlocked from the outside," Conn said, pointing to a second metal latch visible across the gap of the door jamb. Looking around, she spied a board on one side of the shed that had warped so that its bottom end had pulled loose from its nails. "Let's see if we can get out that way."

They picked their way carefully over to that wall and pushed against the loose board. It gave way some as long as someone kept pressure against it. "I think it's big enough," Jed said. He squatted down and wriggled his way through while Conn pushed as hard as she could to widen the opening for him. Once he was outside, Conn shrugged off the rucksack and handed it and the extinguished oil lamp out to him, and then began to squeeze through the gap as Jed pulled on the board from the outside.

"Ouch!" One of the nails protruding from the bottom of the board had caught her left shin, carving a deep gouge in her leg. Moving more carefully, she wriggled the rest of the way through and emerged outside the shed.

"Damn," Jed muttered as he squatted down to inspect the cut on Conn's leg. The blood was running freely down her shin.

"I'm fine," Conn said stoutly, stuffing the oil lamp back into a pocket of the rucksack. "Where are we?" she asked, looking around.

Jed stood up and surveyed their surroundings. "Criminy," he breathed, crouching low as he recognized the small house sheltered in a nearby copse of hemlocks. His eyes widened suddenly.

"Run!" he yelled.

Just as he hollered, there was an enormous boom and a large belch of smoke rose from the trees. A load of buckshot hit the rock face behind them, and Conn was peppered with bits of rock. Jed took off running. Conn tried to follow, but with her first step, there was a searing pain in her left leg and it collapsed under her. She lay on the ground, staring in terror at the figure emerging from the deep shadows of the hemlocks.

CHAPTER 20

An old woman stepped into the sunlight, wearing faded dungarees and a men's shirt with the shirtsleeves rolled up to her elbows. The sunshine glinted off her short silvery hair as she drew near, keeping her shotgun trained on Conn as she approached.

"What are you doing on my property?" she called out while still a distance away.

Conn lay on the ground, gaping helplessly as the woman drew near. "I'm sorry," she squeaked. "I didn't know I was on your property."

The old woman's sharp black eyes took in the bloody cut on Conn's leg. "You're Elizabeth's daughter," she said, a little more gently.

"And you're Miss Molly Peregorn," Conn returned, her voice a little stronger as her racing heart began to slow.

Molly broke the shotgun open and set it on the ground as she squatted next to Conn. "Let me see that leg," she said, laying her gnarled hands on Conn's shin and gently prizing the edges of the wound apart to see how deep it went. "Can't tell until it's clean, but this looks like it goes all the way into the muscle. Let's get you into the house," she said. "Can you walk?"

"I think so," Conn said, getting to her feet and taking a tentative step. If she moved slowly, she could hobble, though it hurt like crazy. Molly picked up her shotgun and carried it hung over the crook of one elbow as she took Conn's rucksack in her other hand.

As they stepped into the dark shade of the hemlock grove, Conn could feel the sudden coolness. The house she had barely been able to see from where she had fallen was a cottage, ornately decorated with lots of gingerbread adorning the eaves and the portico. Conn suppressed a nervous giggle as she thought of the witch's house in Hansel and Gretel.

Painfully, Conn climbed the porch stairs and gasped in wonder as she entered. Nearly every square inch of wall space and most of the furniture was covered with sketches and paintings — some framed, most not. Several chairs had stretched canvases stacked six or seven deep.

An old black and white Border collie struggled to his feet with a half-hearted bark at their entrance. He was missing most of one ear which gave him a grizzled appearance, but his tail wagged as he came to greet them.

"Hush, Vincent," said Molly.

He followed them stiffly into the kitchen where the woman pulled out a chair for Conn. She repositioned another chair and said, "Prop your leg up here."

Vincent sat next to Conn, laying his head in her lap as Molly gathered bowls and clean cloths.

"Who was that with you?" Molly asked as she poured some water into one of the bowls and spooned a yellow powder into it.

"Jed Pancake," Conn replied, watching Miss Molly as she stirred the powder in, turning the liquid brown.

"Sam Pancake's boy?" Molly asked sharply. "Not very brave is he? Leaving you on the ground while he skedaddled."

"Well," Conn said, rubbing Vincent's soft head, "getting shot at would have made me run, too, if I could have."

Molly stared at her for a few seconds and then she burst into laughter. "Yes, well… sorry about that. I've had some troublemakers around here, so I've learned to shoot first, ask questions later. Keeps most folks away," she added pointedly with a slight lift of one eyebrow.

Conn looked at her skeptically. "Isn't that a little dangerous? What if you'd hit us?"

Molly pulled up another chair and sat. "If I'd wanted to hit you, I'd have hit you." She dipped one of her cloths in the brown liquid and swabbed the gash on Conn's leg.

Conn caught her breath as the liquid burned and stung, but she didn't complain or pull away.

"Good girl. Not many can take the sting without yelling."

"What is it?" Conn asked, blinking to stop her eyes watering. Vincent licked her hand as if trying to comfort her. "It smells like turpentine."

Molly chuckled. "Just a little something I mix up to disinfect. And it does have pine tar in it."

As the burning subsided a little, Conn said, "Jed is working with Mr. Greene on the Peregorn barn. That's not yours, is it?"

Molly shook her head. "My brother has the family place." She jerked her head. "Over yonder." She continued dabbing at Conn's leg. "I prefer the witch's house," she smiled.

Molly sat back and looked at her. "What were you and Jed doing in that shed?" she asked. "How did you get in there?"

Conn wondered how honest to be. Looking into Miss Molly's dark eyes, she had the feeling that the older woman already knew the answer. "We came through the tunnel."

Molly nodded. "I thought so." She looked at Conn appraisingly. "I didn't know anyone knew about the tunnel."

"I discovered it by accident," Conn said. She wondered if Miss Molly knew about all the tunnels.

Molly pulled a small crock near and lifted the lid to reveal a thick black paste. She dipped her fingers into it and spread a dollop of the gooey stuff over the cut. To Conn's surprise, the pain immediately diminished.

"Better?"

"Yes, Miss Molly," said Conn gratefully.

Molly picked up a rolled up cloth and began to bandage Conn's leg. "Doc Jenkins would have wanted to put stitches in that, but I think you'll heal up just fine," she said as she wrapped the cloth neatly up Conn's skinny leg. "There," she said, surveying her handiwork as she applied a long piece of duct tape to keep the bandage in place. "I think that'll do."

Conn fingered the duct tape. "I didn't think anyone outside the military knew about this stuff. My dad always had some."

"Oh, you can find it if you know where to look," Molly said. She stood up. "How about a glass of cold milk?"

"Yes, please," Conn said. She glanced back out to the other rooms. "Did you do all those?"

Molly nodded as she handed Conn a glass.

"May I look at them?"

"If you like," Molly said with a shrug.

Conn got to her feet and limped out to the dining room, Vincent hobbling along behind her.

"You two are a matched pair," Molly chuckled. "He's paying you quite a compliment. He doesn't like many people."

Conn grinned down at him, her hand dropping to his head, feeling the remaining nub of his right ear. She looked back up at Molly, smiling bigger. "I get it. Vincent."

Molly laughed. "Not much gets by you, does it?"

Conn grinned again, but said nothing as she leaned to get a closer look at some of the canvases. Most of the scenes were of woods and wildlife. There were amazingly detailed studies of chipmunks and birds, the paint gleaming as if feathers and fur were reflecting summer sunlight. Conn paused before a painting of a stream.

"It looks so real, I expect to see a fish jump out of it," she said.

Just then, they heard a car come up the drive and brake to a stop. A moment later, there was a rapid knock on the door. Molly opened it to find Elizabeth standing there with Will peering out from behind her.

"Hello, Miss Molly," Elizabeth said breathlessly. "Jed Pancake said my daughter is here and that she was hurt."

"Hi, Mom," Conn said brightly as she hobbled into the entryway.

"What happened?" Elizabeth demanded as she spied the bandage on Conn's leg.

"Uh..." Conn stammered, looking uncertainly up at Molly.

"Connemara and Jed wandered onto my property by accident," Molly said, and it occurred to Conn that she had not told Molly her name, "and she cut her leg on one of those old pieces of equipment I have lying around."

Conn looked at her gratefully as Molly added, "It was a deep cut, but I disinfected it and washed it. It's got one of my salves on it and should heal up fine." She went back to the kitchen and returned a moment later with the small crock. "Here's some to take home. Good for all kinds of cuts and scrapes. Reapply some a couple of times a day."

"Thank you, Miss Molly," Elizabeth said in relief. "I'm sorry she bothered you."

"She was no bother, Elizabeth," Molly said. "No more than you used to be."

Elizabeth blushed and smiled sheepishly. "Well, we'll get out of your way."

"Just a minute," Conn said, limping back to retrieve her rucksack and give Vincent a last pat on the head. When she got back to the entryway, Will was already sitting in the car. "Thank you, Miss Molly."

Molly looked down at her for a moment. "You are welcome. And you can come back anytime, Connemara Ní Faolain."

✳ ✳ ✳

As Conn climbed into the car, she was bursting with questions about Molly Peregorn, but guessed that she would get more forthright answers from her mother if she waited.

Elizabeth, meanwhile, had questions of her own which did not need to wait. "What were you and Jed doing on Miss Molly's property?" she demanded as she drove.

Conn, watching carefully which route they took home since she had lost all sense of direction in the tunnels, replied, "We didn't mean to trespass. We got lost and came out of the woods on her land."

Elizabeth glanced over at her. "Jed Pancake got lost in the woods around here?" she scoffed. "More likely he talked you into teasing Miss Molly by sneaking around her house. It's always been a favorite thing for kids around here to do."

"I would never do that," Conn protested, stung to think her mother would suspect her of such a thing.

"Jed said that old lady shot at you," Will piped up most unhelpfully, standing up in the back and hanging over the front seat.

"Shut up," Conn said crossly.

"Watch your language, young lady," Elizabeth scolded.

"She fired her shotgun to scare us off," Conn explained, but hastened to add, "But she fired way over our heads. She wasn't trying to hit us." She was beginning to recognize the road they were on.

"You leave the house before dawn; you're gone for hours; you don't leave any indication of where you are," Elizabeth began, and Conn could tell she was just getting warmed up.

"Well, if we're going exploring, we don't bloody well know where

137

we're going or how long we're likely to be, do we?" she retorted sarcastically.

Elizabeth braked hard, stopping the car in the middle of the road. Will quickly sat back in the back seat, trying to get out of the line of fire.

"What has gotten into you?" Elizabeth asked angrily.

Conn set her jaw mulishly and didn't respond.

Elizabeth continued driving home, her mouth tight. She didn't speak again until they were pulling into their drive. "I think you need to spend the rest of the day in your room and think about a few things. Go."

Conn limped into the house and up to her room, feeling confused. She wasn't sure what had come over her in the car. She never spoke to her mother like that. She threw herself down on her bed. The day had warmed up and she could hear the drowsy buzz of bees outside her window. She would apologize to her mother later....

❧

There was a renewed flurry of activity as Lord Playfair made preparations to return to England. The three months he had been at Fair View had been almost pleasant, Caitríona had to grudgingly admit, owing mostly to the fact that while the masters were there, Batterston had been kept in his place. And without the wives, there was not nearly as much extra work for the servants.

Orla had been right. Lord Playfair did seem to suspect some dishonesty on Batterston's part. He insisted on riding out most days, accompanied by Hugh and Batterston, to inspect nearly every acre of the plantation and do a detailed study of their current crop rotation. When they returned to the house each day, Orla was called in to transcribe Lord Playfair's notes into the plantation's ledgers.

"Things look very different now to how they looked before," she whispered to her sister. "I think it's going to be obvious if Batterston tries cheating the books again."

One day not long after his arrival, Orla had come rushing to find Caitríona. "He wants to see you!" she said.

"Who?" Caitríona asked, looking up from the dishes she was washing.

"Lord Playfair! Who else?" Orla exclaimed in exasperation. "Come quickly."

Caitríona dried her hands on her apron as she removed it and followed her sister back to the study. There, she found Lord Playfair seated at the massive walnut desk that occupied one end of the room while Hugh sat in a chair near the fireplace, reading. She stood there for three or four minutes before he looked up and acknowledged her.

"I require an inventory of the slaves," he said, sliding a small ledger across the desk. "You will record their names and ages if they know them. If they have bred and produced off-spring, you will record those names and ages as well. See that this is returned to me within two weeks."

Orla could see the color rising in Caitríona's cheeks and rushed forward to take the ledger. Thrusting it into her sister's hands, Orla ushered her from the room.

"Did you hear him?" Caitríona finally burst out when they got back to the kitchen. "They're no more to him than cattle!"

"We already know that. That's how he thinks of us, too," Orla reminded her. "Perhaps Hannah will help you."

Caitríona turned away quickly to hide the flush Orla's suggestion brought to her cheeks. Fumbling with her apron strings, she said, "That's a good idea. I'll ask her."

She hardly noticed as Orla returned to the study. She'd hardly seen Hannah since the night at the gazebo, but for some reason, the tingling she had felt in her middle as she gazed at Hannah that night had returned every time she thought of her. She hadn't told Orla about it. Instinctively, she knew she shouldn't talk about this.

That evening, after supper, she went to Ruth and Henry's cabin, and found Hannah there. Ruth was peeling bark from some branches she had collected for one of her medicines. Caitríona sat down at the table and began helping. She explained the task she had been set, and asked Hannah if she would help.

Hannah glanced worriedly at Ruth. "What about the laundry I've got to wash?"

"I'll help you with that first thing," said Caitríona, "and then while it's drying, we'll go start the... I can't call it inventory. It's just too degrading. English bastard."

Henry smiled. "Miss Caitríona, I love it when your Irish comes out," he chuckled as he sat sharpening some of his planes and chisels.

Over the next several days, Caitríona and Hannah visited the slave cabins and the fields. The cabins, mostly built to accommodate four or five people, held instead seven or eight, with sleeping mats stacked up in a pile to be spread out upon the dirt floors at night. She hadn't realized how much work Henry had done to improve their cabin in comparison to these.

Having become accustomed to being friendly with Hannah, Ruth and Henry, Caitríona was dismayed at the surliness with which she and Hannah were greeted as they talked to the other slaves, numbering over a hundred in all. The slaves answered their questions, but in as few words as possible.

"I can understand why they wouldn't trust me," she said, "but why do they resent you so?"

Hannah glanced over at her. "Because I work with the white folks up at the house, and because I'm mixed," she explained as if this should be obvious.

"What do you mean 'mixed'?" Caitríona asked, frowning.

Hannah laughed. "Do you see any others with light eyes? I'm not all African. They say my father was probably my mother's master."

Caitríona stopped dead in her tracks, looking rather stupid as this fact hit her for the first time. It suddenly seemed obvious, and she felt childish for not realizing sooner that things like that happened. She glanced down at her ledger.

"I'm confused. That last woman we talked to, Bertha, said she has three children, but said she has no husband. So who was the father?"

"Her husband was sold a year ago," Hannah said.

"What?" Caitríona exclaimed, trying to remember. "But the masters weren't here a year ago. I don't recall anyone being sold."

"A lot happens that no one knows about," said Hannah darkly. "Batterston sells slaves every now and again. Last year, he sold Bertha's husband and three other men to a slave trader who came through here."

"Do you remember their names?" Caitríona asked as she made notes.

* * *

"He did what?" Lord Playfair asked sharply, his eyes narrowing angrily as Caitríona presented him with the ledger, including a list of slaves Batterston had sold over the last few years. "Send Mr. Batterston to me at once," he said, looking the ledger over.

The tension in the house was thick enough to cut with a knife as Lord Playfair's fury burst through the closed doors.

"You have no more leave to sell my slaves than you do to sell my land!" he bellowed.

Batterston's oily voice could also be heard, attempting to placate his irate employer. "But, my Lord, the slaves I sold were trouble makers or laggards. I was told by young Master Playfair to deal with them as I saw fit."

"By disciplining them or sending them to work on another part of the plantation," roared Lord Playfair, "not by selling them!"

"And," he added, his voice dropping to a dangerously quiet level so that Caitríona had to strain to hear outside the study door, "I see nowhere in the plantation's ledgers an entry for the sale of those slaves."

As Batterston was dismissed some minutes later, Caitríona barely had enough warning to move away from the door and begin scrubbing another part of the floor. Batterston stopped, looming over her with his fists tightly clenched. She stared back up at him defiantly as he said through clenched teeth, "You will pay for this."

"Why didn't you have him arrested? Or at least discharge him?" Hugh Playfair was asking back inside the study.

"This is something you will learn," Lord Playfair said. "No one is honest. If I replaced him, I'd be dealing with the same problem, just a different man. But Batterston now knows I could have him hanged," he said in a satisfied voice. "He won't cheat us again."

Lord Playfair's dissatisfaction with the overall state of the plantation extended to his son. His anger with Hugh had not been lost on the servants.

"I sent you here to protect our investment," he could be overheard as he and his son were out on the veranda one evening not long before his departure. "Instead, you've been drinking and gambling in Richmond."

"But, Father, the plantation runs itself. My presence here is not necessary. And there is no society in this god-forsaken wilderness," Hugh complained.

Lord Playfair fixed his cold stare on his son. "The estates in England and Ireland will go to your brother. You have an opportunity to gather yourself a greater fortune than he will have, and you whine about having no society!" He paced past the window, churning clouds of smoke from his cigar. "You will stay here and supervise the running of the plantation. I will return in three years, and if you have not increased our production, there will be a change in my will."

"Three years!" Hugh protested.

"Yes, three years," insisted Lord Playfair. "It's not too great a sacrifice for a lifetime's security. I shall return in the summer of 1863."

☙

Conn awakened to find her mother sitting on her bed, shaking her gently. Startled, she sat up, looking around her room.

"You were really asleep," Elizabeth was saying. "I've been trying to wake you."

Conn rubbed her eyes and lay back on her pillow. "Strange dream."

She looked up at her mother, remembering why she was in her room. Her mother had never sent her to her room before. "I'm sorry I worried you," she said sincerely.

Elizabeth smiled, running a hand tenderly through her daughter's hair. "I want you to enjoy being here as much as I did when I was your age," she said. "I ran around like a wild Indian, but," she grasped Conn's hand, "I don't know what I would do if anything happened to you."

Conn sat up again, throwing her arms around her mother.

CHAPTER 21

When Conn woke up the next morning, her leg ached something awful. The cut muscles pulled painfully when she moved her ankle. Wincing, she limped downstairs to the kitchen.

"Let's take a look," Elizabeth said as she pulled the duct tape off and unwrapped the bandage, exposing the gash. The skin around the cut was mildly red and swollen, but otherwise looked pretty good. Gingerly, she reapplied some of the black gooey ointment Miss Molly had sent home with them and rewrapped Conn's leg.

"I think you'll be climbing trees and running around soon enough," she pronounced as she pressed the duct tape in place. "In the meantime, how about some oatmeal?"

After breakfast, Conn took a book out to the back yard where she saw some digging tools lying in the yard. "What were you doing?" she asked her mother.

"Well, now that we've got most of the inside work done, I thought I'd start cleaning up the yard, maybe plant some flowers," Elizabeth said.

"Want some help?"

"I'd love some help if you feel up to it."

"So," Conn said a few minutes later as she began digging up a weedy flowerbed with a hand trowel, "you knew Miss Molly when you were growing up?"

"Umm hmm," Elizabeth replied as she pulled out some dead plants. "She and Nana were good friends, so we were often over there or she was over here."

"She called her house 'the witch's house'," Conn said. "What did she mean by that?"

Elizabeth laughed softly. "I'd forgotten. The Peregorn witch."

143

"That's what Jed called her," Conn said. "Why do people call her that?"

"It's silly, but for generations, one Peregorn woman has never married, learning how to make medicines using herbs and roots and things. It probably started a couple hundred years ago, but that woman is always known as the Peregorn witch," Elizabeth explained. "All because they've passed down old knowledge that other people have forgotten."

Conn was reminded of the *seanmhair* who made the prophecy to Caitríona.

"But I think Molly enjoys the whole witch mystique," Elizabeth continued with a fond smile. "I think Nana and I were the only ones she allowed around her house." She sat on her heels, reminiscing. "It was fascinating being around her. She knew so many things about animals and the forest. I learned so much just sitting and listening as she and Nana talked."

"Like what?"

"Well," Elizabeth closed her eyes, trying to recall, "I could be wrong, but I think there was a Peregorn witch who befriended Caitríona when she first got here."

"What?" Conn asked, stunned. Could this be the missing connection she needed to find out what happened to Caitríona?

"I'm pretty sure I remember Nana and Molly talking about it."

Trying to hide her excitement, Conn said, "She invited me to come back. May I go visit her?"

Elizabeth nodded her consent. "As long as you don't make a pest of yourself."

❋ ❋ ❋

Later that evening, after they had eaten dinner and dusk was falling, Jed came by. Will was running around the yard, catching his nightly quota of faerieflies and Conn was sitting on the porch swing, her leg still too sore to run. She saw Jed's untidy blond head appear at the curve in the drive. He stopped there, uncertain as to his welcome.

"Hey," he called hesitantly.

"Hey," Conn replied. "Come on up."

She scooted over on the swing as he approached.

"You okay?" he asked as he sat down beside her.

"I'm fine," she said.

Jed fiddled with a loose thread where one of the seams on his overalls was coming apart, winding and rewinding it around his finger as he mumbled, "I'm sorry I ran out on you."

Conn looked over in surprise. "You didn't run out on me. You went to get help. What do think you could have done against a shotgun if Miss Molly had wanted to hurt us?"

Jed slumped a little in relief. "Was she scary?"

Conn shrugged and said, "At first she was, but then she took me in her house to put medicine on my leg. She makes all kinds of medicines herself. She was friends with my Nana."

Jed was staring at her in amazement. "You went in her house? I heard there are bones and dead things in there for her witch's brews," he whispered.

Conn laughed. "Where did you hear that?" She shook her head. "Nothing like that. She's an artist. She does the most beautiful paintings of animals and plants. I think you would like them." She glanced over at him. "But maybe you shouldn't tell anyone about this. I think she likes to be left alone."

Jed snorted. "Who'm I gonna tell? No one 'round here would believe me."

"Time to get washed up for bed," Elizabeth called as she came out onto the porch. "Oh, hello, Jed. I didn't realize you were here."

Jed stood. "I was just leavin', Miz Mitchell. I just wanted to see how Conn's leg was doin'." He gave a half wave. "See ya."

"Bye," Conn said, getting to her feet, stifling a yawn.

☙❧

"Watch yourselves, dears," said Ellie, her plump bosom heaving as she carried a still-laden tray back into the kitchen. "He's drinkin' again. Didn't eat a lick of dinner."

Hugh Playfair was not dealing well with his "exile," as he frequently muttered, especially when he was drunk. For awhile after his father's departure, he had continued riding out, keeping a close eye on the plantation per his father's mandate. But within a few months, as summer gave way to autumn, the solitude of his situation began to take its toll. Despite occasional visits from the owners of neighboring plantations, there was no one else at Fair View with whom he could socialize or converse. His wife, the servants gleaned from his valet, had refused to return to America, and his friends were managing their affairs in India or Hong Kong or elsewhere in the Empire.

Batterston did not regain his former level of authority or autonomy as Hugh did not trust him, and spent as little time with him as possible. The one person he seemed to gravitate toward was Orla. He called upon her frequently under the pretext of reviewing the plantation's accounts, but, once she was in his presence, he usually began speaking of other things.

"I just listen, really," she said in reply to Caitríona's queries about what they did in the study for hours. "He's lonely. He's not cold like his father. He's not cut out to be by himself."

"You like him!" Caitríona said in a repulsed tone.

"No," Orla protested, but the color rose in her pale cheeks. "Only, I… I feel sorry for him."

"You feel sorry for the man who keeps us held captive on this cursed plantation," Caitríona scowled.

"I miss our family, too, but is life here really any worse than it would have been back home?" Orla asked. Caitríona opened her mouth with a retort, but Orla cut her off. "I'm serious. With Mam dead and Da God knows where… I'll be twenty-one this year. Back home, I'd have who knows how many children of my own by now. Here, we've got plenty to eat, work enough to keep us from being idle. We're not treated as cruelly as others are. Things could be worse for us."

Caitríona could think of nothing to say, though she would have died rather than admit it. She contented herself with not speaking to her sister for two days.

Despite Hugh's assurances to his father that America would not go to war, the rumors were becoming more persistent. Every trader, every courier, every visitor brought tidings of the increased tensions between North and South, and there was talk that the South would secede from the Union.

As Hugh felt more isolated, he began drinking more heavily, sometimes not eating for days at a time. He stayed closed up in his study, or up in his room, bellowing at anyone who interrupted him. Except Orla. She, it seemed, was the only one who could penetrate the fog of whisky and melancholy that surrounded him.

✳ ✳ ✳

Caitríona waited until everyone scattered after supper. Orla had not returned from taking Hugh's tray to him, but that was not unusual lately. She hugged the shadows as she made her way through the grounds to the gazebo. It was an unexpectedly warm evening for October as she waited in the shadows, listening to the frogs down by the water. Just as she was beginning to think Hannah wouldn't be coming, she saw a shadow of movement approaching in the dark.

Hannah was breathless when she got there, the moonlight slanting into the gazebo illuminated the rapid rise and fall of her chest.

"What's wrong?" Caitríona asked, pulling Hannah down to sit beside her.

It was a minute or two before Hannah could speak. "William asked me to marry him," she said.

Caitríona's breath caught in her throat. She turned away, staring toward the stream. "What did you say?"

"I didn't say anything," Hannah answered.

Caitríona felt as if her heart was being ripped from her chest. For a long time, she had known that her feelings for Hannah had changed, though she hadn't put a name to those feelings — until now.

"Don't do it," Caitríona whispered.

"Why not?"

She could feel Hannah's gaze, though she refused to meet it.

"Give me a reason I shouldn't marry him," Hannah insisted, leaning toward Caitríona from her perch on the bench.

The blood was pounding in Caitríona's ears so that she wasn't sure she'd be able to hear her own voice. "Because I love you," she said softly.

For long seconds, Hannah said nothing. Flooded with shame at admitting her feelings, Caitríona lurched off the bench, preparing to flee, but Hannah caught her hand and held it fast. Caitríona stood, not sure what Hannah's gesture meant, but reveling in the feel of Hannah's warm hand in hers. She could feel Hannah rise to stand next to her.

"I love you, too," Hannah said.

Caitríona turned to look at her. "You do?" she asked doubtfully.

Hannah smiled, and Caitríona thought she had never seen anything so beautiful. "Yes, Miss."

Caitríona laughed and pulled Hannah into her arms. With Hannah's body pressed into hers, she thought she could have died contented that very moment. She had no idea how long they stood thus, holding each other, neither willing to let go, but eventually, they did. Caitríona was surprised to find that it was still hard to meet Hannah's eyes, only now it was because she was afraid the intensity of her feelings might scare Hannah away.

"I have to get back," Hannah said reluctantly.

"Me, too."

They walked together down the gazebo steps, but before they parted, Caitríona asked, "So, what will you tell William?"

Hannah smiled. "I'll tell him no."

Caitríona kissed her impulsively, surprising Hannah as much as herself. Laughing, she ran lightly back to the house, feeling more like she was floating. She slipped quietly through the empty kitchen and up the servants' stairs. She fell giddily onto her bed and wrapped her arms around herself. As Orla wasn't yet upstairs, she took out her journal and made a hasty entry. She changed and got into bed, sure she would never be able to fall asleep, but she was awakened sometime in the middle of the night by Orla slipping quietly into their room. Within seconds her giddiness soured.

"What's wrong with you?" Orla asked the next afternoon as she and Caitríona cleaned the dining room. "You've been grumpy as a goose all day."

Caitríona flared at once. "I'll tell you what's wrong with me," she spat. "I could smell him on you when you came in! And I could smell you in his room when we cleaned it this morning."

Orla did not attempt to deny it. Her cheeks burned scarlet, but she bravely faced her sister and said, "I love him."

Caitríona's jaw dropped. "You love him! He's married, you fool! You'll never be anything to him but a... but a whore he can bed when the mood strikes."

In a flash, Orla's eyes blazed with a temper equal to her sister's. "At least what I'm doing is natural," she shot back.

Warily, memories of last evening with Hannah racing through her mind, Caitríona asked, "What do you mean?"

"Do you think I've not seen the way you look at Hannah? How stupid you are when she's about? You're a... you're... unnatural!"

Without thinking, Caitríona slapped her sister hard across the face. The red outline of her hand burned on Orla's cheek.

Orla's eyes filled with tears. "I hate you," she whispered, raising her hand to her cheek.

Caitríona turned and stalked upstairs. She gathered up her few possessions and clothes, tore her bed linens from the mattress and carried them all to another room in an otherwise empty wing of servants' rooms. There, she threw her clothes onto one bed and began making up the other. "I... hate... you," she seethed in rhythm with her vicious tugs on the sheets.

༄

Conn awakened to night sounds as crickets chirped and, far off, an owl hooted. A near full moon was lighting her room as she lay there, feeling a powerful sense of exhilaration. She had always, from the time she was little, insisted that she would never marry. She never questioned how she knew it; she just did. But now, feeling Caitríona's love for Hannah....

She was filled with a fierce joy at the realization of this kind of love. It didn't matter that she wasn't a boy. And she felt fiercely proud of her connection to the line of women who had descended from Caitríona. This, she now knew, was what she would feel someday. She knew it as certainly as she knew her name.

CHAPTER 22

"Don't you let him ride too fast and get tired out," Elizabeth cautioned as she gave her permission for the children to take their first bike trip to town since Will's illness. "And don't forget, your leg is still healing."

A few minutes later, they were coasting down the dirt road into Largo, small rocks squirting out from under their bicycle tires as they rolled over the hardpack. They pulled up at Walsh's and parked their bikes along the far side of the porch.

"Hello, children," Mr. Walsh called out as they entered the store. He was restocking the shelves with canned goods while Mrs. Walsh abruptly ceased whispering to a woman Conn recognized as one of the women who had ignored her mother the last time she'd been there.

"Here's your mail, Wanda," Mrs. Walsh said, a little too loudly.

Will immediately went to the candy counter while Conn wandered back to the fishing equipment.

"Hi, Mr. Greene!" Conn heard Will say as the bell tinkled.

Conn was on her way up front to greet Abraham when she heard Mrs. Walsh say, "What can we do for you, Abraham?" There was a coolness in her tone that made Conn stop in the maze of shelves and listen.

"Let's see," came Abraham's deep voice. "I need a couple of pounds of two-penny nails, five hundred feet of twelve gauge wire and some groceries," he said.

"Sorry, but we're all out," said Mr. Walsh.

Conn frowned, looking down at the large barrel of two-penny nails standing beside her.

"Excuse me," said Abraham, "but, you're out of what?"

"Everything on your list," Mr. Walsh said.

"Everything on my list," Abraham repeated in a flat voice.

Conn edged to the end of the aisle where she could see Abraham and the Walshes.

"If we're not sold out, it's been spoke for by other folks," Mrs. Walsh said as the woman named Wanda stood nearby watching everything.

"I see," Abraham said, his jaw clenching. Even from a distance, Conn could see that his scar had turned red. He refolded his list and tucked it back into his pocket as he turned toward the door. "Good day, William."

The store's screen door swung shut as Conn stomped, fuming, up to Will. "Come on," she said, staring daggers at Mrs. Walsh.

"But I wanted —"

"No," Conn cut him off. "We're not spending another penny in this store." She took Will by the hand and led him out onto the porch just in time to see Abraham's truck pull away in a cloud of dust.

Forgetting that she wasn't to tire Will, and ignoring the pain in her cut leg, Conn pedaled furiously, Will following as best he could, so that they both arrived home red-faced and winded.

"Well, that was a quick trip," Elizabeth called from the sitting room as she heard them storm into the kitchen. She looked up from the clean laundry she was folding as they rushed in, sweaty and hot. "What's wrong?"

Quickly, Conn relayed the encounter at the general store, Elizabeth's dark eyes becoming stonier and her face flushing angrily as she listened. "Those people," she muttered.

"What's Mr. Greene going to do?" Will asked worriedly.

Elizabeth blinked down at him. "He'll have to drive to Marlinton for his shopping. And we will do the same. No more shopping at Walsh's."

"What about the mail?" Conn asked.

"I don't think even Mrs. Walsh would tamper with the mail. She could get in too much trouble with the government," Elizabeth replied. "Come on, I want you both to splash some cold water on your faces and let's get some lunch."

"I don't understand," Will spluttered through the water he was splashing on his face in the bathroom. "Why did the Walshes do that to Mr. Greene?"

"I think they're trying to punish him for not staying in his place. For having dinner with us, things like that," Conn said.

Will looked up from scrubbing his face with a towel, his cheeks still flushed. "But we like him. He's nice."

"You're right. He is a very nice man," Elizabeth agreed. "And I am so proud of both of you for walking out of the store. Maybe we can't change how people around here think, but we don't have to go along with it, either."

Conn picked at her food during lunch, still upset to think of how Abraham had been treated. Suddenly, she looked up. "May I go visit Miss Molly today?"

"Yes, I suppose," Elizabeth replied. "But you ask her when you get there if this is a good time so you're not a bother."

"I will," Conn grinned, wolfing down the rest of her sandwich.

⁂ ⁂ ⁂

A little while later, Conn pedaled up to Molly's gingerbread cottage. Lowering her kickstand, she parked her bike under one of the hemlocks and climbed the porch steps. Her knock brought an outbreak of startled barking from Vincent. A moment passed, and then Molly opened the door.

"I thought I might be seeing you again," she said. Though she wasn't exactly smiling, there was a twinkle in her eyes that let Conn know she wasn't unwelcome.

"I don't mean to bother you," Conn said. "I can come back another time…"

"No need," said Molly, standing back to let her in, though Vincent's enthusiastic welcome made it difficult to get through the door.

"Come on to the kitchen," Molly said, leading the way.

Conn wrinkled her nose a little as she followed. "What are you making?" She sincerely hoped it wasn't something she would be invited to eat.

"It's a kind of tea," Molly explained, stirring whatever was simmering in the large pot on the stove. "It will make a poultice to draw out infection. One of my brother's cows got cut on some barbed wire and her leg is infected."

"Do all your medicines have to smell bad to work?" Conn asked hesitantly, afraid Molly might be offended, but Molly burst into a hearty laugh.

"I suppose it seems that way, doesn't it?" She glanced over. "How's your leg doing, by the way?"

Conn held her leg out so Molly could see. "Almost healed," she said. The cut was still shiny and pink, but was nearly closed up.

"Good," said Molly. "We can't have you laid up now, can we?"

"What do you mean?" Conn asked.

Instead of answering, Molly said, "Pull one of those chairs over here, would you?"

Conn did as she was asked. Molly handed her the wooden spoon. "Keep stirring this while I get the last ingredients."

Conn climbed up onto the chair. "'Double, double, toil and trouble; fire, burn; and, cauldron, bubble'," she intoned as she stirred the thick brown liquid bubbling in the pot.

Molly chuckled as she brought a fistful of crushed black leaves and a small piece of some type of bark. She dropped both into the brew. "Keep stirring now," she said.

Conn was surprised to see the mixture begin to turn green within a couple of minutes. "What's happening?"

"The willow bark and the leaves are releasing their chemicals into the tea," Molly replied.

"How did you learn all this?" Conn asked in wonder.

"My aunt taught me, and her aunt taught her, back and back," Molly said.

Conn bit her lip. "Back to Caitríona Ní Faolain?"

Molly looked at her with a penetrating gaze. "That far and beyond."

"How do you know?" Conn asked excitedly. "That your ancestor knew Caitríona, I mean."

Molly ladled some of her tea into a couple of canning jars and screwed the lids on tightly. "They told me," she said mysteriously.

Conn tilted her head. "Told you? How?" She wondered if there were more ghosts than just Caitríona.

"There are letters and journals," Molly said.

"Really?" Conn's eyes lit up. "May I see them?"

Molly pursed her lips for a moment as she put the jars in a basket with a towel tucked around them to prevent their tipping over. "Yes, I think you should," she said at last. "They may help you."

"Help me?" Conn asked, her heart beating fast. Could Molly know? "The last time I was here, you called me Connemara Ní Faolain. Only one other has ever called me that."

Molly sat down at the table. Conn hopped down from her chair and came to the table. "I know," said Molly.

Conn sat also. "You've seen her?"

Molly nodded. "She comes to me sometimes. She's waited a long time for you for you to come along."

"But why me?" Conn asked in dismay. "There was Deirdre and Nana and my mother's mother — why couldn't one of them do... whatever she needs doing?"

Molly sat back appraising her. "I don't know, Connemara. I don't know why it has fallen to you to complete this task, but you've come farther than I realized. You found the tunnels, and you found me. I don't think any of that is by accident."

Conn looked up at Molly, not sure if she was allowed to ask certain questions. "Do you know what happened to her?"

Molly shook her head. "I don't. But I've never known such a troubled soul."

Conn looked down at her hands and said quietly, "I see things. Things only she would know. Like dreams, only more real. It's starting to happen more often." She looked up, expecting to see skepticism or ridicule on Molly's face. Instead, she saw sympathy.

"Don't be afraid, child," Molly said. "You have a good heart. You'll know if something feels wrong."

They regarded one another for a long moment. At last, Molly asked, "Would you like to come with me to put the poultice on the injured cow?"

Conn nodded and helped Molly carry the basket out to her old truck. Vincent followed. He placed his front feet up on the running board and waited, looking back at Conn expectantly.

"He needs a boost," Molly said. "Just hoist his back end," she added when Conn looked at her questioningly.

Conn grinned and lifted Vincent's rear up into the truck. He scrambled onto the seat and sat between them, looking around eagerly.

Conn draped an arm over his back as Molly pushed the ignition button and the truck rumbled to life. She shifted into first gear and drove carefully, trying not to slosh the contents of the jars.

She turned left at the road, away from Conn's house. Presently, a large farm came into view, situated in a broad valley with a river meandering through fields dotted with grazing cattle. Three huge barns sat off to one side of a beautiful old house.

"This is our home place," Molly said. "My brother just had a new roof put on the bull barn, the middle one, there," she pointed.

"I know," Conn said. "Mr. Greene and Jed Pancake did the work."

"I didn't know you knew Abraham," Molly said.

Conn nodded. "He's done a lot of work around our house, too."

The truck stopped with a squeal of the brakes. "The hurt cow is by herself in a stall," Molly said, getting out of the truck.

Conn and Vincent got out and followed as Molly let herself in through a gate to a small corral outside one of the other barns. Entering the barn, they saw the cow standing in a stall, holding up one of her rear legs.

"There, there," Molly crooned. She put a little feed in the bin and pinned the cow's head at the stanchion with a board she slid into place so the cow couldn't back out. Then she went to get a bucket of clean water from the pump.

"You keep her calm," Molly said, squatting down and washing the infected cut with a wet rag.

The cow started at the touch, but Conn patted her and talked to her in a low, soothing voice. She watched as Molly soaked another rag in some of her brew and wrapped it around the injured leg, securing it with another dry cloth and more duct tape. "There, that should do for now," she pronounced, getting to her feet. She placed the jars of tea up on a nearby shelf. "I'll come back later today to change that."

Conn followed her back out to the truck where she again helped Vincent inside. They rumbled away, back toward town.

"I just need to pick up a couple of things before we go home," Molly said, pulling up in front of Walsh's.

Conn sat still, a stony expression on her face.

"What's wrong?" Molly asked.

"I won't go in there," Conn said.

"Whyever not?" Molly asked.

Quickly, Conn told her what the Walshes had done to Abraham earlier that morning. "We won't buy from them anymore," she added. "Mom says we'll go to Marlinton from now on."

Molly started the truck up again. "And so will all the Peregorns," she said with a stubborn set to her jaw.

"Really?" Conn asked, surprised. "My father always said principles are easy to talk about until they require sacrifice. Then most people do what's convenient."

Molly laughed. "You're a real rabblerouser, aren't you?"

As she drove back home, she asked, "Are you and your mother and brother going to the fireworks tonight?"

Conn's mouth fell open. "I completely forgot today is the Fourth of July." Her gaze fell. "I don't know if Mom will want to go. This was always a big holiday on base, but now..."

Molly cleared her throat. "I don't normally go in for such things, but this year... in honor of your father, I'd be glad to pick you all up and drive you to a good spot where we can sit in the back of the truck and see everything."

Conn beamed, but all she said was, "Thank you, Miss Molly."

CHAPTER 23

"He's a bloody coward," Caitríona grumbled to Fiona and Dolly as she cut up potatoes for the evening's dinner.

"He's not stupid," observed Fiona. "He knows what's coming and he wants no part of it."

A couple of weeks previously, Burley had managed to get hold of a Richmond newspaper detailing the secession in February of seven states to form the Confederate States of America, and predicting that Virginia would join them if the newly-elected Lincoln followed up on his declaration to raise troops. War seemed imminent. Almost immediately, Hugh Playfair had announced plans to leave, and had done so two days ago.

"So, he runs off to England, leaving Batterston in charge again," Caitríona said, whacking at a potato with her knife.

"He's really goin' back to England?" Dolly asked. "Did Miss Orla tell you?"

"Orla didn't tell me anything," said Caitríona flatly. It was true, though Orla's tears over the past several days had been enough to confirm what the staff guessed.

Fiona and Dolly exchanged looks. It was no secret that Caitríona and Orla barely spoke to one another anymore. What no one knew was that, aside from the necessary communication for work, they hadn't spoken at all since their argument. Caitríona stayed in her wing when upstairs, not wishing to know when Orla was or wasn't in her room.

The only light for Caitríona during these dark days was the brief bits of time she got to spend with Hannah. It was only a moment here and there, but the look in Hannah's eyes was enough to gladden Caitríona's heart. Her only other consolation was her journal, nearly full now, in which she reminisced about Ireland and their family, remembering happier times. Strange, though, that they should seem happier when there had been so much misery.

"Where is Miss Orla?" asked Dolly now. "She should be in here helpin'."

Ellie heard this last as she bustled into the kitchen. "She was sick again. I sent her upstairs to rest." She gathered up some clean dishes to carry out to the hutch and left.

Caitríona's head snapped up as Fiona mumbled, "Sure, and it's the nine months' sickness or I'm much mistaken."

By April, the war had begun and Virginia was indeed joining the Confederacy. Fiona's instincts proved to be accurate. Orla was clearly pregnant, becoming, if possible, even more beautiful. Caitríona often caught Batterston watching her wistfully, wishing to possess something that could never be his.

Ellie had wanted to write Hugh Playfair and tell him of the baby, but Orla refused. "That would be a wonderful letter for his wife to find," she said.

Perhaps it was the impending arrival of a new Faolain, but Orla broke down and approached her sister one evening, saying, "Caitie, this rift between us has gone on long enough. Can't we let bygones be bygones?"

Caitríona averted her eyes from her sister's swollen belly and said coldly, "You've made your choices, but you'll not drag me into your shame. I want nothing to do with you or your bastard child."

Walking away, she could feel her heart harden as she heard Orla's heartbroken sobs.

✳ ✳ ✳

Though war had been declared, it felt far away from Fair View. As the summer passed, the plantation saw occasional movement of newly-conscripted Confederate troops in their gray uniforms marching east. Batterston eagerly did business with the officers, selling them provisions despite Burley's protests that there was no guarantee more would be coming.

In August, screams rent the air, but it wasn't the war. It was Orla.

Ellie rushed into the kitchen carrying an armful of clean sheets and towels. "Take these up to Ruth," she said, handing the bundle to Caitríona.

Ruth, as the only healer for miles about, was also the only midwife. She had been summoned when Orla went into labor early.

"She should have at least another month," Ellie fretted as she took Ruth up to the bedroom where Orla lay struggling. "The baby hasn't turned."

Batterston had protested. "You know these rooms are for the family."

Ellie puffed up like an angry hen as she retorted, "Well, seein' as there's none of them here now, we're usin' that room! We don't need to be runnin' all the way to the top of the house."

Orla's labor had so far lasted over thirty-six hours. Apprehensively, Caitríona carried the linens upstairs, stopping in the hall as another horrendous scream could be heard.

Hannah rushed out, calling, "Where are —" She stopped as she saw Caitríona's waxen face. Taking the linens, she hurried back into the room with one more quick glance at Caitríona as she shut the door.

For Caitríona, time ceased to exist. It might have been hours, or days. People came and went from the room, but finally, Orla's screams stopped. Vaguely, Caitríona became aware of the squalling cries of a newborn. From where she sat in the hall, her arms wrapped around her knees, she raised her head hopefully. This was a sound she'd heard many times at home, with each new brother or sister. The bedroom door opened and Ellie came out, carrying an armful of bloody linens. She paused as Caitríona got stiffly to her feet.

"I'm so sorry, dear," she said, her eyes filling with tears. She laid a gentle hand on Caitríona's arm. "Don't go in yet."

But Caitríona pulled away and entered a nightmare. Hannah gasped and hastily pulled a blanket over Orla's splayed body, but not before Caitríona saw the massive pool of blood in which she lay.

Ruth had the baby wrapped in a tight bundle, an unbelievably small bundle. "It's a little girl," she said, tears running down her cheeks. "A beautiful baby girl."

Caitríona glanced down at the tiny face with a shock of black hair peeking out from under the blanket.

"She needs to eat, Miss Caitríona," Ruth said gently. "I'll take her to a woman who can nurse her, all right?"

Caitríona nodded dumbly, and turned to the figure lying in the bed. Hannah hesitated a moment, and then backed out of the room, pulling the door shut.

Lying there, with the blanket covering her, her long black hair cascading over the pillow, Orla looked as if she were asleep. Gazing at her sister's beautiful face, Caitríona was struck by her resemblance to their mother. The beads of Orla's rosary were visible under the neck of her nightgown. Caitríona came to the bed, and gently worked the rosary over her sister's head, untangling it carefully from her hair, not wanting to hurt her. Bent close, she could see Orla's eyes under her half-closed lids, already becoming cloudy and dull. How was it, she wondered, that a body could be alive, a light burning behind the eyes one minute, and the next... nothing. Just... nothing but a shell. Lungs that would never breathe again, eyes that would never look at her....

Caitríona slipped the rosary over her own head. Clutching the crucifix, the sharp corners dug painfully into the flesh of her hand, stopping her from thinking about how she'd never told her sister she was sorry, about how she never got to say good-bye....

Behind her, she heard the bedroom door open and shut, and suddenly Hannah was there. She folded Caitríona in her arms and Caitríona clung to her as tightly as she could, trying to quell the grief and darkness rising within her — shadows so deep, she felt they might engulf her completely, leaving her no more than a wraith upon the earth.

ɞ

Conn woke with a gasp, sitting bolt upright in bed. Breathing hard, she wiped tears from her face. Deirdre hadn't been Caitríona's child at all. She was Orla's. She sat there, digesting this new information, wondering what else had been passed down in error. She could still feel Caitríona's horrible regret and her despair.

Wide awake now, she quietly closed her bedroom door and got her flashlight. From the bottom drawer of her nightstand, she took the oil cloth bundle containing Hannah's pages. Flipping through them, she paused at a sketch of Orla, her long black hair pulled back to reveal her beautiful face and graceful neck. Near the back of the assembled pages was a series of quick sketches of Deirdre, maybe a year old.

She rewrapped the pages and put them away. Turning off her flashlight, she lay back in bed, thinking. She was just beginning to drift back off to sleep when, suddenly, she sat up again as she thought she heard whispered voices coming through the screen.

"I don't think —" said one voice.

"Just do it!" a second voice cut across the first one.

Then there was a crash of broken glass, followed quickly by another crash of more glass.

Conn jumped out of bed and met her mother in the hall. They both ran downstairs in their nightshirts and bare feet. Seeing nothing amiss in the sitting room or dining room, they rushed through the swinging door into the kitchen where they could see the window over the sink was shattered. A flickering light was coming from the bathroom.

"Stay back!" Elizabeth commanded as she ran to the bathroom and saw flames licking up the log walls of the room toward the roof, fueled by some kind of liquid that appeared to be splashed onto the logs. She grabbed a bucket from under the bathroom sink and ran to the tub. Turning the water on full blast, she threw bucket after bucket of water on the flames, eventually dousing them, leaving the wood charred and blackened, with smoke and steam billowing through the broken window and out into the kitchen.

Coughing, Conn made her way to the back door to open it, treading carefully to avoid stepping on the broken glass. She flipped on the light switch next to the door and saw a paper-wrapped object on the floor. Picking it up, she untied the paper from a weighty rock and unfolded it to read, scrawled in nearly illegible writing, "NIGER LOVERS."

"What happened?" Will asked in terror, peering through the swinging door.

"Stay there," Conn said. "There's broken glass everywhere."

Elizabeth emerged panting from the bathroom, tears streaming from her eyes, both from the acrid smoke and from her fury. "What's that?" she demanded, snatching the paper from Conn's hand.

Her lips compressed to a narrow line as she walked across the kitchen to the telephone.

"Ouch!"

She lifted a bare foot to find a piece of glass embedded in her heel. Conn turned to Will. "Go upstairs and get our shoes, will you?"

"And my robe," Elizabeth added.

Will ran to do as they asked.

"Sit down," Conn said, bringing a kitchen chair for her mother, watching where she stepped to avoid the glass.

Elizabeth gritted her teeth as she pulled the shard from her right heel. Conn handed her a towel to stem the flow of blood. Elizabeth pressed the towel to the cut.

Will returned quickly and tossed shoes and robe from the doorway, staying on the dining room side. Conn put hers on and helped her mother slip her left shoe on as well as her robe.

"Can you dial for me?" Elizabeth asked. Conn passed the handset to her mother, stretching the cord nearly its entire length as she dialed the operator on the telephone.

The kitchen clock read five a.m. as the flashing lights and sirens of the volunteer fire department's only truck pulled up. Three firefighters came rushing in, hose unfurled, ready to go to work, only to stop abruptly as they realized the fire was already out.

Dejectedly, a couple of them began winding the hose back up as the third, who seemed to be in charge said, "You better wet that roof real good so it doesn't spark and get goin' again."

They brightened somewhat, eagerly hauling the hose back outside to turn on the pump on the truck and begin dousing the shingles over the bathroom as the third man checked out the remnants of the bottle that had smashed against the logs, igniting everything.

Sheriff Arnold Little arrived in his cruiser a few minutes after the fire truck. Belying his name, he grunted as he tried to dislodge his immense belly from behind the steering wheel. The buttons of his hastily donned uniform shirt were strained to the point of bursting as he hitched his pants up, only to have his gun belt immediately pull them back down again.

Peering into the bathroom, he said in a slow drawl, "Now, Danny, don't you go messin' with evidence."

The firefighter straightened up. "Smells like it was filled with kerosene, Sheriff," he said, pointing to the shattered remains.

"Well, don't touch it, case we can lift some fingerprints," the sheriff replied, yawning. Turning to Elizabeth, he asked, "Any idea who did this, Miz — ?"

"Elizabeth Mitchell," she responded. "And, no. I do not have any idea who would do this." She hobbled to the table, where the crumpled piece of paper lay. "There was this, also," she said.

He peered at the paper, turning it over in his hands. After a long moment of apparent thought, he drawled, "Well, this is interestin', but I'm not sure what we'll be able to tell from it."

"Don't you think there might be fingerprints on it, too?" Conn asked pointedly.

Sheriff Little frowned, puckering his lips as he put the paper back on the table. "I doubt it," he said dismissively.

A new set of headlights flashed through the window as they heard another vehicle pull up. A minute later, Molly Peregorn burst into the kitchen, carrying a canvas bag over her shoulder.

"How did you —?" Sheriff Little began, but Molly pushed past him to Elizabeth.

"Are you and the children all right?" she asked. "What happened?"

Quickly, Conn and Elizabeth told her about the voices, the smashed glass and the fire. Turning to Sheriff Little, Molly said, "Arnold, I assume you've already written this down?"

"I'm getting' to it," he blustered, patting his pockets for a small notebook and pencil.

He began jotting the details, but before he could ask any questions, Molly asked Conn, "Did you recognize the voices?"

Conn shook her head. "No, they were kind of whispering, but loud. But there was this," she said pointing to the scribbled note.

Molly looked at and shook her head. "What a pity," she said.

"What?" Sheriff Little asked, frowning.

"That they don't know how to spell," Molly said drolly as Conn burst out laughing. "You're obviously looking for someone pretty stupid, Arnold." She knelt in front of Elizabeth, taking a small bottle from her bag. "Not that that helps much around here," she added in an undertone, as she swabbed the laceration on Elizabeth's foot with an antiseptic. She bandaged the foot as best she could, and Elizabeth gingerly forced her foot into her shoe.

She and Elizabeth went to the bathroom to survey the damage. "What a pity," Molly repeated, sincerely this time. "I don't think it's beyond repairing, though." She turned to Elizabeth. "It's a good thing you got down here as quickly as you did, or the whole house could have gone up."

Elizabeth's eyes filled with tears as she considered that possibility.

"There, there," Molly said consolingly. "You've got more folks looking out for you than you know," she said with a meaningful glance toward Conn.

Sheriff Little asked for a grocery bag for the bottle fragment in the bathroom. "I'll be in touch, Miz Mitchell," he said, his face red with the effort of bending over, "but I don't 'spect we'll have much luck findin' out who done this."

The fire truck tore up a good bit of grass maneuvering to get back down the drive, and Sheriff Little's cruiser followed after them.

"Sit down," Molly said, "and let me make you some coffee."

She expertly fired up the wood stove and put the pot on while Conn got the broom out and began sweeping up all the broken glass. "You don't think..." Conn began.

"What?" Elizabeth asked.

"You don't think Jed's father would have done this, do you?" Conn asked. "He hates Mr. Greene, and probably us, too."

Molly shook her head. "Sam Pancake can be an ornery cuss, but he'd never do anything this dangerous. No," she mused, "this sounds like the work of some of those boys who like to dress up in white hoods."

Elizabeth's head snapped up at this. "They're here?" she asked in disbelief.

Molly raised one eyebrow. "West Virginia may have left the Confederacy, but that doesn't mean the people here are any less ignorant when it comes to race."

"Can I come in now?" Will asked, still standing in the doorway.

"Yes," Elizabeth said, holding her arms out to him. He rushed to his mother for a hug as he cried. "It's okay. We're all okay."

"Well, it's a cinch no one's going back to bed now," Molly said. "We might as well have breakfast, too."

Conn helped her fry up some bacon and eggs while Will was put to work making toast.

"How did you know we were in trouble?" Elizabeth asked as they ate.

Molly's eyebrows raised as she said casually, "Oh, a ghost told me."

Will's eyes were enormous as he repeated fearfully, "A ghost?"

"Oh," Molly said, waving her hand dismissively, "this is a friendly ghost." Her gaze met Conn's for a moment and she winked.

At the reference to Caitríona, Conn recalled her dream, and the tragedy of Orla's death. "Deirdre was Orla's baby, not Caitríona's," she blurted without thinking.

"What?" Elizabeth asked, startled.

"I… I had a dream last night," Conn said, kicking herself for not keeping quiet, "that Orla died when she had Deidre. Caitríona raised her, but she wasn't her baby." She cast a quick glance at Molly, begging for help.

"We've always held that it's a great gift to receive glimpses into the lives of our ancestors," Molly said as Elizabeth's expression darkened with worry. Deciding that this was a good time to change the subject, she stood and carried her plate and Elizabeth's to the sink. "Would you like for me to stop by Abraham's place and let him know you'll need his help?" She turned to look back at Elizabeth. "Unless you're too scared to have him back," she added.

Her taunt had the desired effect as Elizabeth's eyes blazed angrily. "Too scared my — eye," she quickly amended with a glance at the children. "They are not going to tell us who we can and can't have as our friends."

"Good for you," Molly said with satisfaction as Conn and Will grinned at one another. "Then I'll have Abraham stop by as soon as he can."

CHAPTER 24

"I'm afraid I have bad news."

Abraham had done a thorough inspection of the damage in the bathroom.

"How bad is it?" Elizabeth asked, bracing herself as Conn stood nearby listening.

"The roof will have to be replaced," he said. "There's just too much damage. And these two walls, also." He squatted down. "And the floor boards as well. The water damage is already causing them to warp, see?"

Elizabeth expelled a worried breath. "I guess it's a good thing I took out an insurance policy on this house when Nana left it to me."

Abraham looked at her sympathetically. "Are you absolutely certain you want me doing these repairs?"

Elizabeth's temper, easily roused these last days, flared at once. "Mr. Greene, we are not giving in to these tactics. No one is going to intimidate us or frighten us away from our friendship with you."

Conn's pride at her mother's declaration was dampened as Abraham said pragmatically, "Mrs. Mitchell, we are not talking about just gossip anymore. What if that bottle had been thrown where it blocked the stairs? How would you and the children have gotten out of the house?"

In an instant, Conn understood exactly why Caitríona and the others had needed the hidden stairs and the tunnel. The black people had lived in this house, too — Conn was sure of it. And if anyone hostile had come their way, they would have needed an escape route. She bit her lip, wondering if she should say something.

"I've got a way out," she said.

Elizabeth stared at her for a few seconds and then laughed. "I forgot." Conn's heart leapt. "You found a way down off the porch roof, didn't you?"

Conn laughed, too.

"Very well," Abraham said. "I'll write up an estimate for you to give the insurance company. I can start right away if… if you can afford the materials. I wish I could —"

"Of course I don't expect you to front those expenses for us," Elizabeth cut in. "But your offer was very generous. And we will pay you as we have always done."

"Until tomorrow then," he said. "I'm afraid you'll be without a bathroom for at least a week."

"Back to the outhouse," Conn sighed.

※ ※ ※

The next morning, Abraham and Jed showed up bright and early to begin demolition of the damaged portions of the roof.

"I'm sorry this happened," Jed said to Conn. "Must have been scary, havin' your house on fire."

"It was," Conn agreed.

"Your ma really ran in there in her bare feet and put the fire out?" he asked incredulously.

Conn nodded with a renewed sense of pride in her mother's bravery. It seemed much grander when someone else said it. "She did."

Abraham and Jed climbed up onto the roof to begin prying the shingles off and tossing them down to the ground, where Elizabeth and the children piled them in the back of Abraham's truck to be hauled away later. As the sheathing boards and rafters were dismantled, Abraham showed them how to pull the old nails so they could reuse anything that was salvageable.

The work went quickly, and by mid-morning, the old log portion of the house stood open to the summer sky.

"Now for the hard part," Abraham said as they took a short break for a cold drink. "We've got to get the bathroom fixtures out so we can get to the floor and then the walls."

Just as they were preparing to resume work, a truck rumbled up the drive and two black men got out. Doffing their caps, they approached Elizabeth and said, "'Scuse us, Missus. We was sent to bring you new logs for to replace the burnt ones," said the taller of the two. He bobbed his head in Abraham's direction.

"Good morning, Lemuel," said Abraham.

Elizabeth frowned, puzzled. "But, who sent you?"

"Mr. Peregorn, Missus," said the one called Lemuel.

"Where do you want we should put 'em, Abraham?" asked the other man.

"How about over there, Buck," Abraham replied, pointing to a spot on the side of the yard. "We'll need enough space to plane and dovetail them to fit."

Within a few minutes, with Abraham and Jed helping, the men had the truck unloaded with the logs, already rough sawn into squares, stacked neatly off to one side of the yard. The two men rolled up their sleeves and began pulling tools out of the truck.

"I don't understand," said Elizabeth.

"We're staying to help," said Lemuel.

"But… but I can't afford to pay you," Elizabeth stammered, blushing furiously in her embarrassment.

Buck doffed his cap again. "We don't want pay, Missus. We heard what happened and asked Mr. Peregorn could we come help. He said we're yours as long as you need us."

"Oh," Elizabeth said, blinking rapidly. "Oh."

"What we will need," said Abraham to cover the awkward moment, "is a big lunch. I've heard your Johnny cake and beans are the best around."

Elizabeth laughed. "Johnny cake and beans it is."

As she was turning to go inside, they heard a new voice. "Could y'all use some extra help?"

"Pa!" Jed exclaimed as they turned to see Sam Pancake standing near the corner of the house.

※ ※ ※

"Well, I'll be," Molly Peregorn said in astonishment a couple of hours later when she stopped by to see how work was progressing.

More people had come, white and black both, including several women who brought breads, pies, fried chicken, potato salad and casseroles, so that soon the kitchen table was overflowing with dishes. Several children had come also, shyly saying hi to Conn and Will and helping carry tools and supplies for the adults. All were strangers to Elizabeth and the children, but had heard about the fire and wanted to help. Interestingly, none of the gossipers from down at Walsh's were among those who came to volunteer. Conn, who thought the other girls were silly, remained aloof, though Will gladly played with some of the boys.

With Abraham acting as foreman, two log walls had been carefully disassembled to allow the bathroom fixtures to be disconnected and carried outside, and now floorboards were being pried up and stacked while Sam Pancake and Buck were using adzes to cut notches into the ends of each new log in preparation for fitting them together.

"I never thought I'd see the like," Molly said, shaking her head as she surveyed the scene before her.

"What?" Conn asked, not understanding. Only she and Will seemed brave enough to talk to her and she noticed that the other children melted away when Molly was near.

"All these people, working together," Molly said. "I don't think this would have happened anywhere but here."

Conn tilted her head as Will asked, "Why?"

"You're too young to understand, but when someone like your mother takes a stand, refuses to be bullied or scared away from doing the right thing, it sets a powerful example for other people," Molly said. "The black folks around here know what it's like to live with the threat of being beat up if they step out of line, or having their homes or their families threatened. They understand the chance your mother is taking, and they're paying her tribute." Her eyes narrowed as she talked. "But Sam Pancake, I must say that surprises me most. Look at him, all shaved and cleaner than I've seen him in years. I never thought I'd see him working alongside a black man in my lifetime. Hmmph."

Will wandered off to watch from a closer vantage point with a few boys about his age, leaving Conn to ask the question she'd been dying to ask. "Caitríona really warned you? That's how you knew about the fire?"

Molly nodded. "She came to me, said you were in danger. I didn't know what until I got to your house." She peered down at Conn. "And you're continuing to have dreams of her life? Like the one about Orla and Deirdre?"

"Yes," Conn said. "I've tried to make them come faster so I can figure out what happened to her, but I can't control it." She looked up at Molly. "Do you think I should tell Mom?"

Molly shook her head. "Not now. She's got enough to worry about. This would really scare her, I think."

"Sometimes, I get the feeling she knows, like maybe she remembers dreams like these from when she was a girl," Conn said.

"Maybe Caitríona has shown herself to all the women in your family," Molly mused, "but there is something about you that makes you the one she's been waiting for." She turned toward the house. "I'll go see if your mother needs any help."

Conn sat down in the shade of one of the trees, watching all the activity.

❧

"Look what our little angel has picked for you, Miss Caitríona," said Ruth.

Deirdre, almost two, was clinging to Ruth's finger as she walked proudly up to Caitríona, holding a bunch of dandelions in her other hand. "Here, Mam," she said.

"Why they're beautiful," said Caitríona as she bent down to pick Deirdre up, carrying her into the kitchen.

"Would you like some sweet peas, darlin'?" Fiona asked.

Deirdre held out her plump little hand for the early June peas and clapped her hand to her pink lips. She looked so like Orla with her wavy black hair and big blue eyes. Caitríona set her down and gave her a small canning jar filled with water. She plopped down on the floor and began carefully placing her flowers, one crumpled stem at a time, into the jar.

"When is Burley due back?" Caitríona asked as she returned to shelling peas.

Ellie looked up at the clock worriedly. "He should have been back before now," she said.

Trips to town were much more dangerous now. Not only was there no guarantee there would be anything available to buy, there was a good chance Burley might run into roving bands of troops who would commandeer whatever he had been able to acquire. Union or Confederate — it didn't matter anymore. By all accounts, the war was horrible, with huge costs in terms of goods, infrastructure and lives lost. The new stretch of railroad coming into Buckingham County had been blown up twice, once by each side. Several skirmishes had been fought on plantation land, and the house had been briefly occupied a few times by the officers of whichever side had the upper hand at the moment. The house itself had suffered as well, with some of its wrought iron having been stripped by Union soldiers to melt down for cannon balls. As soon as they moved out, Burley, Henry and some of the others had removed all the rest of the iron and buried it far out on the property. "We'll put it back on soon," Burley said confidently.

But two years into the war, there was no sign of its ending. Despite Lincoln's issuance of the Emancipation Proclamation in January, the war dragged on with no change for the slaves in the South. Batterston had been eager to sell off provisions early in the war when both sides could afford to pay, but after two bloody years, neither side had money and the soldiers were desperate. The plantation staff had learned to grow their vegetables in remote patches of plantation property, and to quickly pick and preserve what they could grow, hiding the canned goods in a secret cellar under the pump house where the spring kept it cool year round. The few remaining cattle and horses were herded onto some of the hillier pastures not normally used as they were more difficult to get to. Ewan, Nate and the others who looked after them could quickly move them if troops came through looking for fresh mounts or meat.

Though Fair View was in Virginia, no one on the plantation felt any particular loyalty to either side in the war. Burley saw the practical aspect of running a five thousand acre plantation without slaves. "The Proclamation means he'll have to pay them, if the North wins," he said as they discussed the issue one evening.

"That's ludicrous," Batterston said disdainfully.

"It's reality," said Burley sagely. "If the North wins, and they probably will, the slaves will all be freed. If Lord Playfair was smart, he'd start paying 'em now, so they'll want to stay when the war is over."

Caitríona scoffed at this. "He thinks it's his God-given right to own people, no matter what color they are." The momentary expressions of hope in Dolly, Ruth and Henry's eyes faded as she spoke, and she was sorry she'd said anything.

Neither Lord Playfair nor Hugh had returned to America since the onset of the war. Post delivery was even more unpredictable than normal — they'd had only one letter from them in the past year, instructing Batterston to maintain the plantation's typical rota of tobacco, wheat and cattle.

"He's daft," said Burley as Batterston had read the letter aloud. "We can't eat tobacco, and he's not caught in the middle of this madness."

Burley did get back to Fair View, hours later than expected. He had detoured around a Confederate encampment and it had taken him miles out of his way.

"And wait till you hear," he said as he swung down from the high wagon seat as Nate and Ewan unharnessed the horses. "Virginia has split!"

"What?" the others exclaimed in unison.

Burley nodded. "It's true. The western part has decided to break off and re-join the Union. West Virginia, it's called."

"I don't believe it," Batterston scowled, snatching the newspaper Burley had brought with him.

"Then it will be a non-slave state?" Caitríona asked.

"Yep," said Burley. "Folks out that way are mostly just small farmers who work the land theirselves anyhow. Not many of 'em have slaves."

Everyone but Batterston helped carry the supplies Burley had been able to procure into the root cellar — salt, flour and a little cane sugar.

"Is this all you could get?" asked Fiona worriedly.

"It was like pullin' teeth to get this," Burley told her. "Not much is makin' it past Richmond anymore, and the folks who can get these supplies are chargin' five times what they're worth."

Caitríona pulled a small ledger out of her apron pocket and recorded Burley's purchases, making a point of asking him how much he'd had to pay or barter for everything, as he handed the surplus gold back to Batterston. No one was accepting Confederate paper money any longer, and no shop keepers in the South could exchange Union paper money without looking as if they were trading with the enemy. Gold and silver had become the most desirable currency.

The others all assumed that Caitríona had simply taken over Orla's duties of keeping the plantation's books. Only she and Batterston knew that she was keeping her own records as a safeguard.

"I'm not afraid of you anymore," she had said to him soon after Orla's death. "I know that Lord Playfair was this close," she held up her thumb and finger an inch apart, "to having you hanged for stealing. Now that Playfair is gone, you may be thinking you can go back to your old ways, but I'm warning you, I'll be watching."

Batterston had glared at her and, for a moment, she thought he might strike her, but then he turned on his heel and stalked away.

"He's dangerous," worried Hannah, to whom Caitríona had confided everything, including where to find hers and Orla's account books in the event something did happen to her.

"I know he is," Caitríona agreed. "That's why we're keeping these as security."

❦

Conn blinked to find herself still sitting under her tree. She had no idea how much time had gone by, but the men were putting their tools away for the day, and the dismantled floorboards were being put to use as makeshift tables, set on sawhorses out in the grass. Soon, everyone was gathered round, eating and talking. Conn watched her mother forego food herself to wander among the others, thanking each and every one for his or her contribution.

After everyone had eaten and the leftover food was wrapped up and put away in the refrigerator, people filed away with promises to return the following day. Soon, only Abraham and Molly were left.

"Well, that was unexpected," Abraham said, his scar pulling his face to the side as he smiled.

"I'm astonished," Elizabeth said, her hands falling limply at her sides as she shook her head.

"It felt like a barn-raising," Molly observed.

"Mmmm, more like a latrine-raising," Conn said.

CHAPTER 25

In less than a week, the bathroom was nearly rebuilt. The new logs fit seamlessly with the old. All that remained to be completed was the roof.

Elizabeth took a break to drive to the general store to collect the mail, the first time she'd been there since the day the Walshes had snubbed Abraham. Conn and Will decided to tag along.

Mrs. Walsh was behind the counter as they entered the store. "Hello, Elizabeth," she said. "What can I get for you?"

"Just my mail, please."

"Nothing else?" Mrs. Walsh asked. "You haven't been in for two or three weeks."

"That's right," Elizabeth said sweetly as the doorbell tinkled behind them.

"Mrs. Mitchell?"

Conn turned to see a tall man removing a fedora to reveal thick gray hair, with a matching gray beard along his jawline, like Abraham Lincoln, she thought.

"I don't expect you'll remember me," the man began. "Obediah Peregorn, Molly's brother."

"Of course I remember you, Mr. Peregorn," Elizabeth said, shaking his hand. "And I cannot thank you enough for sending Lemuel and Buck with those logs. They've been such a help to us. It was so generous of you."

He waved off her thanks. "Not at all. Glad to do it. As a matter of fact, that's kind of what I wanted to talk to you about. I've got extra roof shingles from when Abraham repaired my barn, and if you could use them, I'd be more than glad to send them your way."

"You are so kind," Elizabeth said sincerely. "At the risk of taking advantage of your generosity, yes, we could use them."

He chuckled. "Good. I'll send them today with Buck and Lem."
He turned to Mrs. Walsh. "Mail, please, Betty."

"Nothing else?" she asked, sounding displeased.

"No, no, I got everything I needed last Tuesday in Marlinton," he
said. "Ran into Abraham there," he said to Elizabeth as Mrs. Walsh
gathered his mail in a bundle. "He said you were there earlier."

"Yes, we were," Elizabeth smiled.

Conn's eyes darted back and forth between her mother, Mr.
Peregorn and Mrs. Walsh.

"Well, why in the world would you do your shopping there?" Mrs.
Walsh asked in a voice much higher than normal, forcing a smile onto
her face.

Elizabeth and Mr. Peregorn glanced at one another before she said,
"You and your husband are perfectly free to do business with whomever
you choose, Mrs. Walsh. And so are we."

"Why, whatever do you mean?" asked Mrs. Walsh, no longer attempting to sound friendly.

"I mean that I will no longer tolerate the vicious gossip that you
and your husband and your friends have propagated," Elizabeth said,
keeping her voice neutral. "Gossip that caused someone to want to set
my house on fire. Nor will I do business with people who could treat
Mr. Greene the way you and your husband have."

"I'm afraid that goes for me, too, Betty," Obediah Peregorn added
genially, as if he was discussing the weather. "Abraham Greene is one
of the best men I know. You won't see any business from any of the
Peregorns or any of our people. Not until you and Walter change your
ways."

He reached forward to retrieve the two bundles of mail Mrs. Walsh
had set on the counter, handing one to Elizabeth.

"And that includes an apology to Mr. Greene," Elizabeth said, sliding her mail into her purse.

"If it comes to that, I think you owe Mrs. Mitchell an apology as
well," said Obediah. "I've heard some mighty nasty talk in here the last
good while. You should be ashamed. I know I am. I should have spoken
up long ago."

Conn grinned as Mrs. Walsh stood with her mouth hanging open.
Mr. Peregorn held the door for Elizabeth and the children as they left
the store together.

"Those roof shingles will be out your way later this morning," he called, tugging the brim of his hat respectfully as he got into his truck.

"Thank you," Elizabeth said as he pulled away.

She hummed as she drove home. "Isn't it a beautiful morning?"

Conn smiled broadly.

※ ※ ※

"Oh, Mr. Greene," Elizabeth said a couple of days later as she inspected the finished bathroom, "it's just like new. That fire might never have happened to look at the place."

Jed blushed furiously as she hugged him, saying, "And you were a tremendous help."

Her eyes filled with tears. "Everyone who helped was so kind," she said. "I just don't know how to thank them all enough."

"I think they were happy to do it, Mrs. Mitchell," Abraham said, surveying the new structure proudly. He turned to Conn. "I say we deserve an afternoon off for some fishing."

"Yeah!" Jed grinned happily.

Within the hour, Abraham and all three children were piled into his pickup and bouncing along a dirt road to the river. Abraham got Will set up where he could sit on a rock and drop his line into the water while Jed and Conn waded out into the stream. They spread out, standing knee deep in the crystal clear water. Conn made a couple of casts, but her eye was drawn to the flashes of sunlight reflecting off the water....

❧

By July, the weather was again sweltering, and tempers were running as short as the food supplies.

"Not grits again," groaned Burley as he came in for breakfast.

"You'll eat it and be grateful," said Fiona irritably. "We could tell you stories —"

"I know, I know," he grumbled. "The horrible famine." He stuck a spoon in his bowl of thin, watery grits. "But I dream of a big breakfast of bacon and eggs, and real coffee..."

Caitríona smiled as she gave Deirdre a small bowl of the grainy cereal and a tiny spoon. She was as tired of their meager rations as everyone else, but the horror of the famine would never fade for anyone who lived through it. She might grimace, but she would never complain.

"You might like it this mornin', Mr. Burley," said Dolly. "I put a little bacon grease in for flavor."

Batterston came into the kitchen and helped himself to a bowl. "I want the slaves to work in the southwest field today," he said.

"Then you take 'em," said Burley. "We've got corn needs pickin'." He waved his arm in a vaguely southern direction, toward the sheds. "I don't know where you think you're gonna put more tobacco. The sheds are full to the rafters from the last season you couldn't get to auction. We need food, not more tobacco."

"I could fire you for saying that," Batterston threatened.

"You just try," Burley returned, knowing it was an empty threat. "When this dadblasted war is over and life gets back to normal, then we'll worry 'bout tobacco. But for now, we need to get through this comin' winter. And to do that, you need all of us. Or there won't be no plantation for Lord High 'n' Mighty to come back to."

Batterston scowled and went back to his small house, calling over his shoulder as he did so, "I don't know why we even keep so many god-damned niggers on the place."

A couple of days later, everyone at the house, including several slaves, were mustered to husk the huge pile of corn that had been picked. Deirdre rocked away on the wooden horse Henry had made for her as Caitríona, Hannah and Ellie worked at an outdoor table, cutting the kernels off the cobs into large pots so that Fiona and Dolly could blanch them in preparation for canning.

They all paused and watched as a rider approached the house. He was rough-looking, with a dirty, unkempt beard and a shirt stained with perspiration under his suspenders. A rifle was visible in a scabbard buckled to his saddle, and he wore a pistol on his belt. As he drew nearer, they could also see large coils of rope strapped to the pommel of his saddle and hear the clank of manacles strung behind the cantle.

He touched a finger to the brim of his sweaty hat and said, "Afternoon, ladies. I need to see the owner of the place, if I may."

The politeness of his speech created a better impression until he spat a large quantity of tobacco juice on the ground.

Looking up at him disapprovingly, Ellie said, "You'll have to settle for the overseer, Mr. Batterston."

Batterston appeared at that moment, and invited the stranger into the study. Suspicious, Caitríona carried a pot of corn into the kitchen and, ignoring Fiona's complaint that it was only half-full, crept quietly down the hall.

"… could use ten to fifteen if I can get 'em," the stranger was saying.

There was a long silence.

"I could probably do that," Batterston said at last. "Got more than I know what to do with anyhow."

"I'll make it worth your while," the stranger said, and Caitríona could hear the clink of coins.

"All right." Batterston seemed to have made up his mind. "But we'll need to do it after dark."

The stranger laughed. "Just tell 'em to smile, so's we can see 'em. I'll have men with me to make sure there's no trouble."

"There's a drying shed about a quarter mile down the lane," Batterston said. "I'll round up fifteen good, healthy ones and meet you and your men there at ten tonight. I'll keep this as a deposit." Caitríona could hear coins clinking again. "You'll have the rest tonight?"

"I'll have it."

Caitríona's heart was pounding as she went back to the kitchen. Batterston was planning on selling fifteen of the Negroes. She was only half-aware of what she was doing as she returned to the pile of corn.

"What's wrong?" whispered Hannah.

Caitríona gave a tiny shake of her head. It wasn't until later in the afternoon as she rocked Deirdre's cradle in the shade and fanned her to sleep that she had an opportunity to tell Hannah what she'd overheard.

"He can't do that!" Hannah exclaimed as Caitríona shushed her. She continued in an angry whisper, "Lord Playfair told him he wasn't allowed to sell any more of us."

"I think he'll not be worrying about that any longer," said Caitríona grimly. "He knows there's nothing Lord Playfair can do from England."

Hannah's eyes filled with angry tears. "It's not right," she said bitterly. "You said that the proclamation meant we're not property anymore."

"I know," Caitríona said. "But who in the South is going to care about that? This trader will buy and sell those men and no one will ask questions."

All that day, Caitríona stewed, trying to think of how she could stop Batterston. The only thing she could think of, and even she had to admit it was weak, was to threaten to write to Lord Playfair. But she had to find a more immediate way to thwart him in case the threat didn't work. Later that evening, she went to find Ruth and Henry.

"Hannah told us," Henry said quietly.

"We've got to keep those men from going with him," Caitríona said. "Do you know who he picked?"

Henry nodded.

"If they ran away, they'd just be caught," she said. "Could you tell them to go to the far pastures, spend the night in the woods there. They can say they were sent to move the cattle and horses."

"He'll just find them the next day," Ruth said.

"But it will give me more time," said Caitríona.

"For what?" asked Henry.

Caitríona didn't answer. She asked Ruth to keep Deirdre and went to check on Batterston's whereabouts. He stayed in his house all evening, emerging only to get a dinner plate and take it back with him.

Caitríona waited until after the kitchen was cleaned up, and then went to the overseer's small house. She knocked and was startled when Batterston jerked the door open.

"Oh, it's you," he said nervously. "What do you want?"

Caitríona looked past him and saw a stuffed valise sitting on the floor. "Going somewhere?" she asked, pushing by him and entering the small parlour.

"What do you want?" he repeated in a more menacing tone.

"You're not going to sell those men," she said, deciding to take the upper hand with a direct approach.

If Batterston was startled to hear that she knew of his plans, he hid it well. He closed the door and walked to the window that faced the big house.

"Are you going to stop me?" he asked quietly as he pulled the curtains closed.

Mustering as much bravado as she could, Caitríona said, "I've already written Lord Playfair."

Batterston chuckled and turned to her. "By the time he gets any letter and tries to do anything, I'll be long gone. I'm not going to stay here and wait for this damn war to kill me or starve me."

Caitríona had known her bluff had little chance of succeeding. "Well, the ones you were going to sell aren't here," she said. "I sent them away."

Batterston's eyes widened. "You sent them… you!" His face twisted into a snarl, his lip curling as his teeth were bared. "I've had enough of you!"

He lunged across the room, reaching for her throat. Caitríona ducked, but Batterston managed to grab her dress at the shoulder. He slammed his other fist into her face, knocking her to the floor. In his rage, he dropped to his knees, pinning her and pummeling her with his fist. It felt as if her nose was broken as blood gushed over her face, choking her.

He grabbed a handful of her hair and slammed her head back against the hearth stones. Caitríona saw lights pop behind her eyes as her head hit the stone. Batterston placed his hands around her throat. Gasping for air, she tried to prize his hands from her throat as she looked into his crazed eyes. Desperately, she reached out, her hands flailing about, searching for something, anything that might help. Her hand hit a heavy earthen crock used for kindling. She floundered for a moment, trying to get a grip on the heavy pot, and finally managed to swing it up, smashing it hard against the side of Batterston's head.

He crumpled to the floor beside her and didn't move. Caitríona lay there, still gasping. She rolled to the side and spat out the blood from her mouth. She struggled to her hands and knees, prepared to fend Batterston off when he got up. She looked over at him, and saw that the side of his head was sunken in where the crock had hit him. His lifeless eyes stared up at nothing as blood trickled from his ear.

She sat heavily on the floor, trying to gather her wits. Batterston was dead. It seemed to take a long time for that fact to sink in. The mantel clock indicated it was nearly nine o'clock. What would that trader do when Batterston didn't show up at ten?

She staggered to her feet, so dizzy that she almost went back down. When she finally felt steady enough to walk, she slipped out Batterston's door, making her way to Ruth and Henry's cabin, trying to keep to the shadows so no one would see her.

She knocked softly and Henry opened the door.

"Good lord, girl," he gasped, pulling her inside.

Hannah was sitting in a rocking chair, holding a sleeping Deirdre. Her hand flew to her mouth at the sight of Caitríona's bloody, bruised face.

"Sit down," Ruth whispered, taking Caitríona's arm and leading her to the table. "What happened?" She poured water from a pitcher into a shallow bowl.

"He… he went crazy," Caitríona said hoarsely. "He was all packed. He was going to run off with the gold. He didn't care if Lord Playfair knew." She rubbed her throat which clearly showed bruises. "He was choking me. I had to stop him. I… I hit him. I hit him with a crock." She looked at all of them. "He's dead."

Ruth paused in the midst of wringing out a cloth she had soaked in water. "He's dead?"

Caitríona nodded. Ruth began sponging the blood from her face as Hannah put Deirdre on one of the beds.

"I don't know what to do," Caitríona said numbly. "Should we report this to the law?"

Ruth and Henry looked at each other, and Caitríona could see the fear in their eyes. "Of course, I can't involve you with the law," she realized.

"I don't know you'd be much better off yourself," Henry said.

"What about Burley? Should I tell him?" she wondered.

Henry squatted down in front of her. "Miss Caitríona," he said as if talking to a child, "you're the only one heard what he was plannin'. You got no proof, and now he's dead."

"But look at her face!" Hannah said indignantly.

"Since when has the law cared if a white man beats a nigger or a woman?" Henry asked. He paced as Ruth finished washing the blood from Caitríona's face and began applying one of her salves to the gashes and bruises.

Henry turned to her. "Where is he?"

"He's where I left him, in front of the fireplace," Caitríona said.

"That trader might come lookin' for him when he doesn't show up," Henry said. "We best get him buried and fast."

Hannah retrieved a sheet from the laundry pile and the four of them went to Batterston's house. They rolled him up into the sheet, and

Henry hoisted him over his shoulder as Hannah hastily scrubbed the blood from the floor. Caitríona grabbed the stuffed valise and, together, they made their way to a deep patch of woods on the plantation property, digging far into the night.

❧

"Connemara!"

Conn came to as her face hit the water. Abraham lunged toward her, but Jed got there first. Grabbing her by the back of her shirt, he hauled her up coughing and sputtering, water streaming from her hair down her face.

"What in tarnation were you doin'?" Jed yelled.

"I... I lost my balance," she lied, avoiding Abraham's eyes.

"Are you all right?" Abraham asked.

"'Tis nothing," Conn said, trying to laugh it off. "Just a wee bit clumsy."

"Hey!" Will hollered indignantly. "Doesn't anyone care I caught a fish?"

✳ ✳ ✳

"She killed him."

Almost beside herself at this latest glimpse into Caitríona's life, Conn forced herself to continue fishing for awhile, though Abraham quickly realized she was not focused on the fishing when he looked over to see that her rod was almost bent double as she stood, oblivious to the fish on the other end.

"Let's call it a day," he said gently, reeling her fish in and releasing it.

He kept glancing at her worriedly as they packed up and got back in the truck.

"I'm all wet," she protested.

"It's all right," he assured her. "You won't hurt anything in this old truck."

She stared absently out the window as he drove, not speaking until she suddenly called, "Stop!"

Abraham braked and Conn flung the truck door open. "I've got to go to Miss Molly's," she said.

"Connemara," Abraham started to protest, but Conn looked him dead in the eye as she shut the truck door.

"I've got to go to Miss Molly's," she repeated. "If my mother wants me, that's where I'll be. I'll be home for dinner."

With one last look, she hopped down off the running board and took off through the woods.

"Women," Jed said, shaking his head.

Running all the way to Molly's house, Conn breathlessly banged her fist on the door. When she heard no bark, and no one answered, she ran around the house. There, she saw that the door to the shed connected to the tunnel was standing ajar, with most of the contents of the shed sitting in the grass. Sprinting across the yard, she saw Molly and Vincent inside. Molly was sorting through the tools hanging on the walls.

Vincent gave a welcoming bark as she skidded to a stop, clutching the stitch in her side.

Molly turned to her in surprise. "Connemara? What's wrong?"

It was a couple of minutes before Conn could answer. "Had... had another vision..." she gasped. "She killed someone."

"Caitríona?"

Conn nodded.

"Come to the house," Molly said, looking around to make sure no one else had overheard.

Quickly, they walked to the hemlock grove and into the little house where Molly poured Conn a glass of ice cold water.

"Drink," she said, "and then tell me what you saw."

Conn gulped the water, nearly choking on it in her eagerness to tell someone what she'd seen.

"Batterston — he was the overseer of the plantation Caitríona and Orla were sent to — he was going to sell some more slaves..."

"Caitríona and her sister?"

"No," said Conn impatiently. She realized she needed to back up. "Orla was already dead in this vision, because Deirdre was about two. This was during the Civil War and Lord Playfair and his son were back in England, so Batterston knew they couldn't do anything to him. He had already gotten in trouble for selling slaves and keeping the money." She took another drink and continued, "Anyway, a slave trader came by, and Batterston agreed to sell him some slaves, but Caitríona heard them talking and she tried to stop him. First, she told him she'd written to Lord Playfair, but he said he'd be long gone before they could do anything. Then she said she'd sent the slaves away and he... he went crazy and started hitting her and choking her and... she grabbed this jar thing, like one of those," she said, pointing to a heavy crock Molly had sitting on her kitchen counter, "and hit him in the head with it and killed him."

Conn got up and began pacing agitatedly around the table. "She didn't mean to, but she did."

Molly was staring at her. "I didn't realize your dreams were this detailed," she said.

"It's like I'm in her head, like I see everything she saw, feel what she felt," Conn said. "She told me, she said, 'tis a terrible shame I've brought on our family.' This must be what she meant."

"Maybe," Molly agreed, somewhat doubtfully. "But it sounds like this was self-defense, and you said she didn't mean to do it." She thought for a moment. "Who else knew about this?"

Conn stopped pacing. "Only Henry, Ruth and Hannah. They decided not to tell anyone else."

"Who were Henry —"

"The black people, the other slaves that she was friends with," Conn said impatiently. "More than friends," she added.

Molly's eyes narrowed. "What do you mean, 'more than friends'?" she asked carefully.

"Caitríona loved Hannah," Conn explained, pacing around the table again. "They loved each other."

"She showed you this?"

Conn stopped again and stared at Molly. "You think I'm too young to understand about two girls loving each other?" she asked, almost challengingly.

"No," Molly said slowly, looking at Conn with new eyes. "But I'm beginning to understand why she's been waiting for you."

Conn wasn't listening.

"She told Henry, Ruth and Hannah," Conn repeated. "And they buried him in secret. That's when I fell in the river and woke up."

"What do you mean you fell in the river? I wondered why you were wet," Molly said. "I thought you usually had these dreams when you were asleep."

"I used to," Conn said, rubbing her eyes. "But, lately, more of them have been happening when I'm not really asleep, but I can't really remember anything, either…"

She sat down heavily, suddenly looking exhausted. Vincent laid his head on her lap and she rubbed his soft fur absently.

"Have you told anyone else about your dreams, or about Caitríona?" Molly asked.

Conn shook her head. "No. But I think Mr. Greene suspects something. He keeps asking me if I'm in any kind of trouble."

She looked up at Molly. "What were you doing in the shed?"

It was Molly's turn to look bewildered as she shook her head. "I'm not sure. I just woke up this morning with this feeling that I should clean out the shed so the entrance to the tunnel is clear. I couldn't shake it, so I figured I'd better listen."

Conn's shoulders slumped. "How am I supposed to figure all this out? How am I supposed to make it right?" she asked imploringly.

Molly looked at her sympathetically. "I don't know, child. But I believe you will find a way."

CHAPTER 26

Conn lay in the dark in her bedroom, staring at the patches of moonlight streaming in through the windows. Unable to concentrate on anything she tried to read that evening, she'd finally told her mother she was tired and had come up to bed early. Hours after her last vision, her heart was still beating rapidly with the fear and dismay Caitríona had felt during Batterston's attack and its aftermath. She felt racked by a terrible guilt at the thought that she had killed him — "that wasn't me", she had to keep reminding herself. Caitríona's emotions were becoming so enmeshed with her own, that she couldn't easily separate them any longer.

She could hear the muffled sounds of her mother saying good night to Will, and then there was a soft knock on her bedroom door as Elizabeth opened it and came in.

"Are you awake?" she whispered.

"Yes," Conn said, rolling to face her.

"Are you feeling all right?" Elizabeth asked, sitting down on the side of the bed.

Conn didn't answer immediately.

"What happened at the river today?"

"I lost my balance and fell in," Conn said evasively.

"That's not what Mr. Greene said," Elizabeth said.

"What do you mean?"

Elizabeth shifted on the bed, leaning sideways and bracing her arm on Conn's other side. "He said before you fell in, you had a strange look on your face. Your eyes were kind of unfocused, and when he called to you, you didn't answer. He said you didn't stumble or anything, you just... fell." She reached with her free hand and smoothed Conn's forehead. "I've noticed similar things lately. There are times when you seem like you're in some kind of trance or something."

Conn looked up at her mother's face, half-shadowed in the dim light.

"What's going on, Connemara?"

Her mother almost never called her by her full name. Conn suddenly sat up, hugging her mother tightly, wanting to leave all this business of the prophecy behind, wanting to just be eleven. Elizabeth held her, waiting.

"Caitríona comes to me," Conn whispered at last. "Sometimes, she really comes, but mostly, I have dreams about her, showing me things."

Conn waited for her mother's reaction. Elizabeth didn't say anything, but Conn could hear her mother's heartbeat quicken against her ear. She pulled away and looked up into her mother's eyes.

"You've seen her, too, haven't you?" she asked.

Elizabeth nodded. "A few times, when I was your age. But not since we came back here."

"So, you believe me," Conn asked hesitantly. "You don't think I'm making this up?"

"I believe you," Elizabeth said. "But what does she want?"

Conn bit her lip, trying to decide how much to tell. "There really is a curse on our family. It was told to Caitríona by an old woman who knew things, could foresee things, before she left Ireland. Her name was Brónach."

Elizabeth looked hard at Conn for several seconds. "What does this curse say?"

Conn closed her eyes and intoned,

"Ill-fated shall your progeny be;
From each generation after thee
Only one girl child shall survive
To carry on and keep alive
The hope to right a grievous wrong,
Until the one comes along
Who may set the past to rights.

None may help her in her quest, or
Ease the burden laid by her ancestor
On shoulders much too young to bear such sorrow.
Not since barren fields stole all hope for tomorrow

Has such a one been needed,
When father sold daughter for land he was deeded,
And plunged his soul into endless night.

Hatred is poison, like blood on the fields,
Father to daughter, a blackened soul yields
Naught but mem'ries of what once was good.
A child, ne'er soiled by hate or greed could
Bring forgiveness and healing to those long gone.
With the dead laid to rest, the living move on,
Freed at last by a soul blessed with light."

When Conn finished, there was a long, strained silence. She opened her eyes and looked up at her mother, waiting.

"Will almost died," Elizabeth whispered.

Conn nodded solemnly. "No boy has lived. Only one girl from each generation."

Elizabeth pressed a hand to her cheek. "But what happened? What was the 'grievous wrong'?"

"I don't know yet," Conn said. "The dreams have been taking me through her life, like a story, but I don't know how it ends."

They sat, each lost in her own thoughts for long minutes.

"That's how you knew Deirdre was Orla's daughter?" Elizabeth asked. "And the stories you were telling Will about how they almost died on the boat here?"

Conn nodded. Elizabeth lapsed into silence again.

"Miss Molly sees her, too, sometimes. It was Caitríona who told her we were in danger the night of the fire," Conn said, hoping this would mollify her mother, helping her to see this as maybe a good thing, too.

Elizabeth opened her mouth a couple of times before saying, "Can you call her?"

Conn's eyes opened a little wider. "Do you want me to?"

Elizabeth nodded slowly, not truly sure she wanted to see what would appear.

Conn closed her eyes again, concentrating hard and said, "Caitríona Ní Faolain."

For several seconds, nothing happened, but then there was a sudden chill that raised goosebumps on their arms. Nothing more happened for a while and Conn began to think nothing would, but slowly a mist gathered in the center of the room and Caitríona's form took shape.

Elizabeth gasped, as if she still hadn't truly believed it was real. "I remember you," she breathed.

"Yes."

"You came to me when I was a girl."

"Yes," Caitríona said again. "But you weren't the one I was waiting for." Her eyes shifted to Conn. "Connemara is the one."

"But why?" Elizabeth demanded. "She's only a girl."

"She's a girl and a woman both," Caitríona said, her brogue undiminished by time. "She is innocent, but wise beyond her years. She can feel and understand things, things others would never understand."

"You killed Batterston," Conn said.

"Yes," Caitríona answered at the same time Elizabeth exclaimed, "What?"

"He was trying to kill you," Conn said.

Caitríona nodded.

"Was that the thing you need forgiveness for?"

Caitríona's eyes filled with ghostly tears and ran like quicksilver down her cheeks as she shook her head. "It was my hatred..." she whispered.

"But... but you loved," Conn said, hesitating to say more in front of her mother. "I know you did."

"But my hatred was greater," Caitríona said. "What I did... was unforgiveable."

With a heartrending cry, she vanished, leaving behind her the bone-penetrating cold of her misery.

Elizabeth clasped her hands to her chest. She and Conn both jumped as the bedroom door was flung open.

"I heard noises," Will said, rubbing his eyes as he stood there in his pajamas. "Why is it so cold in here?"

CHAPTER 27

"Where in the world do you suppose he went?" Ellie asked for probably the hundredth time.

It had been four days since Batterston had simply disappeared. The mystery and speculation over why he had gone had helped to minimize the curiosity over Caitríona's bruises from tripping down the servants' staircase.

Only Burley seemed dissatisfied with that explanation. "Funny how the banister managed to wrap itself round your neck," he said quietly so that no one else would hear.

Caitríona's face reddened, but she said nothing.

A few days later, Burley had to go to High Acre, the closest neighboring plantation, to see if they could trade some sugar for fresh corn and beans.

"I need to talk to you, private," he whispered to Caitríona when he got back.

She met him at the pump house.

"They're talkin' over there," Burley said in a low voice, "Said a slave trader came by, lookin' to buy some slaves. Said he had a deal to buy some of ours, but Batterston never showed up. The folks at High Acre are askin' all kinds of questions. I told 'em I didn't know nothin' 'bout sellin' any of our slaves. 'S far as I know, Batterston headed to the river, tryin' to find a buyer for our tobacco this fall. That's what I'm tellin' Ellie and the others."

He looked down at her, a kindly expression on his face. "I don't know what happened, an' I don't wanna know. From what I can see, he deserved whatever he got. But," he glanced around to make sure they were alone, "I don't think it's safe for you to stay here. If anyone pokes around and starts askin' questions…"

He laid a gentle hand on her shoulder. "You've worked here eight years now. I think eight years' worth of wages an' a horse to travel with ain't askin' too much."

Caitríona stared up at him, stunned. As much as she had chafed at being bound to this plantation, the thought of being turned loose after all this time was terrifying.

"You think on it," Burley said, leaving her.

Caitríona had to wait until evening to tell Ruth, Henry and Hannah about that conversation. "I don't know what to do," she confessed as she finished. She looked up at them, but had to quickly avert her eyes from the expression on Hannah's face. "I'm thinking about West Virginia. It's the closest state to where we are. I think Deirdre and I could get there in a few weeks."

"Just you and that baby, travelin' alone?" Ruth asked indignantly. She looked over at Henry who was looking back with a questioning expression. Ruth nodded.

Henry turned to Caitríona. "How would you feel if we came with you?" he asked.

"And why would you want to be doing that?" she asked incredulously.

"Because I want my baby to be born free," he said with quiet conviction.

Hannah's mouth fell open. "You're going to have a baby?"

Ruth's face reflected her happiness only for a moment. "Do you think we can do this?" she asked worriedly.

Henry came to her and placed his hands on her shoulders. "We can do anything as long as we're together." He turned to Caitríona. "And you'll have a better chance of making it safe with us helping you."

Hannah stepped forward. "You're not going without me," she said, glaring at Caitríona as if daring her to contradict her.

Caitríona's face was radiant as she looked at them. With a sudden rush of affection, she realized that, besides Deirdre, these three were the people she loved most in the world.

"So," she said, more bravely than she felt, "we're off to make a new life for ourselves."

☙

Conn lay in bed, listening to the soft rain falling outside, mourning doves calling to each other from the trees. "Why do they always call each other in the morning?" she wondered. For three days, she had been waiting impatiently for the next dream. When none had come, she'd begun to wonder if she and her mother had angered Caitríona somehow.

Finally, she knew why they had come to West Virginia. And, remembering Hannah's last journal entry, she knew when they had left — August 1863.

Kicking off her covers, Conn went to her mirror and stared at her reflection. Even in the dim early light, she could still see the bruises and healing cuts on her face and neck. Like the welts on her back, she'd known that these marks would appear soon after her dream of Caitríona's beating at Batterston's hands, faintly, like an echo of the original injuries.

In alarm, Elizabeth had taken Conn over to Molly Peregorn's when they appeared. "Why is this happening?" she demanded, glancing back out to Will, who had opted to stay in the car.

Fascinated, Molly held Conn's face, turning it this way and that as she studied the bruises. She also inspected the welts on her back, still faintly visible, like scars. "I don't understand exactly why this is happening," she mused, "but there is some connection between them that we cannot comprehend. Caitríona and other spirits have appeared to me over the years, but I've never seen a situation this... this entangled."

"Well, I want it to stop," Elizabeth said.

Molly and Conn both looked up at her in surprise.

"Mom," Conn said, "if it stops now, the curse continues. Will —"

"I can protect Will," Elizabeth said determinedly. "But you're being hurt."

Molly pulled another chair out. "Sit down," she said. Elizabeth sat. "First of all, you can't protect Will — not from everything. You couldn't protect him from polio," she said gently. "Second of all, even though we don't understand what's happening between Connemara and Caitríona, the only way to end it is to let it play out to the finish."

"But what will the finish be?" Elizabeth asked, her voice and eyes troubled.

"I don't know," said Molly, "but we can see what the beginning was."

She went to a sideboard where she retrieved a stack of papers and leather-bound books. "I've not looked through these in decades. They're my predecessors' journals and letters. Let's see what we can discover."

Spreading the documents out on the table, they began reading and sorting, trying to figure out who wrote when and put things in chronological order. For several minutes, they read in silence, then Elizabeth said, "Listen to this."

Holding a very battered, very old journal, she said, "This belonged to Lucy Peregorn. Her entries began..." she flipped through the early pages, "in the 1820's. But here..." she flipped back to a page she had marked with her finger, and read, squinting to decipher the cramped handwriting, "in January of 1863, she wrote,

'Last night I had a most peculiar dream. I was led to Jacob Smith's abandoned cabin and there, a family of doves be living. Two white doves there be, and three black. There, they built a nest. And as I watched, rocks were thrown, and one black dove was sorely injured. She lay as one who was dead, but she was not dead. One of the white doves flew at the attacker and led him away from the others, but she did not return.

A most strange dream.'"

She turned several pages. "And here... in September of that same year,

'People have come to the cabin. A white woman and girl, and three colored people. I think they be the doves of my dream.'"

Elizabeth slid the journal across the table to Conn. "I think this is the one you need," she said quietly.

Conn took the journal as if holding a treasure. "Lucy Peregorn," she murmured. She looked up at Molly. "May I borrow this? I'll take good care of it."

Molly nodded. "There may be things in there that will help you."

✳ ✳ ✳

Conn got dressed and went downstairs, carrying the fragile journal. No one else was up yet. She made herself a piece of toast, slathering it with peanut butter and jelly, and went out onto the front porch to eat, sitting on the porch swing, and leafing through the journal. Most of Lucy's entries were brief descriptions of where she had found certain plants or roots she was searching for, or who had been sick or what new baby she had delivered. There were a few Pancakes mentioned, as well as a reference to a William Greene, who had been ill with some kind of fever that Lucy had treated. Conn wondered if this was one of Abraham's ancestors.

She found the entries her mother had read aloud, and then there were more entries concerning Caitríona and her family.

10ᵗʰ November 1863
I was called to help Ruth deliver her baby. A boy, named Moses. Henry be proud to have a free son.

and

30ᵗʰ April 1864
Today I came upon Caitríona, crying in the woods. She told me it be her mother's birthday. Such sadness for one so young. I did not remind her there be more sadness to come.

Conn closed the journal as her mother came out and joined her with a cup of coffee. She had been unusually quiet the past few days, and Conn knew she was struggling to accept all that she had learned the night Caitríona came to them and in the days since. Conn was glad she hadn't revealed everything — the tunnels, Caitríona and Hannah. She wasn't sure how much her mother could deal with. Grown-ups were funny that way.

"So," Elizabeth said, a forced casualness to her voice, "what are you learning?"

"Oh, nothing else big," Conn replied. "Ruth's baby was a boy, Moses. I haven't gotten to these parts in my dreams yet."

"Did you —?"

Conn nodded. "I had one last night. People were starting to ask questions about where Batterston disappeared to, so they decided to leave the plantation."

They sat silently, swinging for a few minutes.

"Have you thought about writing these down?" Elizabeth asked.

Conn glanced up at her. "I have been. In the journal you gave me. I didn't want to forget anything."

Elizabeth shook her head. "Who would believe all this?"

"No one," said Conn pragmatically. "Which is why it's probably a good idea not to tell anyone else."

CHAPTER 28

Conn and Will lay on their stomachs in the dark hallway at the top of the stairs, listening to the voices coming from the sitting room.

"Elizabeth, it isn't right for you and the children to be here all alone when you could be with us."

Elizabeth's voice was clipped as she replied, not for the first time, "I've told you, Mother, we aren't alone. We have friends here. This is my home."

Earlier that afternoon, Conn and Will had been mowing the grass and Elizabeth weeding the flower beds when a car had pulled up the drive. Looking up curiously, Elizabeth's face had turned a peculiar blotchy red as her in-laws got out of their Cadillac convertible.

"Uh oh," Conn murmured, pausing the mower.

"Well, aren't you glad to see us?" said Grandma Mitchell, wearing a luridly floral dress with enormous sunglasses and a scarf to keep her hair from flying away.

"Doesn't she look just like Grace Kelly?" Grandpa Mitchell asked loudly.

Will ran to them.

"Hey, Willy-boy," Grandpa said, giving Will a rough shake of the shoulders.

"Come on," Elizabeth said to Conn in an undertone as she pulled off her gardening gloves, "I'm not doing this alone." To the Mitchells, she said as she forced a smile, "What are you doing here?"

"You all sounded so lonely when we talked on Connemara's birthday," said Grandma Mitchell. "We said we should come for a visit."

"I told you we were fine," Elizabeth reminded them. "Why didn't you call?"

"Oh well, you know how it is on these hick roads," Grandma Mitchell said. "You never know where you're going to find a sign of civilization. I said to Harold, 'Harold, aren't you going to stop so we can call?', but he said we didn't need gas, so we didn't need to stop." She smiled, and kissed Elizabeth on the cheek, then held her at arms' length. "Why, Elizabeth, whatever are you wearing?" she asked, looking disapprovingly at Elizabeth's slacks, marked with grass stains at the knees, her worn canvas sneakers covered with dried mud.

"That's right," said Harold, hoisting up the waist of his Bermuda shorts over his ample belly, revealing white knees above black socks and deck shoes. "Gets twelve miles to the gallon. I told Clara we're not stopping till we have to." He gave the hood a pat. "There's my Connie," he said in an overly jovial tone, holding his arms out to Conn.

Conn just stood there, looking at him.

"What's the matter with her?" Clara asked.

"There's nothing the matter with her," said Elizabeth, hiding a smile, "but don't call her Connie if you expect a response. She hates being called Connie."

"Well, I never," said Clara, but Harold covered the moment with a gruff cough and said, "C'mon, Willy, you can help me carry in the suitcases."

"Um, how long are you planning on staying?" Elizabeth asked as Harold retrieved two enormous suitcases and several smaller bags from the Cadillac's cavernous trunk. Conn could detect the note of panic in her mother's voice, though the Mitchells seemed not to have noticed.

"Why, Elizabeth, someone might think you weren't glad to see us," Harold said with a guffaw.

"Don't be silly," Elizabeth replied weakly as Will began dragging the smaller of the suitcases through the grass toward the house.

"We have nowhere we have to be," Clara said, "so we can stay as long as you need us."

"Where are they sleeping?" Conn asked, laden with the straps of two cases hanging from her shoulders and her hands filled with the handles of two more small bags.

"In your room, I suppose," said Elizabeth, taking the suitcase from Will and carrying it with some difficulty up the porch steps. "You can sleep with me."

Dinner was somewhat haphazard. Elizabeth had not planned for two extra people and while she, Will and Conn shuffled things in the bedrooms to accommodate their unexpected visitors, Harold played with the controls on the oven, declaring he had never seen such an antique, with the result that the roast that had been slow-cooking all afternoon burnt.

"I don't know how you put up with the heat of that monster," Clara said, fanning herself with the latest issue of *Look* magazine. "Why don't you get something modern?"

"It was my grandmother's and her mother's before her," Elizabeth said, trying to control herself as she pulled the charred meat from the woodstove and set it outside.

Conn could see the tension in her mother's jaw, and said, "Let's just have BLTs, Mom. We've got fresh tomatoes, and we'll only have to fry up the bacon. And we have more potato salad in the frig."

"Sandwiches? For dinner?" Clara sounded scandalized. "Do you and the children always eat like this?" she asked disapprovingly.

"Only when someone ruins the dinner," Elizabeth replied snappishly. Forcing herself to smile, she said, "You've both had a tiring drive. Why don't you go sit and we'll call you when everything's ready."

Will made a pile of toast and Conn sliced the tomatoes while Elizabeth fried the bacon. When everything was done, Will went to call his grandparents.

Seated around the table, Harold said loudly, "Well, it's the funniest dinner I've had in a month of Sundays, but I guess beggars can't be choosers."

Conn saw her mother bite her lip to avoid a retort. She reached for the bowl of mayonnaise and....

❧

"We've got to stop and rest," Hannah said. "Ruth can't go any farther."

Though Caitríona wouldn't have asked to stop, she was grateful for the excuse to rest.

For nearly two weeks, they had pushed west, guided by a map Caitríona had taken from Lord Playfair's study.

"Here," Burley had said, counting out money from the strongbox and pushing it into her hands. "This is a fair wage for your years here, plus some for Orla."

Caitríona blinked up at him. "I don't know what to say. From the day we met you, you've been so kind."

"Don't be silly," he blustered, though he looked pleased. "Now, I think it's best if we don't tell anyone you're goin'. If we tell 'em, they'll be askin' all kinds of questions."

"But what will they say about Henry and Ruth and Hannah?" Caitríona asked worriedly.

"Well," he frowned, rubbing the stubble on his chin. "There'll be a fuss, for sure. Might even be a search party. If there is, I'll try to head 'em to the river."

"God keep you, Burley Pratt," Caitríona said, standing on her tiptoes to kiss his cheek.

"You'd best be keepin' those prayers for yourself," he said with feigned gruffness. "You'll be needin' 'em."

And so the small party had slipped away in the night, taking one of the draft horses from a far pasture. Deirdre rode or was carried, and the horse was laden with their pathetically small bags of possessions and the provisions Burley could spare.

Caitríona, who had arrived in America with so little, had no difficulty leaving with nothing more than her journal and a change of clothes for herself and Deirdre, but Henry had stood in his shop, agonizing over what few tools he could afford to take with them.

"You'll make new ones," Ruth said, patting his arm. She herself had packed only a few jars of medicines and herbs she thought they might need.

At first, the going wasn't too bad, but the terrain became wilder and more mountainous the farther west they pushed. Though they tried to avoid towns and settlements, they occasionally ran into other travelers or bands of soldiers.

"My husband was killed in the war," Caitríona would say if she was pressed for an explanation as to why a white woman was traveling with a baby and three Negroes. "He wanted us to go to his people if anything happened to him."

Which side her fictional husband had fought on changed depending on who was asking. One trader had been particularly irksome, asking uncomfortably probing questions about where they came from and where they were headed.

"We're going to Charleston," Caitríona lied. They had no intention of going that far west, but if Burley was right about a possible search party hunting for them, she wanted no chance of laying a trail they could follow.

When they did run into fellow travelers, she tried to glean some information as to their whereabouts. Her map pre-dated West Virginia's split from Virginia, and they weren't sure where the new boundary was. One farmer driving a small herd of swine pointed to a distant depression in the mountains.

"That's Rucker's Gap," he said. "If you get across there, you're in West Virginia."

The paths leading them to Rucker's Gap were little more than deer trails through the woods. While in the forest, it was impossible to accurately head toward a specific landmark, and they often had to crash through undergrowth in an attempt to correct their direction, using axes and knives to hack paths wide enough for the horse. They crossed innumerable streams, some shallow enough to ford with no difficulty, but others running swiftly through steep canyons that forced them to detour up or downstream, sometimes for miles before finding safe places to cross. Where they found grassy clearings, they were forced to stop to allow the horse to graze.

"Are you sure we're doing the right thing?" Caitríona asked Henry in a low voice one night as they pored over their map yet again after a lengthy detour to cross a stream.

"This is hard now, Miss Caitríona," he replied, "but it will be worth it when we can breathe free."

His confidence reassured her. Their food stores were getting low, and they were all battered and bug-bitten and weary, but she reminded herself that she had endured worse. She glanced over at Deirdre who was lying on a blanket next to Hannah. Watching the two of them sleeping together, she knew she would do anything to keep them safe. Anything.

"Conn? Conn!"

Conn became aware of her brother prodding her. Blinking, she looked around. Her grandparents were staring at her as if she had sprouted horns, but her mother was shaking her head, her hand over her eyes.

"Day dreaming," Conn shrugged with a half-laugh. She realized she was still holding the mayonnaise. She passed it on to Will. "Sorry."

Lowering her eyes to her plate, she breathed a sigh of relief that this dream had not been a bad one. She was not really listening for a while, so she was jolted when the conversation between the adults began to penetrate her preoccupation.

"The whole family thinks it would be for the best," Clara was saying.

"They do?" Elizabeth said, trying to keep her tone neutral.

"Of course they do. Why shouldn't you come back to Indiana to be near family?" Harold interjected. He waved a hand in the air. "I can't see how anyone would be sorry to leave this old place."

Conn looked up, panic in her heart. Surely, her mother would never — but Elizabeth met her eyes and Conn knew it was okay.

"Mark would want you to be with family," Clara said.

A shadow immediately fell over Elizabeth's features, but she calmly said, "Mark wanted us, if anything happened to him, to be where we felt at home. This is our home and we are with family."

"What family?" Clara demanded.

"Oh, you'd be surprised," Conn said.

After dinner, Elizabeth insisted that Harold and Clara go sit on the porch while Will entertained them by catching faerieflies. As she and Conn were clearing the table, she whispered, "And you tell Caitríona, her timing could be better!"

CHAPTER 29

"Hey."

Conn looked up to see Jed sliding down off Jack's back.

"Hey," she returned in surprise. "How'd you know where I was?"

"Your ma said she thought you was fishing."

Jed tossed the reins to the ground and let Jack graze. He clambered up onto the rock where Conn was sitting, dangling her bare feet in the creek while her fishing rod lay idle next to her. Jed sat on her other side.

"What's wrong?" he asked.

"My grandparents got here a few days ago," she said. "My dad's mother and father. They just showed up from Indiana and they're driving us crazy."

Jed plucked a small purple flower growing in one of the cracks of their rock and dropped it, watching it swirl in the eddy circling at the base of the boulder. "What're they doin'?"

Conn expelled an exasperated breath. "They keep trying to tell Mom that we shouldn't be here. They want us to move back to Indiana with them."

"Your ma won't do that, will she?" Jed asked, aghast. "You can't leave."

"I don't want to," Conn said. She leaned back on her hands, splashing her feet in the water. "I don't think Mom will do it."

Jed's shoulders slumped in relief. "It just wouldn't be the same 'round here without y'all."

Conn grinned. "I didn't think you liked me."

Jed said seriously, "You're my best friend."

Conn blushed. "You're my best friend, too."

"You wanna do some more explorin' in the tunnels?"

Conn shook her head. "I can't. If anything happens with them here, it'll make things worse for Mom." She sighed. "I've already been gone for a while. I should get back."

She started to get to her feet, and Jed followed. "Why don't they think y'all should be here?" he asked curiously.

"Daddy was —" She caught herself, and bit her lip for a second as she climbed down off the rock to where she'd left her shoes in the grass. "Daddy is their only son, and mom says having us closer would be like having him back with them. But we belong here. We can't leave." There was a determined note in her voice as she spoke.

Jed whistled and Jack shuffled over to them, a large clump of succulent grass hanging from his mouth as he chewed. "How about we ride back?" he asked, leading Jack to a tree stump. There was no answer, and he turned to see Conn on her hands and knees.

❧

"Have we gone far enough yet?"

They had passed through Rucker's Gap six days ago. As close as Caitríona and Henry could tell, they were now in West Virginia, but Caitríona had insisted they push deeper in, wanting to get farther away from slave territory.

As they walked through a lightly forested area, they came unexpectedly upon a log cabin. Caitríona and Henry hid the others behind a dense thicket while they cautiously approached the cabin. There was no smoke coming from the stone chimney, and there were no signs of any people about.

"Hello?" Caitríona called out, but there was no answer.

The door was hanging crookedly on rough hinges so that it juddered as she pushed it open to reveal a single room, empty and seemingly abandoned. There were a few old pieces of broken crockery lying about, and some dry firewood stacked next to the hearth, but no other sign of recent occupants.

"What do you reckon?" Henry asked.

Caitríona turned to look at him hopefully. "I think we should stay here a few days, see if anyone turns up. If they do, we'll just say we were resting before moving on."

The relief was plainly written on Ruth and Hannah's faces as they were told they would be stopping for a while. Ruth was far enough along in her pregnancy that she was riding most of the time, and was getting more and more uncomfortable. Even the horse seemed happy as he carefully lowered himself onto the grass to roll and scratch his back. A nearby spring provided water for horse and humans. When Ruth found an old cast iron pot in a corner of the cabin, she lit a fire and set to work making a sort of stew using wild onions she found nearby. Hannah made small loaves of bread with some of their last remaining flour and set them to bake in the coals.

Days passed, and no one came by to demand they leave or question who they were. Henry managed to trap a couple of rabbits, providing them with the first meat they'd had in weeks. They explored the land surrounding the cabin. Hannah found a large patch of blackberries which Deirdre delighted in picking, though she ate as many as she put in the basket.

There was a rocky outcropping about fifty yards away from the cabin. As Caitríona explored this one day, she suddenly disappeared from view. Yelling for her, the others crowded round the spot through which she had fallen.

"Wait," she called up as they lowered a rope to her. They stood there, waiting anxiously until she reappeared, saying, "There are tunnels down here. We need to see where they go. One heads toward the cabin."

Once back up on solid ground, she looked at the others and said, "I think we've found our new home."

They began cleaning out the cabin, making it habitable. Henry fashioned a simple ladder and climbed up to repair some of the wooden shingles that had broken, allowing water to leak in during the previous night's rainstorm. Ruth and Hannah began foraging for wild asparagus and turnips.

"We found another abandoned cabin nearby," they announced after one such trip.

"Why would we need another cabin?" Caitríona asked.

Hannah tilted her head, looking at Caitríona as if having to explain the obvious to a child. "If anyone else comes around, we cannot look like we're all living together. We can fix the other cabin up just enough to look like someone lives there, and then if anyone gets nosy about why we're here, we can say we only work here for you."

Caitríona opened her mouth to protest, but Ruth cut her off. "Miss Caitríona, most white folks don't look at things the way you do. This is for the best."

Grudgingly, Caitríona acquiesced.

One morning, they opened the cabin's door to find a basket containing smoked bacon and fresh baked bread with a crock of butter. Caitríona looked around, but could see no one.

"Can't we just be grateful for someone's kindness?" Hannah asked when Caitríona seemed upset by the gift.

"We can't trust anyone," Caitríona insisted worriedly. "Who knows we're here?"

She got her answer a couple of days later. Each morning since the first basket, fresh food had been deposited on their doorstep. Caitríona, determined to find out who was leaving it, stayed outside one night, perched in the crook of a nearby tree that gave her a view of the cabin. Drifting off for a few minutes at a time, she was startled by movement off to her left just as the eastern sky was beginning to turn a lighter gray.

A stooped figure stepped out of the woods, making its way quietly to the cabin. There, it deposited another basket near the door, picking up the empty basket they had left outside.

Caitríona cautiously climbed down from her tree and cut the figure off just before it reentered the woods. "Who are you?" she asked.

The figure stopped and turned to her. An ancient woman peered at her in the half-light. "Come."

Mystified, Caitríona followed the old woman through the woods, apparently following a path only she could see as darkness closed around them once more. Caitríona had no sense of time as they wandered, eventually coming to a small cottage tucked under a grove of hemlocks. The old woman beckoned her to follow as she entered the little house.

"Please, who are you?" Caitríona asked again as the woman led her into the kitchen.

The woman gestured to the table and chairs, bidding Caitríona to sit as she made tea for the two of them. Caitríona was reminded forcefully of Brónach as the old woman pushed a cup of tea into her hands, her wizened face so wrinkly that her eyes were mere slits.

"I know who thou be," said the woman, in a rasping voice that sounded rusty from lack of use.

Caitríona's heart pounded. How could this woman know anything? "What do you mean?" she asked.

The old woman smiled, at least Caitríona thought it was meant to be a smile. "Raising a child of thy blood but not of thy womb," she croaked, "and protecting those who would be defenseless." She nodded. "Aye, I know who thou be." She reached out and pushed Caitríona's cup up toward her mouth as she took a sip from her own cup. "I be Lucy. Lucy Peregorn. I have been waiting for thee."

The hot tea scalded Caitríona's throat as she choked upon hearing the old woman's words. "How do you... how can you know these things?"

Lucy sipped her tea, her cup held in both her gnarled hands, not answering for a long moment. "Some things there be, things that be truth if thou knowest how to listen," she said. "Whether thou be in Ireland or here." Caitríona stared at her with frightened eyes. "Thou hast naught to fear from me, child," the old woman told her. "I have been asked to help thee."

"Asked? Asked by whom?" Caitríona whispered.

But Lucy did not answer. She got up and brought a loaf of bread and a small wheel of cheese to the table. Cutting them, she placed some on a plate and slid it across the table to Caitríona.

"Thou hast found the tunnels," said Lucy.

Caitríona nodded as she chewed on a piece of cheese.

"Use them. Build on them. Thou wilt have need of them one day," Lucy said.

"Why? What will happen?" Caitríona asked.

"That be not given to me to know," said the old woman. "Only this have I been shown — that thou and those with thee wilt face grave danger one day, and that thou wilt sacrifice thyself to save them." Lucy looked at her with eyes that seemed to pierce her. "And that thou wilt need another's help to redeem thy soul."

☙

Jed's face looked scared as Conn blinked and found herself on the ground.

"Are you okay?" he was asking, shaking her gently.

She sat back on her heels, pressing her fingers against her eyes, and said, "I'm okay." But it was a few minutes before she let Jed pull her shakily to her feet.

"C'mon," he said, leading her to the tree stump where Jack stood, waiting patiently.

Jed helped Conn onto the horse's back and climbed up behind her, wrapping an arm protectively around her waist as he nudged Jack with his heels and reined him toward the Mitchell house.

Will greeted them as they entered the yard. "Hi, Jed!" he called out.

Conn slid down off Jack's back. "Where is everyone?"

"In the kitchen," Will said. "Mom told me to go play outside."

Conn's eyes narrowed a bit. "Why?"

Will shrugged. "I dunno. They're arguing about something."

"Wait here," she said, letting herself quietly in the front door. She paused outside the swinging door to the kitchen, listening.

"This is not normal," Grandma was saying.

"She's always had a vivid imagination," Elizabeth replied heatedly. "Regardless of what's in it, you should not have read it."

Conn shoved the door open and stepped into the kitchen. Sitting around the table, her mother and grandparents started at her unexpected entrance. Her journal was lying on the table.

Conn's face drained of all color. "How dare you!" she demanded.

"Don't you take that tone with me, young lady!" Clara said.

There was a roar in Conn's head that drowned all other sound. "You've no right!" she shouted. She looked at her mother accusingly. "You told me journals were private." There was such a tone of hurt betrayal in her voice, that Elizabeth couldn't meet her eyes.

"They are. Your grandmother was wrong to read it," she said.

"You're eleven. You don't deserve privacy," Clara cut in, waving her hand dismissively as if the whole idea was absurd. "If this is what's going on around here —"

Conn rushed to the table and snatched the journal. "You are an evil, wicked old —"

"Connemara Faolain!" Elizabeth stood, holding her hands out as if physically pushing everyone apart. She took a deep breath. "Conn, go upstairs, please." Conn glared at her. "Please," she repeated.

Conn spun on her heel and stomped from the kitchen. As the door swung shut behind her, she heard her grandmother say, "This would never have happened when Mark was —"

"Well, Mark isn't here!" Elizabeth shouted, losing her composure at last. "He isn't here, and this is my house to run as I see fit!" Conn paused to listen. "I'm sorry you don't approve. Maybe it's best you leave."

"Now, Elizabeth," Harold said placatingly, "there's no need to be hasty."

"You showed up here with no warning, no invitation," Elizabeth said. "You've violated my daughter's trust and her privacy. You owe her an apology."

Clara began to sputter a protest, but Elizabeth cut her off, repeating, "I think it would be best if you left."

"When?" Harold asked in shock.

"Now," Elizabeth said firmly. "See how far your Cadillac can get you and you can find a hotel when you feel like stopping for the night."

"Well, I never," said Clara.

Conn could hear chair legs scraping, and she scampered up the steps to her mother's room. She wondered how much of that exchange Will and Jed had heard from outside. She went to the window, and saw Jed mounting Jack to leave. He looked up and she waved. He waved back with a sympathetic shrug and nudged Jack into a trot.

She went to the bed and crawled up, sitting cross-legged as she listened to the activity down the hall. Her grandparents were soon packed. She could hear the sound of heavy suitcases thumping down the stairs, as well as a great deal of unintelligible grumbling.

The door opened a short while later and Elizabeth came in. "I would like for you to come say good-bye to your grandparents, please."

Conn stared at her mulishly for several seconds. "I'll do it for you. Not for them," she said at last.

Elizabeth nodded in acknowledgement. "Thank you."

Conn followed her mother downstairs and stood off to the side as awkward farewells were said.

"Good-bye, Elizabeth," Clara said, her voice high as she blinked back tears. "We only meant —"

"Good-bye, Mother Mitchell," Elizabeth said calmly. "Tell everyone in Indiana that we send our love."

Harold gave Will's head a tousle before he grumbled a muffled good-bye to Conn.

"Good-bye, Grandpa," she said. She looked at her grandmother, who pursed her lips primly and gave Conn a curt nod before getting into the car.

The Cadillac backed up and then rolled away in a cloud of dust, and Conn breathed a huge sigh of relief.

Elizabeth also looked relieved, but she muttered, "Oh, we're going to hear about this for a long time." She looked down at Conn, one eyebrow raised, and said, "Please hide your journal in a better spot."

Despite the more relaxed atmosphere in the house now that it was just them again, Conn knew that the argument had brought up a harsh reminder of Daddy's absence.

But, later that night, when she tiptoed down the hall to her mother's room, she didn't hear any sounds of crying. Instead, she could hear the soft sound of her mother's bare feet pacing, pacing back and forth in her room. Conn sat listening and wondering. It seemed like a long time before she heard the bedsprings squeak as her mother went to bed and things eventually got quiet.

CHAPTER 30

"Hello, Mrs. Mitchell."

"Why, Mrs. Thompson," said Elizabeth as she got out of the car, "how are you?"

"Very well, thank you," said Mrs. Thompson, who was the wife of Buck Thompson, one of the two men who had brought the logs from Mr. Peregorn when the bathroom was being re-built. Mrs. Thompson had contributed her wonderful fried chicken to the impromptu meal they had all enjoyed.

"We can get the mail," Conn had said to her mother that morning.

"No," Elizabeth replied. "There's still too much tension. I don't want you down there alone."

There had developed a clear schism in Largo between those who were boycotting the general store and those who weren't. If the Walshes were feeling the financial pinch, they weren't about to admit it.

They had become mildly hostile to Elizabeth during recent trips to collect her mail. The men sitting in the rockers, playing checkers and gossiping stared without making any attempts to hide it. The women were more snide, dropping their voices to whispers when Elizabeth and the children entered. Elizabeth continued to offer a polite "Good morning" to all, though she received no response.

"They're in a state this morning," Mrs. Thompson confided now, her mail in hand. "Mr. Walsh was talking about a large order that Obediah Peregorn cancelled with them and took his business to the farmers' co-op in Marlinton."

"Oh, dear," said Elizabeth. "They didn't give you a hard time, did they?"

"Oh, no," Mrs. Thompson said. She smiled down at Conn and Will. "Are you enjoying your summer, children?"

"Yes ma'am," they replied in unison.

"Have a good day, Mrs. Thompson, and thank you," Elizabeth said as Mrs. Thompson went on her way with a wave. "Stay with me, please," she said to Conn and Will as they climbed the store's steps.

"Good morning, Mrs. Walsh, Mr. Walsh," she said as she entered.

Mr. Walsh ignored her as he continued talking to a small knot of men gathered around the hammers.

"Mail, please," Elizabeth said to Mrs. Walsh.

Mrs. Walsh silently gathered their mail. The bell tinkled again as she was handing the bundle to Elizabeth, and Abraham Greene walked in. In an instant, the atmosphere crackled with tension.

"Well, hello, Mrs. Mitchell, Connemara, William," he said genially, ignoring the others.

"Hi, Mr. Greene!" Will said. "When are you coming back to our house?"

Conn closed her eyes and groaned internally.

Before Abraham could answer, one of the men standing near Mr. Walsh said, loudly enough for everyone to hear, "You know, Joe, some folks just ask to be put in their place."

The man called Joe nodded, spitting tobacco juice toward the spittoon on the floor, but missing. He said, "I know what you mean, T.R. Some folks are just plain stupid."

Elizabeth stepped toward the men and retorted, "Yes, they are, T.R. Watts. Some people are stupid enough to think that skin color is justification for treating people badly. Now, I know no one here would be that ignorant and that backwards, would they?" she finished with a smile.

Abraham hastily stepped up to the counter and asked for his mail as the men scowled at Elizabeth, but said nothing further. He and the Mitchells left the store together.

"I don't know that it's worth it to keep coming here for our mail," Abraham said as he walked them to their car.

"Those cowards are not going to chase us out of here!" Elizabeth declared. "You haven't been threatened directly, have you?"

"Only the kind of thing you heard in there," he said, shaking his head. "I'm more worried about you."

Elizabeth glanced back up at the men still sitting on the porch.

"We're fine." Speaking low so that she could not be overheard, she asked, "Can you join us for supper tonight?"

He smiled his crooked smile. "There's a difference between being brave and asking for trouble," he said. "I will decline until things calm down, but thank you."

She nodded.

"Bye, Mr. Greene," Conn said as he turned back to his truck.

He winked as he climbed onto his running board. A moment later, he rumbled off down the road.

"Mom, may I go to Miss Molly's this afternoon?" Conn asked on their way home. "I want to show her that journal entry I found."

Elizabeth nodded. "Yes, but —"

"— make sure I'm not bothering her," Conn finished for her mother. She grinned. "I will."

A couple of hours later, she was riding her bicycle to Molly's house. Coasting into the hemlocks, she retrieved the journal from her basket, ran up the porch steps, and knocked. Vincent whined, announcing her. Molly answered, wearing an old shirt covered in splashes of paint, a trio of artists' paintbrushes in her hand.

"Come in," she invited.

Conn followed her into the dining room where Molly had a canvas set on an easel. She picked up her palette and resumed dabbing a cloud on a painting of a mountain that Conn recognized.

Conn sat on the floor silently, letting Molly work. Vincent lay down beside her and settled his head in her lap. She stroked his silky black and white coat for several minutes.

Molly stepped back, critically scrutinizing her work. "What do you think?" she asked.

Conn tilted her head. "I like it," she said, "The trees look... real."

"Thank you," Molly said, pleased. She set her palette down and cleaned her brushes in a jar of turpentine, wiping them dry. "So, what brings you this way?"

"I found another journal entry," Conn said. "An important one, I think."

Molly nodded. "Read it to me."

Conn carefully opened the journal to the page she had marked, and read,

"'20th November 1865

Hannah recovering, but inconsolable. Her wounds be severe, but her body wilt live. Less certain be her soul. No sign of Caitríona or the men. I believe this be the fulfillment of my dream, and we wilt hear naught of her again.'"

Molly pulled up a chair and sat. "What men? Did she say?"

Conn shook her head. "No. The last entry before that one was in October, and had nothing to say about any kind of trouble."

Molly frowned, thinking. "It's still a mystery, but I think you're getting closer."

✳ ✳ ✳

Conn fell asleep that night, still puzzling over Lucy's entry and who the men could have been. She was awakened by a sound outside. She slipped out of bed and crept to peer out her window. There was movement in the front yard. She could see light-colored shapes and then a sudden burst of flames rose from the ground to ignite a crooked wooden cross which had been planted in the grass. By the light of the flames, she could see figures, maybe four or five of them, wearing white hoods.

"We'll teach you to respect your betters!" one of them shouted. "And we'll give that nigger a lesson he won't soon forget!"

There was a bang downstairs that sounded as if the kitchen door had been kicked in. Conn heard someone outside yell, "What're you doin'?" She grabbed a flashlight and raced out into the hallway where Will and her mother were emerging from their rooms, panicked.

Conn clapped a hand over Will's mouth as he was preparing to cry out. "This way," she said, taking his hand and leading him to the hidden door.

She popped the moulding and the door swung open. "Be very quiet," she breathed, handing her mother the flashlight and gesturing for her to go down first. Will followed, and then Conn, who carefully clicked the door shut behind her.

"Keep going," she whispered.

They could hear loud footsteps ascending the regular stairs on the other side of the plaster wall as they crept down the winding hidden staircase.

Once at the bottom, Conn held her finger to her lips to signal silence and took the flashlight, leading them along the tunnel to the fork below the barn. Pausing, they listened, but heard nothing.

"How did you —?" Elizabeth began.

"They needed this escape," Conn said, knowing her mother would understand who "they" were. She pointed up the ladder. "This goes to our barn, on the bottom level."

She crouched down at the small alcove and retrieved a candle and an oil lamp. She lit both and handed her mother the candle. "I don't know how long the battery in my flashlight will last, so use this. Wait until you hear help coming. If it doesn't come, I think you can stay down here and be safe. There are more candles if you need them."

"Where do you think you're going?" Elizabeth demanded, still shaken from the shock of the break-in and the discovery of this tunnel.

"I can get to Miss Molly's through the tunnels," Conn explained. "We can call the sheriff and get help over here."

"I don't think we should split up," Elizabeth said as Will cowered next to her.

"Mom," Conn said calmly, with a glance toward Will, "We can't do anything against that many men. I've been all through these tunnels. You know I'm not alone. I can go faster on my own."

After what felt like an agonizingly long time, Elizabeth nodded her consent. "Please, be careful," she said, hugging Conn tightly.

"I will."

Conn took the oil lamp and headed into the darkness.

CHAPTER 31

Conn's bare feet were scraped and bruised and she was out of breath by the time she got to the tunnel's opening into Molly's shed. Feeling immensely grateful that Molly had cleaned the junk out of her way, Conn pushed the shed's door open and raced down to the house, her feet slipping on the dewy grass. Her knock brought frenzied barking from Vincent and a startled call from an upstairs window, "Who is it? I'm armed."

Conn stepped back off the porch so she was visible. "It's me, Connemara," she gasped.

"I'll be right down," Molly said. A moment later, the door was yanked open and she stood there in her nightshirt, shotgun in hand as Vincent wriggled out the door to greet Conn. "What's the matter?"

"Men. White hoods," Conn gulped, still out of breath. "They lit a cross in our yard and kicked in the door."

"Your mother and brother?" Molly asked, heading back into the house. Conn followed.

"Safe for now, down in the tunnel under our barn," she said. "Can you call the sheriff and get him over there as soon as possible?"

"Of course." She turned to see Conn heading back toward the door. "Where are you going?"

"To Abraham," Conn said. "They shouted something about teaching him a lesson. I've got to warn him."

"Conn," Molly called. "Conn!"

But she was gone.

"Damn that girl," she muttered as she rushed into the kitchen to call Sheriff Little.

✳ ✳ ✳

215

By the time Conn got to Abraham's house, she knew she was too late. Forcing herself to ignore the cuts on her feet that were now bleeding freely, she limped closer. From where she crouched in the undergrowth, she could see a crudely made cross already burning in the yard, and she could see movement in the house where lights were on. A moment later, Abraham was pushed out the door, wearing only pajama pants, his hands bound behind him. Seeing them closer, Conn could tell that the white hoods worn by his assailants were just pillowcases with slits cut in them.

"Over here," someone called. "I've got a rope already strung over this beam."

They herded him toward the woodshed at the edge of the yard. In the light from the burning cross, she could see a rope dangling from the center beam of the peaked roof. They forced him to climb up onto a stack of firewood, and slid a noose around his neck.

"We didn't say nothin' 'bout stringin' him up," one of the hooded figures said.

"The world won't miss one more nigger," said another.

"I ain't havin' no part of this," said the first man.

"Then you go pour the kerosene on the house, Grady," said the second man disdainfully. "Joe, give me a hand!"

"We weren't gonna use our names," said Joe.

The other man, whom Conn was now sure was the one called T.R., laughed harshly and said, "Who's he gonna tell?"

Conn watched in horror as the one called Grady picked up a fuel can and began splashing liquid on the house while Joe and T.R. took hold of the other end of the rope around Abraham's neck. A couple of other men stood in the yard, watching and weaving a little on their feet.

"I ain't so sure about this, neither, T.R," said one of the men and Conn recognized Mr. Walsh's voice. Abraham seemed to have recognized him as well, for he turned his head and looked at him, though Conn couldn't tell if he could actually see any eyes through the holes in the pillowcase.

"Are you going to be able to live with yourself, Walter?" he asked in his soft voice.

"You shut up," Joe said, punching Abraham in the gut so that he doubled over as much as the rope would allow.

Turning to Mr. Walsh, T.R. growled, "You're just chickenshit. You talk all big down at the store, but when it comes to doin' somethin', you turn yella."

He wound the rope a few times around his hands and called, "Ready, Joe?"

Joe rushed over and wrapped the rope behind his back and together they pulled, hoisting Abraham into the air. As he swung, his feet kicked out, toppling the stack of wood upon which he had been standing.

Swallowing a scream, Conn ran behind the house and around to the woodshed from behind. Joe and T.R. had tied off the rope to one of the posts supporting the roof and were now hooting and clapping as they watched Abraham swing, gurgling noises coming from his throat as he kicked spasmodically.

Conn saw an axe stuck in a broad stump which was used for splitting firewood. Yanking it free, she chopped at the rope where it was tied off against the post. As it split, Abraham crashed down onto the wood below him, still unable to breathe.

"What the hell?" T.R. yelled as Conn clambered over the wood and loosened the noose.

Abraham took great, rasping breaths of air, only partially conscious. Conn tried to untie his hands, but was only able to get the knot loosened a little before she was grabbed roughly by the hair and pulled to her feet.

"It's that Mitchell brat," said Joe. Conn swung her fists wildly, trying to punch him. He laughed. She got hold of the pillowcase and ripped it off his head. She could smell the alcohol on his foul breath as he leaned close and said, "You like this nigger so much, fine. You can die with him."

"Wait a minute, Joe," said Mr. Walsh, real fear in his voice now. "You can't. She's just a kid."

Even T.R. hesitated, saying, "This changes things, Joe."

"She knows who we are!" Joe roared. "What're you gonna do, let her tell the sheriff who all was at this little party?"

He grabbed Abraham's bound hands and yanked him to his feet. Abraham yelled in pain as the motion nearly dislocated his shoulders. Still holding Conn by the hair, Joe forced both of them toward the house. Shoving them inside, he pushed them roughly to the sitting room floor. Looking around at the books, he pulled a couple off the shelves, ripping pages out and throwing them at Abraham, the loose pages fluttering to the floor like injured birds. "You think you're better than the rest of us," he leered. "You and your books can burn together."

From outside the house, they heard a chorus of yells, "Grady, no!"

Through the windows, Conn saw flames leaping up the exterior walls of the house. Every direction she turned, the house was on fire, the flames greedily lapping the kerosene that had been freely thrown at the wooden frame.

"You idiot!" Joe screamed in panic. He rushed toward the front door, looking as if he might try running through the wall of fire, but the flames lunged inside, reaching for him.

He fell backward onto his rear. Looking about wildly, he saw the entrance to the kitchen and began crawling in that direction.

Conn shook Abraham. "Get up," she said. "We've got to get out of here!"

Abraham sat up, coughing. In the minute it took Conn to finish untying his hands, he seemed to have fully regained consciousness.

The old, dry wood of the house was being rapidly consumed by the fire.

"Upstairs!" Abraham croaked, pushing Conn toward the stairs. They ran up to the second floor, and into one of the bedrooms where there was a tree a few feet away from the house. He forced the window open as wide as it would go and pushed the screen out. Hastily, he pulled back inside as flames were now licking up nearly as high as the second story.

"We're going to have to jump across to that tree," he said. "Can you do that?"

Conn nodded, terror making her mute.

Abraham picked up a chair and used it as a battering ram to break out the entire window, glass and sash, so that they could stand on the sill. He picked Conn up and placed her on the sill where she could feel glass underneath her feet. Gritting her teeth, she looked down and saw a solid wall of fire below her. The heat was incredible and the flames were already reaching up to her.

She turned back to Abraham, throwing her arms around his neck and cried, "I can't do this!"

He held her for a second, kneeling on the floor and then took her arms and pulled her free so that he could look her in the eye. "You can do this," he said calmly. "You are the bravest person I know. I'll help you."

Making up her mind, she nodded. Abraham placed her back on the window sill and said, "On the count of three, you jump, all right?"

The flames were higher than the sill now, and burned her feet as he counted. Instinctively, she withdrew first one foot then the other. When he shouted, "Three!" she leapt awkwardly as he threw her toward the tree.

Flailing wildly, she grasped at the tree branches, trying to get a solid hold on one. Branches cut her face and chest as they broke under her weight and she began to fall. She continued clawing and was able to grasp one larger branch that was strong enough to hold her. Scrambling farther onto a stouter part of the branch, she turned to see Abraham already standing on the sill, ready to jump.

He gave an enormous leap, and fell further than Conn before he was able to grasp a limb strong enough to support him. Vaguely, she could hear shouts from below as the others saw what they were doing. She could also see the flashing lights of sirens as both the sheriff's car and the firetruck pulled up to the house.

Inside the house, a shout could be heard. A moment later, Conn saw a shadow through the flames now almost completely obscuring the window.

"Help me!" Joe called from inside the bedroom.

Conn hesitated for a moment, as a part of her felt a cold wave of hatred. All she had to do was... nothing, and he would get what he deserved. It only lasted a couple of seconds, and then she shouted, "You have to jump! I'll help you!"

She could see Joe approach the window, terror in his face. "You're not strong enough to catch me!"

Suddenly, Abraham was behind her on the branch. He leaned out as far as he dared, reaching toward the house. "Come on!" he yelled. "We'll catch you, but you've got to jump now!"

Even through the flames, Conn could see the hatred twist Joe's face as he hesitated. Without warning, the floor gave way and he disappeared with a scream. She pressed her face into Abraham's shoulder as the screams continued to rip the fabric of the night. When they finally stopped, all that could be heard was the roar of the flames as they devoured the house.

CHAPTER 32

The war was over.

What was good news for most was a renewed sense of worry and anxiety for Caitríona and her family, which now included little Moses. Lucy and Hannah had assisted Ruth with the birth. Henry had broken into tears of joy as he held his son and declared him a free man.

Life had been good for the little family. They'd slowly explored around the cabin to discover they were in Pocahontas County, near a small town called Largo. The mountain residents had built an iron furnace of stacked stone, and as Henry was the most accomplished blacksmith in the region, he soon was not only making his own tools, but was forging for others as well. By bartering his services, they had acquired nearly everything they needed to be comfortable: cooking utensils, cloth for new clothes, provisions. While they initially downed trees and hand-cut all their own lumber, there was a nearby sawmill whose machinery was in constant need of repair. Caitríona negotiated Henry's expertise in exchange for rough-sawn boards which sped the work on their building immeasurably.

They had no idea if the original owner of the cabin, someone Lucy called Jacob Smith, might return home, expecting to pick up where he'd left off, but if he did, he would not recognize the place. By now, nearly two years after they'd first discovered the cabin, Henry and Caitríona had built a barn over the rocky outcropping where Caitríona had first fallen into the tunnel. She was now nearly as handy with a hammer and saw as he was, having long ago used the material from her dress to make britches for herself. He didn't understand her insistence that they build over the tunnel, making a trapdoor for access, but he did as she instructed. In secret, they worked on the tunnel, enlarging and supporting the one that extended toward the cabin so that it would be accessible under the new house they were adding to the original log structure. Henry came up with an ingenious design for a hidden staircase that would allow access to the tunnel.

Though the people around Largo had accepted Caitríona's story about being a war widow, she was always on guard for strangers. Hannah and the others sensed that there was something she knew that she had not shared with them, but did not press her for an explanation. Hannah would often find her sitting by herself in the evenings, when work had stopped for the day, brooding on thoughts known to her alone. Knowing better than to ask what was wrong, she would simply sit and rest her head against Caitríona's shoulder, enjoying the feel of Caitríona's arms holding her tightly. Without any drama or discussion, Ruth and Henry had accepted that their family now consisted of two couples and their children.

The one person they had met whom Caitríona trusted completely was Lucy Peregorn. Lucy knew everything about these mountains. She helped Ruth learn the local herbs and roots and, together, they exchanged their secrets for making medicines and salves. The old woman no longer surprised Caitríona with the things she knew or gleaned. Lucy had generously given them a milkcow so they were able to have fresh milk and make their own butter and a little cheese.

As weeks went by, more and more men returned home from the war. When none claimed the cabin as his own, Caitríona began to relax a bit.

"Where's Mam?" Deirdre asked one day. Nearly four years old now, she was Orla in miniature.

"I don't know, darlin'," Ruth answered, stirring a pot she had heating over the fire. "She was down below."

She went into the new part of the house to where the hidden staircase zigzagged down to the tunnel and called out, "Caitríona?"

Hannah appeared at the base of the stairs. "She's not here. She's carrying." All the extra dirt and stone from their work in the tunnels had been carried, bucket by bucket, to one of the branch tunnels they had discovered. "We can't have people wondering where this great bloody pile of dirt came from," Caitríona had insisted.

"Come to think of it, she's been gone a long time."

Alarmed, Ruth said to Deirdre, "You stay here with Moses, darlin'. We'll go find your mama and be right back." She quickly descended the stairs. She and Hannah took an oil lamp and headed toward the tunnel where they had been dumping the debris. They found their way clogged by a cloud of dust. Coughing and choking, they came upon a wall of dirt closing off the tunnel all the way up to the roof.

Disregarding the possibility of another cave-in, Hannah screamed, "Caitríona!" Scrabbling at the dirt, she tried to claw her way through, sobbing and yelling.

Ruth grabbed her and restrained her tightly. "Don't. We might be trapped, too. Let's get Henry."

Within minutes, the three of them were back at the cave-in. Henry methodically explored the wall of rock and dirt facing them. "It's too big, and it's holding the roof up now," he said, pointing. "We can't move it without bringing more down on top of us."

"We can't leave her in there," Hannah sobbed.

"We won't," Henry assured her. "We'll bring back some timbers and try shoring the roof up, so we can dig her out."

Late that day, exhausted and covered in dirt from head to toe after hours of work, they climbed dejectedly back up to the house. "We'll eat and rest a little, and then go back," Ruth said.

She and Henry forced Hannah to eat a few bites. "You're gonna need your strength to keep digging," Henry said.

Just as they were lighting more lamps in preparation for returning to the tunnel, Caitríona appeared out of the darkness, limping and bedraggled and caked in mud and dirt, but very much alive.

Hannah cried out in relief and joy, flinging herself into Caitríona's arms.

Sitting shakily, Caitríona told them of being caught in the cave-in. "I didn't have time to run," she said. "It just came down." Ruth handed her a bowl of stew. She ate a few bites. "Thank the Lord, I wasn't buried under the full weight of it. I was able to dig myself out on the far side. We never went further than the underground lake, but that tunnel comes out near Lucy's house. I got back as soon as I could." Deirdre crawled into her lap, clinging to her and crying. "I'm fine, child," Caitríona said, kissing her head and holding her tightly.

"I don't think we should go back into those tunnels," Hannah said.

"No!" Caitríona said vehemently. "No, we need those tunnels. Those tunnels are going to save our lives one day."

&

Conn woke with a start to find herself in her own room. For the past three days, she had been confined to bed, her feet treated with one of Molly's salves and wrapped in bandages to give her burns and cuts a chance to heal. Her arms and chest were also healing from her scratches and cuts from the tree branches. She heard them whispering — her mother and Molly and Abraham and the doctor. They all thought she was distraught over the horrific events of that awful night.

The sheriff had taken the surviving members of the erstwhile Klan into custody. It turned out, they were no more members of the KKK than he was, he reported to Elizabeth. They'd just gotten to drinking and as they got each other all riled up, they had decided to try and scare Abraham and the Mitchells, taking it a step further than Grady and Joe's first clumsy attempt at warning the Mitchells away from their friendship with Abraham. The others hadn't counted on Joe and T.R. getting so carried away. "They're all gonna be charged, though," Sheriff Little said smugly. "Either as accessories or with attempted murder and arson." This was the biggest case of his career, and was sure to get him re-elected until he was ready to retire.

Abraham's house was gone. The firefighters had had no chance of putting out the blaze, accelerated as it was by the kerosene. The most they could do was contain the flames and prevent them from spreading to the nearby woods. Joe's remains had been found, but the fire had been so intense, there wasn't much left for his family to bury.

Molly had found Elizabeth and Will safe in the tunnel where Conn had left them, the men there at the house scattering as Molly drove up, brandishing her shotgun. By the time the three of them drove over to Abraham's house, it was fully engulfed. Conn and Abraham had managed to climb down from the tree that saved them just moments before it, too, caught fire and burned.

What none of them knew, for Conn had confided to no one the thing that was tormenting her, was how close she had come to willfully letting someone die. She had been certain, after watching her trout die, that she could never kill again. But, she had come so close to doing just that. That flash of hatred had been so powerful… And part of her couldn't help wondering if her hesitation had cost Joe the time he needed to jump from that window. The prophecy had said the curse could only be ended by "a soul blessed with light." She felt soiled, stained by that moment, and was sure she could no longer be the one.

Yet… she had just had another dream. She lay there now, remembering. She didn't know if the tunnels had ever saved the lives of Caitríona and the others, but she knew they had saved four lives the other night.

A knock on the door roused her from her reflections. Her mother appeared. "Are you up for a visitor? He's been waiting three days to see you."

Conn nodded and sat up against her headboard as Abraham came in.

"Hello, Connemara," he said, his voice a little hoarse. Dr. Jenkins wasn't sure the damage to his trachea would ever heal completely. She scooted over so he could sit on the edge of the bed. "How are you?"

"I'm okay," she said. "How about you?" She could see the raw stripes around his neck and wrists from where the ropes had bitten into the flesh.

"I am healing," he said.

"Where are you living now?" she asked.

"Miss Molly invited me to stay with her until I can rebuild," he said.

Conn couldn't help but smile. "That must be interesting."

He laughed a little, but then coughed as his throat was still easily irritated. "Yes, it is. She's a little set in her ways; then again, so am I. But, she's a good person."

Conn leaned over to her nightstand. "Here," she said, holding out the little leather-bound volume of *The Song of Hiawatha* that Abraham had given her on her birthday. "You should have this back."

He shook his head. "You keep it. I'll start a new collection of old books once I have bookshelves again. Maybe you'll help me?"

He looked down at his hands, long-fingered and callused. He blinked rapidly as he said, "I can never thank you —"

"You don't have to —"

He looked up at her with soft eyes. "I know how you felt. Out on that limb, when he called for help." Conn stared transfixed into his eyes, wondering if he could possibly know… "Part of me wanted to leave him in there, after what he did…"

"But we didn't."

"No," he agreed. "We didn't. It was his choice."

And to Conn's mortification, she began crying. Abraham hesitated, then reached out to hold her as she cried.

CHAPTER 33

One of the first things they did when Conn could walk again was to go to Walsh's. Molly told them that Mrs. Walsh had come out to her cottage to bring Abraham three pair of blue jeans and some shirts, plus some new underclothes and a pair of boots.

"You'll be needing things to re-build your house," she said, staring at Abraham's shoulder. "I'd... I'd be pleased to get you anything you need. I'll give you a good price."

"Thank you, Mrs. Walsh," Abraham said. "That is indeed generous of you. I'll see you soon."

"You could have knocked me over with a feather," Molly declared. "Though it did look like the words were being dragged out of her."

"It must be hard for her," Elizabeth said, "with everyone knowing what her husband did."

"But he at least tried to stop it," Conn said quietly. "He could have tried harder, but he wasn't part of..."

Elizabeth looked at her closely. "Are you all right with going back to that store? Mr. Walsh is there now, until his trial. You'll probably see him."

Conn sat up straight. "He's the one who should not want to see me."

When they entered the general store, the ceiling fans were humming as the early August heat was oppressive. The change in the atmosphere was once again palpable, but this time, in a different way. Everyone present parted to make way for Elizabeth and the children. The men and women gathered weren't exactly friendly, though there were some respectful nods of greeting. Most of them seemed embarrassed, as Conn felt they should be. She was a bit of a curiosity, as they couldn't seem to help staring at the girl who'd done the things they'd heard about.

It was Mrs. Walsh who boxed up their grocery order. Mr. Walsh gave them a cursory nod and disappeared into the back. As Elizabeth gathered the box in her arms, Jed and his father came in. Conn almost didn't recognize either of them. Jed was wearing new blue jeans and a clean shirt, and his father was newly-shaven and cleaned up as well.

Sam Pancake hurried over. "Let me carry that for you, ma'am," he said.

Conn grinned as she looked Jed up and down. She plucked at the sleeve of his shirt as they followed the adults outside. "Where'd these come from?"

He grinned. "Pa got a real job. He figured I better start dressin' a little better."

"Except when we're fishing," she said, grinning back at him.

His smile broadened. "Yeah."

They were quiet for a minute, and then Jed asked, "Are you doin' okay?"

Conn shrugged. "I guess."

He shook his head. "I just can't believe — everything. I can't believe they did that, tried to string Mr. Greene up, and the way you saved his life. Thank the Lord you got out of that house." He looked down at his hands, cleaner than usual, but still with dirt under the nails. "I don't know what I'd do if you died. You don't know how much y'all have changed things 'round here…"

There was an awkward silence for a few seconds.

"How are things at Mr. Greene's house?" she asked.

"We got most of the burnt stuff hauled away now," he replied. "Gonna start the new foundation next week, he said."

"Ready, Conn?" Elizabeth called.

"You wanna go fishin' tomorrow?" Jed asked as he walked Conn to the car.

"Sure. Early?"

"Yup. I'll come get you."

"See you," Conn said, hanging out the car window.

"See you," he said with a wave as they drove off.

It was the first autumn after the war, and America was still reeling, both from Lincoln's assassination and from the efforts to re-unify the divided country. Things such as sugar and coffee were still scarce, but the continued somber atmosphere could not dampen Caitríona's pride the day they nailed the last clapboard on the new house. "Isn't it grand?" was all she could say.

Hannah's eyes glistened with tears as Caitríona led her inside. "A proper house," she murmured. "A proper house all our own."

For Henry and Ruth, there were no words.

There was still a great deal of work to do inside — plastering and putting mouldings around the doors and windows, but with the exterior finished, the sense of pride was overwhelming. They invited Lucy over for their first real dinner in the house, sitting at a table and chairs that Henry had made.

"We'll have better someday," he promised.

Caitríona showed her the hidden stairs.

"A wise precaution on thy part," Lucy said, nodding her approval.

The autumn days were busy with cutting firewood, and harvesting the potatoes and carrots they had planted. With all the building they'd been doing since they arrived, they hadn't had time to plant much, and would have to buy or trade for most of what they needed to get through the winter, but they all felt immeasurably wealthy.

The first blast of winter arrived in the form of a mid-November snow, driving them all indoors unless they had to be out. Ruth made a large batch of pumpkin bread, setting the little loaves aside to cool. Hannah was reading to the children while Henry worked on trimming out one of the windows in the sitting room where a cold wind was blowing into the room. They already had lamps lit as the dreary afternoon light was giving way to an early dusk.

"I'm going to take a couple of these to Lucy," Caitríona said, wrapping two of the dense, fragrant loaves in a towel.

"You best take a lantern with you," Ruth called. "It'll be dark early."

Caitríona pulled on a heavy wool coat and lit a lantern hanging near the door before stepping into the frigid wind outside, which was blowing the falling snow sideways. Her unruly red curls were blown into her face along with stinging pellets of ice and, as she trudged through a light layer of snow toward the woods, she thought she heard something.

Looking around in the early twilight, she couldn't see anything unusual. Deciding it was only the wind, she continued on her way. When she arrived at Lucy's house, it was dark. Leaving the wrapped bread at the door, Caitríona made her way back through the woods, glad she'd brought the lantern as the trees closed around her.

Nearing the house, she was startled again by a rustling, audible over the wind and this time very close at hand. A shadow moved to her right, and Lucy stepped into her lantern light.

"Put out thy light!" Lucy whispered.

"Why? What's happened?" Caitríona asked, dousing the lantern immediately.

"I came to warn thee... men have come, asking questions," Lucy said.

Caitríona didn't need to ask what kind of questions. "Where are the others?" she demanded.

"Ruth, Henry and the children are safe in the tunnels," Lucy replied.

Caitríona's heart ceased to beat. "Hannah?"

Lucy didn't answer immediately and Caitríona's face drained of all color, looking ghostly in the darkness.

"Where's Hannah?" she repeated.

Lucy laid a restraining hand on Caitríona's arm. "She wanted to warn thee," she said softly.

Caitríona grabbed Lucy's hand in an iron grip. "Where is she?"

Lucy gestured wordlessly toward the house, but "Don't go," she pleaded. "Run, hide. I'll —"

But Caitríona could hear nothing for the blood now pounding in her ears. She tore loose from Lucy's grasp and ran the remaining way toward the house, stumbling and slipping on snowy tree roots.

The front door stood open, throwing an elongated patch of lantern light out across the porch and over the snow-covered grass. And there, lying in the small patch of light was a shadow. Caitríona stumbled to Hannah's body, lying there, her beautiful face bloody where she had been hit, her dress and shift ripped away to reveal her breasts. Dropping to her knees, Caitríona covered her and picked her up, cradling her closely. She was cold, so very cold. Raising her face to the heavens, Caitríona let loose a cry, an animal scream that rent the night — a lament for all that she had lost, all that had been taken from her in her life. Lucy felt the hairs raise on her neck and arms as she listened to that cry and never forgot it for the remainder of her life. But others also heard it. Shadows moved within the house, and men's shouts were heard.

Caitríona gently laid Hannah back down on the frozen earth, and, filled with a blind, driving rage against those who had done this, she knew in an instant what she would do. She ran a few steps toward the woods, giving them time to spot her. She hadn't gone twenty paces when she heard a man's voice yell, "I see her!"

Another voice, deeper, said, "Ames, you call the others and follow as fast as you can. The rest of you, come with me!"

"Remember, they're worth more alive!" yet another voice shouted.

Sprinting, Caitríona tore off through the woods, ignoring the branches that whipped her face and caught at her hair. After a few minutes, she stopped to listen. She could see the dancing light of torches behind her. She wanted to stay ahead of them, but did not want to lose them entirely. Her trail in the snow was easy to follow. She could hear the sound of heavy footsteps crashing through the woods in her wake. She began running again, heading in the direction of Lucy's house. She stayed just far enough in front of them to stay out of their clutches and keep leading them away from the house. If she could just get to the tunnel entrance behind Lucy's house, she could slip inside and they would follow.

She emerged from the woods, but to her dismay, they had gained on her. She had no time now to find a lantern. She knew she would be blind once in the tunnel, and hoped she would remember the way. Deciding she had to take the chance, she sprinted toward the rock face, found the cleft in the wall and slipped inside. As quickly as she dared, she began climbing down the stone stairs, feeling her way, the sound of water growing louder as she descended.

"In here!" said one of the voices above her. "She went in here!"

She could see the flickering light of the men's torches reflected off the damp walls behind her. Her only advantage was that she knew where she was going. Once she was down on relatively level ground again, she began running as fast as she could on the slippery wet rock, trailing a hand along the wall to her left to guide her. She got to the shallow lake and stopped, listening. They were still behind her. In one last moment of indecision, she had to choose which tunnel to take from there. One led to the main cavern where she knew she could lose them and get away, but she and Henry and Ruth would forever be looking over their shoulders; and the other tunnel, she knew, led to the cave-in. Remembering Hannah's cold, beaten body lying in the snow, she made up her mind, splashing through the pool and into the cave-in tunnel. Running along this tunnel, she stumbled over piles of dirt, evidence of other partial collapses since she'd last been there. At one point, she fell headlong, scraping her hands and face on the rocky floor beneath her. Scrambling to her feet, she paused to listen.

The men were further behind her now, she had temporarily lost them at the pool, but it wouldn't be long before they saw her wet footprints and figured out which path she had taken. She knew she was nearing the cave-in; she could feel the timbers she and Henry had put up to bolster the walls and roof from this side when they had thought they might be able to clear the blockage. But every time they dug, more of the roof had caved in on them until they decided it was too unstable to try any further. Dropping to the floor, she felt about and found what she was searching for. There, where they had left it, was the long coil of rope which they had used to hoist timbers into place. Working as quickly as she could in the dark, she coiled and knotted the rope around every post and looped it quickly around the horizontal timbers supporting the roof as bits of earth and rock fell down upon her. Then, climbing and digging her way up the mound of dirt and rock still blocking the tunnel, she waited, the free end of the rope held tightly in her hands.

She could hear them now, whispers and low voices coming in magnified echoes in the dark, but she could not yet see the light of their torches. Digging in further, she created a small bunker she could burrow into that would hide her from their view until it was too late. The darkness was absolute as she waited.

Within a few minutes, she could see flickering lights far down the tunnel. The lights grew brighter and she could hear their voices. It seemed they had been joined by the second group, for there were more torches now.

"This is the devil's work, I tell you," said one.

"I'll give you the devil," growled another. "That red-headed witch is the very devil."

"What the —"

The men had arrived at the cave-in. Caitríona held her breath, waiting for them to step a little closer… just a little closer….

With a scream and a mighty yank on the rope, she brought the timbers crashing down, one pulling the next. Dirt and rock began to fall in large chunks, much of it falling behind the men, trapping them. The men yelled and their yells helped accelerate the fall of debris. The ones closest to Caitríona and the wall of dirt were the first to realize what was happening, but as they turned to run, they found their way blocked by the others trying to avoid the debris falling down on them from behind.

With a savage scream, Caitríona saw them buried by an avalanche of rock and earth. The dust choked her as more dirt rained down upon her and all light was extinguished. Coughing, she covered her head and face with her coat to filter the air. It took a long time for everything to settle, and when it did, she was partially buried in fresh dirt herself. Once again, she was in absolute darkness, the torches having been buried with the men. Carefully, she raised herself up from the earth covering her, shaking the dirt from her hair. Gingerly, she tested the wall behind her to see if any of it had shifted, but it remained as solid as ever it was. Slipping and sliding down the mounded dirt, she made her way over the newly caved-in portion under which Hannah's attackers lay buried. Crawling over the debris, she found that it was piled solidly, but not all the way up. With a new sense of hope, she scrambled forward to see if she could dig her way out the other side.

Her hope died in an instant, as she found that way blocked by a huge chunk of rock that had collapsed down from the tunnel roof, now firmly wedged in place by the surrounding rock and dirt so that it left only a tiny gap through which she could reach a hand, but not large enough for her to crawl through. She dug, trying to enlarge the gap, but her fingers were soon raw and bleeding.

When they search for me, I'll be able to call and signal to them, she thought, but immediately realized that no one knew where she had run to.

She fell back on top of the freshly collapsed dirt, sitting on the bodies of her enemies and realized that she, also, would die. She could feel a small whisper of fresh air blow past her cheek, and laughed at the irony that, unlike her enemies, her death would not be mercifully swift as air ran out, but would be agonizingly slow as thirst and hunger took her.

❦

"Why, Jed, what are you doing here?" Elizabeth asked in response to Jed's knock on the kitchen door.

"We were gonna go fishin'," Jed replied, once again wearing his faded and patched overalls. "Isn't Conn up yet?"

Elizabeth frowned. "I thought she'd already left the house to go meet you," she said. "I'm sure I heard her leave. Come on in."

Jed waited in the kitchen as she went upstairs, calling for Conn.

"Hi, Jed," said Will, coming out of the bathroom still in his pj's.

Elizabeth came back downstairs. "That's odd. She's not here. I can't imagine where she's gone. Do you know where your sister went?" she asked Will.

He shook his head with a shrug as the telephone rang.

"Elizabeth?" came Molly's voice, slightly out of breath. "I think you should get over here as quickly as you can. I'll explain when you get here."

Elizabeth herded the boys into the car, and sped to Molly's cottage, where the front door was standing open.

"In here," Molly called out, and they trooped into her house.

There, in the kitchen, they encountered the strangest sight. Molly was sitting on a struggling Conn, pinning her to the floor.

"I've got to go to her!" Conn was crying.

Elizabeth dropped to her knees and held Conn's face in her hands. Conn seemed not to know she was there as her eyes remained focused on some distant thing, and she kept repeating the same phrase.

"She's been like this since I found her," Molly explained. "That's all she says, over and over." She looked up at Elizabeth. "I think we should let her go and follow her."

Elizabeth met Molly's eyes. "You think —?"

"Yes."

Fearfully, Elizabeth nodded and Molly got up. As soon as she was released, Conn sprang to her feet and sprinted out the back door toward the shed.

"Wait!" Jed called as the others started to follow. "We need a light."

Molly grabbed an oil lamp from her pantry and lit it hurriedly.

"William Joseph, you are to stay right here," Elizabeth said firmly. "Don't you dare follow us. Do you understand?"

Will nodded, sitting down on one of the kitchen chairs.

"Vincent, stay," Molly commanded. "He'll keep you company," she added kindly.

By the time they got to the shed, Conn was nowhere to be seen. Jed took the lamp and led the way carefully down the stone steps.

※ ※ ※

Conn needed no light. She had done this in the dark before. She knew the way. Reaching the shallow pool of icy water, she splashed across, staying near the left hand wall, not bothering to take off her shoes. Groping on the far wall, she bypassed the tunnel on her left, the one that led back to the cavern. Reaching to her right, she found the other tunnel, the one she and Jed had never explored, but which she now knew would bring her to the culmination of her quest.

She moved more slowly now, relying on her feet and hands to guide her. The tunnel curved slightly to the right, and she could see a ghostly light up ahead as the air before her chilled.

Caitríona stood before an immense pile of dirt supporting an enormous vertical slab of rock.

"Here?" Conn asked.

Caitríona nodded. "'Tis the place."

Climbing up, Conn began digging with her hands. She paused, looking at the apparition next to her. "Stay with me."

"I'm with you, child."

The rock slab was too massive and was buried too deeply to be removed. Conn began scratching at the rock-hard dirt near a small opening up high, but made only a tiny increase in the size of the gap. Her nails were soon scraped down to raw nubs and she realized she could not dig an opening large enough to get through.

"Conn!"

"Conn, where are you?"

Conn looked back at the sound of the voices approaching from down the tunnel. "Down here," she called. "Keep coming."

With one last glance, Caitríona vanished and Conn was left in total blackness for a few minutes until a beam of light thrown by their lantern pierced the darkness.

Conn slid down the dirt pile as the others approached. Elizabeth grabbed her and held her tightly. "Are you all right?" she asked anxiously.

Conn nodded. She pointed. "We need tools. She's in there."

✳ ✳ ✳

Within the hour, they were back, accompanied by Abraham. Armed with more lanterns as well as shovels and picks, they worked carefully to enlarge the opening without bringing the roof crashing down upon them.

Before too long, they had an opening big enough for Conn to squeeze through. She wriggled and squirmed until she fell through on the other side. They passed a lantern through to her.

"What is it?" Elizabeth called up. "What's there?"

Conn squatted down beside the mummified remains lying there. "Caitríona."

There was silence for several seconds. "You found her?" Molly asked.

Jed's face appeared in the opening. He squirmed through also as the adults waited anxiously on the other side.

Conn handed the lantern to Jed and turned back to the dessicated remains. There, clutched in the withered hand, was Orla's rosary. Gently, Conn pried the wooden beads from the brittle fingers. "It's her," she said reverently.

"What's that say?" Jed asked, holding the lantern up high. There, a rock had been used to carve a word into the packed dirt wall.

By the illumination of the lamp, Conn read, "Miserere."

CHAPTER 34

"We have to bury her next to Hannah," Conn insisted. She worked for hours with Abraham to make a simple coffin, laboring to carve a simple Celtic cross into the top.

She had sat down and described the last dream in detail for her mother and Molly. "I don't think she ever knew that Hannah hadn't died that night," she said sadly.

After some discussion, the three of them decided against notifying anyone else of the presence of other bodies in the tunnel. "They've been buried there for over a hundred years," Molly argued. "I think it best if they stay there."

"I don't understand," Elizabeth said to Molly later as they sat together on the porch swing watching the children out in the yard.

"You don't understand what?" Molly asked.

"The connection between Caitríona and Hannah."

Molly looked askance at her. "They were lovers," she said matter-of-factly.

The look on Elizabeth's face was comical. "How do you know?" she asked, non-plussed.

"Conn told me."

The expression on Elizabeth's face a moment ago was nothing to the one it wore now. Molly waited for her to process this information.

"What exactly does she know?" Elizabeth asked carefully.

Molly shrugged. "I don't think she was shown anything intimate, but she understands that they loved one another, that they were in love."

"But she's only eleven!" Elizabeth said indignantly.

"Whatever she is, she is most definitely not 'only eleven'," Molly said calmly. "No normal eleven-year-old could have done what she has done."

Speaking very deliberately, she continued, "Elizabeth, I believe that the fact that Connemara was capable of understanding their relationship was the reason she was the one Caitríona was waiting for. She needed someone who could truly understand the anguish she felt when she thought Hannah was dead. It was the thing that drove her to do what she did in that tunnel."

Elizabeth frowned as she considered the significance of Molly's words. "Are you saying…?"

Molly shrugged again and smiled. "Who knows? Does it really matter? Abraham told me that she asked him once why love should be so hard to understand. Good question, don't you think?"

⁂ ⁂ ⁂

A small procession made its way to the Faolain family cemetery. It was a glorious August morning, cool and dewy. Birds were singing joyously. Columbine and morning glory were blooming in profusion, climbing the grave markers and the stone boundary of the tiny graveyard. The Mitchells stood gathered around the freshly dug grave, joined by Abraham, Molly and Jed. Together, they lowered the coffin with ropes, settling Caitríona Ní Faolain at long last into her final resting place next to Hannah.

Elizabeth gave Conn a small nod of encouragement, and she picked up the Bible she had brought from the house. As she opened it, she said, "Caitríona spent her last hours in that tunnel praying for forgiveness. This is the Miserere, the 51st Psalm." And she read,

> "'Have mercy on me, O God, in your goodness,
> in your great tenderness wipe away my faults;
> wash me clean of my guilt,
> purify me from my sin.
>
> For I am well aware of my faults,
> I have my sin constantly in mind,
> having sinned against none other than you,
> having done what you regard as wrong.

You are just when you pass sentence on me,
blameless when you give judgement.
You know I was born guilty,
a sinner from the moment of conception.

Yet, since you love sincerity of heart,
teach me the secrets of wisdom.
Purify me with hyssop until I am clean;
wash me until I am whiter than snow.

Instill some joy and gladness into me,
let the bones you have crushed rejoice again.
Hide your face from my sins,
wipe out all my guilt.

God, create a clean heart in me,
put into me a new and constant spirit,
do not banish me from your presence,
do not deprive me of your holy spirit.

Be my saviour again, renew my joy,
keep my spirit steady and willing;
and I shall teach transgressors the way to you,
and to you the sinners will return.

Save me from death, God my saviour,
and my tongue will acclaim your righteousness;
Lord, open my lips,
and my mouth will speak out your praise.

Sacrifice gives you no pleasure,
were I to offer holocaust, you would not have it.
My sacrifice is this broken spirit,
you will not scorn this crushed and broken heart.'"

No one spoke as she finished. She closed the Bible and said, "I hope you find the peace you were seeking."

✳ ✳ ✳

Later that night, sitting in her bed in the moonlit darkness, listening to the night sounds of summer outside her window, Conn waited. When all was quiet, there came the chill and the light she knew would appear.

"You have done what no other could," Caitríona said. "You fulfilled the *seanmhair's* prophecy."

"I didn't think I was… after the fire," Conn murmured.

Caitríona said, "You could have given in to the hatred, but you didn't." She lowered her eyes. "I was consumed by it. You could never have done what I did."

"Will you be able to… move on, now?"

Caitríona nodded, smiling a little, the first smile Conn had seen on her face. "I hope Hannah will be waiting for me."

"I found a journal entry from 1890," Conn told her. "After Lucy, the next Peregorn witch, her name was Nell, she wrote that Hannah was a soul living with one foot in this world and one foot in the next. I think she'll be waiting."

Caitríona's silvery form faded a bit.

"You won't be coming back again, will you?" Conn asked.

"No, child," said Caitríona. "The bottom step of the hidden stairs is a secret box. There, you will find my journal." She regarded Conn for a long moment. "One last gift am I permitted to give you, though you may think it a curse. Your father will not be coming home. He has gone on." She paused at the tears that sprang to Conn's eyes. Softly, she said, "'Tis the not knowing that tears a soul apart. Farewell, Connemara Ní Faolain."

Caitríona faded away and Conn's room was once again lit only by moonlight and filled with warm night air.

EPILOGUE

Conn stood on the hill, her short red hair blown by a wind carrying the smell of the sea and the heather, and looked down on a small stone cottage. Undiminished by the passage of twenty-five years, the memory of her dreams was as sharp as if she had just lived them that summer. Years of searching through old estate and county records had led her at last to this moment. Grasping the hand of the woman next to her, they walked down to the cottage, which now stood in ruins, its thatched roof falling in in places, the stone walls in need of new chinking, the windows taken long ago by someone with greater need.

She looked around. Over there was the little lean-to where the pony and the cow had sheltered. In the other direction was the hill beyond which the *seanmhair* had lived. She ducked through the low door, stepping into the cottage. It seemed impossible that so many had lived in this tiny place. A couple of blocks of peat still lay next to the fireplace.

"Are you all right?" the other woman asked, gripping Conn's hand more tightly.

Conn nodded, blinking rapidly. "I just can't believe I'm here. Could you take some pictures to show Mom and Will?"

As the woman pulled her camera out of the case hanging from her shoulder, Conn stepped to the window at the back of the cottage. There, up on the next hill, were three small crosses that she had seen before, along with two others that were newer, though still very old.

"I'll be back in a few minutes," she murmured.

She walked up the hill to the graves. The largest of the crosses there had a name crudely carved into the wood, so weathered as to be almost indiscernible. She was able to make out "Eilish O'Faolain." She reached into her pocket and pulled forth a rosary. Kneeling, she wound the wooden beads around the upright post of the cross.

Sighing, she looked out over the cottage, the home that Caitríona and Orla had been forced to leave. Though they had never seen home or Ireland again, it felt to Conn like she had achieved some kind of closure for them, even if it was five generations late.

The woman climbed the hill and knelt next to her, wrapping an arm gently around her shoulders. "Are you all right?" she asked again.

Conn brushed tears from her face. She lifted the woman's hand to her lips, kissing it, and said, "Let's go home."

Made in the USA
Charleston, SC
18 April 2014